His Love Was All I Needed

His Love Was All I Needed

T. Friday

www.urbanbooks.net

Urban Books, LLC
300 Farmingdale Road, N.Y.-Route 109
Farmingdale, NY 11735

ISBN 13: 978-1-64556-670-0
EBOOK ISBN: 978-1-64556-674-8

First Trade Paperback Printing August 2025
Printed in the United States of America

10 9 8 7 6 5 4 3 2 1

Distributed by Kensington Publishing Corp.
Submit Orders to:
Customer Service
400 Hahn Road
Westminster, MD 21157-4627
Phone: 1-800-733-3000
Fax: 1-800-659-2436

The authorized representative in the EU for product safety and compliance
Is eucomply OU, Parnu mnt 139b-14, Apt 123
Tallinn, Berlin 11317, hello@eucompliancepartner.com

Dedication

This book is dedicated to the five most important people in my life: my babies Jordin, Jacob, Jacory, Jakayla, and Jalisa. Please understand that everything I do and every struggle I overcome is so that you guys don't have to worry about a thing. I love you guys, and never forget it.

Also, to my heartbeat and headache, Blunt. Thank you so much for always believing in me and having my back. You have been there to push me even when I felt like giving up. Thank you.

Acknowledgments

To my first publisher, Racquel Williams, RWP, you're the best, Boss Lady!!!! People always say make your first choice your best one, and I can say making you my first publisher was the best decision that I could have ever made. Over the last few years of knowing you, I have learned so much in this industry. No matter what the situation was, you have always had my back every time. You have shown me nothing but love, and for that, I really love and appreciate you.

To my pen sister, Christine Davis, it's because of you that I'm doing something that I love. I really appreciate you and your grind.

To the wonderful ladies of RWP, I really love and appreciate all the support from you guys.

To my wonderful readers and my supporters, I'm nothing without you. For the last five years and thirty books later, you guys have read and reviewed all my books, and I appreciate each and every one of you guys. I really want to say thank you from the bottom of my heart. It really touches my heart when I hear some of you say that I have become one of your favorite authors. You all make me keep going stronger.

To my baby sister, Amanda Jordin Hollis, I love and miss you so much. I swear fifteen years wasn't long enough to have you here with us.

To my mom, Lisa, and dad, David, I wish you guys were here to see that I'm finally doing something that I love. I love and miss you guys so much. Please continue to watch over the family.

Chapter 1

"Malik, you gonna help me with these bags or not?"

"Yeah, Ma," He answered with his attention still on the girl across the street.

Ms. Patt took a seat on the porch while her son brought in her groceries.

"Ma, why you ain't tell me you got a new neighbor?"

Ms. Patt shook her head. Her son, Malik, had always been a ladies' man. "Leave that girl alone, Malik. You don't need her mixed up in your foolishness. You have broken plenty of hearts before. Don't even go over there."

Malik stood in the doorway before stepping completely outside. "Ma, chill on me. Who all stay over there with her? I know you been on that porch, minding her business." Anyone that knew Ms. Patt knew that she stayed in everyone else's business.

Camy had no idea what she was getting herself into, moving on Cortland Street, but she knew it was time for her to be on her own. Camy once thought that she was in love with her high school sweetheart, Jason; he, on the other hand, felt differently. Jason had become a serial cheater, and after finding bitches' panties and earrings in their house multiple times, Camy had had enough and ghosted his ass.

Camy took her last bag out of her trunk.

"Good afternoon. You need some help?"

Camy turned around to see who was talking to her. She had only been on the block for a few days and hadn't paid anyone any attention. She smiled when she saw the handsome guy standing on the porch across the street. "I got it, but thanks anyways."

"Please leave that girl alone. She not even your type."

Malik laughed. "And what's my type, Ma?"

"Boy, now you know you like those wild, big-mouth girls. She seems to be quiet and more into herself."

"How you know that?"

"'Cause she ain't had nobody over there yet. How many females do you know move into a new house and don't celebrate with a few friends?"

Malik soaked up everything his mama said, thinking maybe she was onto something. Malik took a seat, staring across the street, hoping that his mama's new neighbor would step back outside. No matter his mama's warnings, he knew he had to have her. In his eyes, she was too cute not to want her.

"Malik, go ahead and head home."

"Damn, Ma, how you gonna use me for a ride and groceries then try to get rid of me? I ain't even do shit."

"But I know what you are thinking. What you gonna do with Shay ratchet ass if you start getting that girl over there attention?"

Malik shook his head. One thing about his mama was that she would be in your business no matter what.

"Ma, I'm not in a relationship with Shay or anyone else. She ain't got no title to say shit about my business."

Ms. Patt shook her head. She knew all that playboy shit was going to catch up with him eventually, but he was grown and at the age that you couldn't tell him shit.

Malik looked down at his phone to read the text message that popped up on his phone.

Shay: Come fuck me before you leave the hood.

Malik stood up. "All right, Ma, I'm headed out."

"See you, son. Call me later if you are around. I'm about to put this food on."

"All right, I'll be back to get a plate."

Instead of going home, Malik drove around the corner to cater to Shay's request.

"Hey, baby, come on in," Shay said, greeting Malik at the door.

Malik walked in, admiring her frame in the bra and boy shorts that she had on. "You look good today."

Shay made her booty cheeks jump. "Stop acting like I don't do this shit on the regular, nigga." Shay snatched his hand. "Come on, Daddy. Come stretch me out."

Malik let her lead him into her bedroom. They quickly undressed after entering the room. Shay then dropped straight to her knees to show Malik just how much she missed him.

"Damn, girl." Malik moaned, just a little above a whisper.

Shay made his dick disappear in her mouth, knowing that shit drove him crazy.

"Fuck!"

Malik enjoyed the sloppy-ass head that she was putting on him, but his mind was on the new girl on the block. His mind was on hooking up with her. He wasn't worried about shit that his mama was talking about.

"Damn, Malik. If you not feeling it, you could have just taken your ass home."

"Fuck you talking about? Come on, Shay. Get that nut out of me."

"I just asked you if you wanted me to ride it, or did you wanna hit it from the back?"

"Toot that ass up, girl. You already know what I like."

Malik's mind wasn't completely there, and Shay knew it, but with him serving those hard back shots that she loved, she decided not to bitch about it.

"Damn, Daddy, this your pussy!" she yelled out, enjoying every last bit of dick that he was giving her.

"It better be," Malik muttered as he pulled the rubber off and nutted on her left ass cheek.

Shay instantly jumped up to run the water for their shower. After fucking around for three years, everything was so routine with them, and Malik was ready for a change.

Shay gave Malik a peck on the lips. "What's wrong, baby?"

"Nothing."

Malik tried to get his mind back in the game. Picking Shay up, he placed her back against the shower wall. He drilled deep into her pussy, making her dig her nails into his back as she screamed out.

"I love you, Malik!"

Like any other time, he didn't respond. She knew what tip they were on and was trying to cross that line.

After stepping out of the bathroom and getting dressed, Malik texted his brother, Rell.

"So, I guess you about to go?"

"Yeah, I got to go meet up with bro, then go handle some shit."

Shay rolled her eyes before flopping down on the bed. "What are we doing, Malik?"

"Fuck you mean? We doing what we been doing."

"That's the problem, nigga. I'm tired of the same shit with you. You come over and fuck me good, cash me out, then get up and leave like I don't matter."

"And what's wrong with that, Shay?" Malik asked, putting his shoes on.

"What's wrong with it? Really, nigga? We've been fucking around for almost three years now, and I want more."

Malik dug in his pocket. "What you want some more of? How much more do you need?"

"Stop fucking playing with me, Malik. You know what the fuck I'm talking about, nigga. I want us to be more than just fuck buddies," she yelled.

Malik shook his head. "Don't do that shit, Shay. You already know how shit is. Don't try to fix shit that ain't broke."

As Malik started to walk out the door, Shay jumped up. Crying and all, she expressed her feelings. "You keep saying fuck me like you don't know how much I love you. Why you gotta be like that with me? I proved that I'll do anything for you, and you know it. Why can't we just be together?"

"You knew what type of nigga I was when we first hooked up. I'm not changing for shit. You want dick, I give it to you. You need cash, I got you. Fuck wrong?"

Malik kept walking out the door, not paying her tears any attention. He didn't feel bad because he had told her that he didn't do relationships from jump, and she still fucked with him. Now, damn near three years later, she was trying to switch the game up, and he didn't like that.

Malik jumped in his truck, telling himself that he was done fucking with her. She was making his life difficult, and he didn't do drama. Malik then drove toward the east side to drop some weed off to his homeboy. It was just his luck to run into a few more niggas that needed what he had.

Before driving off, he texted his brother to see if he had picked up the new shit because he was all out. After receiving a text back saying everything was in play, Malik drove right back to his mom's crib to see what tip his brother was on.

"What up, bro? Where you coming from?"

Malik took a seat on the porch next to his brother, Rell.

"Shid, I was around there with Shay ass. Then, I had to shoot a move."

Rell then pulled out a large Ziploc bag full of weed. "Check this shit out, nigga."

Malik opened the bag then gave it a good sniff. "Oh, yeah, that's the shit right there. I hope that shit blow good like the last shit we got from that nigga."

Ms. Patt walked out on the porch. "Get off my porch with that shit. I don't need my friends riding up the street seeing this shit."

Rell stood up. "All right, Ma, chill out. We about to leave."

The brothers took their goodie bag into Rell's car. They were eager to test their new product out.

"Aye, bro, have you seen that bitch that just moved over there yet?" Malik asked Rell.

"Hell yeah, that bitch bad as hell. I wouldn't mind popping that li'l bitch."

Malik chuckled. "Nigga, now you know Tiffany would beat your ass if she even thought you were thinking about talking to another bitch. Besides, that's gonna be me, bro."

"How you claiming a bitch and you ain't even talked to her yet? And while you talking, Shay would fuck you up."

Malik laughed. "That ain't my damn girlfriend. I'm free to do as I fucking please. You the one that's tied down with two fucking kids and one on the way and not even thirty yet."

Rell laughed right along with his brother. "When you gonna tell Shay that she ain't your girlfriend?"

"She know what tip I be on, and being cuffed to a bitch ain't what I want out of life. The pussy good, the head fire, but I'm forever single." Malik told his brother before taking a pull from the blunt.

"So, what? She gonna be a forever side chick?"

"If that's what it's called, then that's what she gonna be until I say so."

The brothers continued to smoke while talking shit to one another.

Rell and Malik were only two years apart, but they were best friends, and nothing could get in between them. Rell, being the oldest, tried to give his baby brother the best advice, but Malik was the type who had to fall and bump his head before he learned.

After smoking up the car, the brothers walked into their mama's house, ready to eat.

"Don't think y'all about to go into my damn kitchen and eat up all that food in there."

"Ma, stop all that," Rell told her. Rell was irritated and prayed that she didn't blow his high.

Being serious about them eating up all her food, Ms. Patt got up to fix her boys' plates, so they could eat and go the fuck home.

After a while, Tiffany started blowing Rell's phone up, so he was the first to leave.

"Ma, I'm gone. Can Tiffany get a plate?"

Ms. Patt got up to fix her daughter-in-law's plate. She always cooked more than she needed, knowing that somebody would want to eat.

Once Malik walked off the porch, he saw Camy taking her trash out. "See, that's why you need my number. You could have called me to take that trash out for you." He yelled.

"Thanks, but I got it," Camy replied, blushing.

Malik watched as she went back into the house. He didn't care about the games that she was playing. He could tell by her smile that she wanted him.

Camy woke up early, getting ready to hit the gym up. With moving and trying to unpack, she had been eating a lot of bullshit and neglecting her workout schedule. As she climbed in her car, she could see that someone had pulled her trash can out to the front. She didn't think too much of it as she drove off.

Early morning traffic had her pulling up half an hour later. She shook her head, remembering when the gym was a ten-minute drive from her old place.

Camy turned on her AirPods then got on the treadmill. The treadmill had always been her favorite, and the way she was stacked up, it did her body good.

"Excuse me."

Camy's music had taken her to another world, preventing her from hearing Malik trying to get her attention. It wasn't until he tapped her that she stopped the machine to see who was tapping her.

"What?" she snapped before turning around and taking her AirPods out.

"My bad. I didn't mean to bother you."

Camy calmed down, seeing that it was the guy from her block. "I didn't mean to snap like that. It's just that guys be mad weird, seeing a woman work out. It's like they think that means she's single and looking."

Malik chuckled. "I understand, but it's cool. Anyways, my name is Malik. What's yours?"

"Camy."

Malik reached out to shake her hand. "Nice to meet you, neighbor."

Camy tried not to blush, but his sexiness made it hard. Not only was he good looking, but he also had the prettiest smile, showing off his perfect white teeth. "It's nice to meet you too."

Malik wanted to hang around, but not wanting to look desperate, he excused himself. "I'm gonna let you get back to work, but I might see you later on the block."

Camy smiled as he finally let her hand go. "All right."

Malik walked away feeling good, knowing that he was right about her wanting him. Her smile told on her.

Camy continued her workout but couldn't stop herself from thinking about Malik. She had to admit that he was the shit, and watching him work out turned her on. After seeing him with his shirt off, she secretly wanted to rub on his sweaty chest. Feeling foolish, thinking so hard about a dude that she had just met, made her leave the gym earlier than she had planned. She wasn't ready to jump out of one toxic relationship to start up anything new.

After a long, hot shower, Camy sat on the couch, waiting for her bestie, Mona, to pull up. She had been in her new house for a few days now and hadn't had company yet. A good laugh and wine were needed.

Mona knocked on the screen door.

"Hey, boo," Camy said, opening up the door for her bestie.

The girls took a seat on the couch.

"What's good, bitch? How have you been?"

"Oh, my gawd, Mona, this move has me tired as hell, but I'm so happy to be on my own."

Mona laughed. "You ain't let Jason come over and break in the new house yet?"

Camy was irritated by her question. Mona knew that she wasn't fucking with that dude anymore after the way he played with her heart. "Fuck Jason! The whole purpose of moving out of his house was to get away from him. He had me all the way fucked up, cheating on me then constantly lying. I checked him plenty of times, and he wanted to keep lying and playing in my face. I couldn't stay with him any longer. I needed my own space to get my life back in order."

Mona rolled her eyes. "So, you telling me that Jason can't come give you some act-right?"

"You must have been sipping before you pulled up because you acting like you don't understand. I'm done with that boy. Truth be told, he doesn't even know where I moved and will never have the chance of pulling up."

Mona laughed. "Damn, bitch, you really ghosted him like that?"

"Yes, love don't live here anymore. Now, can we drink this wine and talk about happy shit?"

Mona didn't respond, although she had a bunch of shit to say about her friend and Jason's relationship.

"So, has your dad been by?"

"Not yet, but he sent me some money to make sure I was good. Him and his wife are out of town, so I won't see him for a while."

Mona heard men talking, then got up to look out the door. "Damn, bitch, why you ain't tell me it's some fine-ass niggas living across the street? I see why you ain't tell Jason where you live."

Giggling, Camy walked over to the door to see who she was talking about. "You see ole boy right there in the red shirt?"

"Yeah. What about his sexy ass?" Mona asked.

"He seems cool. I mean, we only talked for a minute at the gym, but he was all right."

Mona took a mental note of what Camy was saying before making an excuse to leave. "Damn, bitch, I forgot I had to go by my mom's today. Let me get out of here."

"Really? I be so lonely here by myself. I thought we were gonna have a girls' day today."

Mona grabbed her purse. "Maybe next time. Besides, you wouldn't be lonely if you wouldn't be playing with Jason like that. You know that man still loves you."

"How you my friend and vouching so hard for that nigga? I'm not fucking with no man that's gonna cheat the whole relationship. I don't care how much a ring costed. I'm not that lonely."

"Damn, I was just playing, but I get it. You and Jason are over for good."

"Hell yeah, and I stand on that!" Camy yelled as Mona walked out to the car.

As Camy watched Mona drive off, she could feel someone watching her. She looked over to see Malik sitting on the porch with another guy. He was staring at her with a slight grin on his face. Being friendly, she smiled back before going back into the house.

"Damn, nephew, that's you?" Davon asked.

"She bad, ain't she, Unc?"

"Hell yeah, and her friend that just left bad as hell too. How you pull that?"

Davon was only a few years older than his nephews, but they all were tight and could talk about anything. Davon was born a little slower than some, but Malik and Rell still treated him normally and would hurt anyone who played behind him.

Malik had no problem telling his uncle the truth. "She ain't mine yet. I want her, though. To be honest, I'm working on it. Just give me a minute."

Davon asked what anyone hearing that conversation would have asked. "What about Shay? Ain't y'all still together?"

Malik shook his head. "Shay is not my fucking woman. I keep telling muthafuckas that. I'm a grown, single man and can do what I want."

Davon laughed. "Shay gonna come around here and fuck you up, nephew. You better be careful 'cause baby girl over there too close to home."

Malik was tired of muthafuckas assuming Shay was his girl just because they had been fucking for some time now. She knew how he got down and how to play her role, no matter if another chick was in the picture or not. Malik wasn't worried about shit, and that was what his people needed to understand.

Malik paid him no mind as he got up from the porch to move Camy's garbage can to the back of her house.

Hearing her doorbell ring, Camy got up from the couch. She was surprised to see Malik standing on her porch.

"Hey, what's up?"

"Hey, the garbage trucks come on Friday mornings over here."

"So, you're the one who took my can out to the front?"

"Yeah, I take my mom's out, so I grabbed yours too."

Camy smiled. "Thanks. That was very nice of you."

Malik stood there, wondering what he could say next that didn't make him seem desperate or like a corny-ass nigga.

After a few seconds of just standing there in silence, Camy assumed that he was looking for some type of payment or something. "So, how much do I owe you?"

Malik snapped out of his zone. "What?"

"Did you want me to pay you for taking the trash can out?"

"Hell nah. I just wanted you to know what day the truck came out." Feeling embarrassed, Malik walked away. Malik could tell that Camy wasn't like the easy chicks that he pulled in the hood. From the looks of things, she had her shit together and wasn't impressed by what a nigga had.

Camy had seen him driving around in two different rides, wearing nothing but designer, with a nice chain and watch, and she still didn't give a fuck. Even after he took her trash out, she treated him like he was a bum-ass nigga looking for change. Malik knew he would have to go harder to get her attention.

Chapter 2

"So, what was your girl talking about?"

Mona moved over so that Jason could walk through the door.

"She on her strong-woman shit. She says she is done for real this time."

Jason shook his head. "That bitch trippin'. I gave her everything she wanted and needed. I spent bands on that engagement ring, too."

Mona was tired of his whining. She didn't see why he was tripping over a bitch that clearly didn't want him when she had been wanting him from day one. How could he not see that she was in love with him?

"She doesn't want to be with a cheater, but who does? You gotta take that L and move on. I'm pretty sure you'll find someone else that would appreciate you."

Jason buried his head in his hands. "That's the thing. I wasn't even cheating on her ass this time. I really loved her, and that ring was to show her that."

While he covered his face, Mona smirked. Camy had him all fucked up behind their breakup, and for the most part, it was all for no reason. Knowing that Jason had a problem in the past with keeping his dick in his pants only made the setup even easier for Mona. She had a ball, leaving panties and earrings around Jason's house so that Camy could find them. In her eyes, Jason was too good for Camy's spoiled ass. Camy had a dad who spoiled her. She didn't need a man who did just the same.

Mona moved over to the couch where Jason was sitting. "It's gonna be all right, Jason. You'll find the right one soon," she repeated, rubbing his thigh.

"She was the right one for me, and I want her back. She moved and changed her number on me. I didn't deserve all that."

Mona tried not to snap and go off. She couldn't take him crying over a funky bitch like Camy. "Look, I gotta go check on my mama. I'll hit you up later."

They walked outside together. Jason called out to her as she walked to her car. "Aye, Mona, if you talk to my baby, please let her know that I'm sorry and I love her."

Mona rolled her eyes. "Yeah, I got you."

"Thanks, Mona. You're a real one."

Before leaving, Mona could hear him mumble some bullshit about missing his baby.

Mona drove off with her attitude on ten. Her harsh reality was that no matter what she did to try to get Jason, he still had his head stuck up Camy's ass.

The next morning, Camy got up early to go to the gym. She was actually hoping that she would run into Malik again. After thinking about what had happened the day before, she felt bad and hoped that she didn't offend him in any type of way.

Camy was doing warmups when Malik walked in. She smiled, seeing him walk her way, but that didn't last too long. Malik walked right past Camy, not acknowledging her presence.

"Damn? Really?" Camy mumbled, assuming that she had offended him the other day and he was pissed at her.

Malik didn't know how he really felt about Camy. Up until yesterday afternoon, he was feeling her, but when she called herself being funny, acting like he was a begging-ass bum, he wasn't sure. One thing he did know was that he wasn't into chasing behind nobody, including her fine ass.

Camy tried to get into her workout, but she couldn't stop looking around, trying to see if Malik would come talk to her. "Girl, stop tripping. You don't even know this nigga like that," she whispered to herself.

As time passed, Malik did manage to be in the same area as her. Camy caught him staring at her as she stared at him.

"You're staring but not gonna speak today?" she boldly called him out.

Malik walked closer toward her. "I didn't want you to think I was looking for some punk-ass change just to speak to you."

Camy tried not to, but she giggled in his face. "I'm sorry. I wasn't trying to offend you or be rude. You were just standing there, not saying anything, and that was the first thing that came to mind. I do apologize, Malik. I'm not trying to have any enemies."

Malik finally gave her a smile, showing off his beautiful teeth. "Maybe I was staring, admiring how beautiful you are. And just to let you know, I'm not trying to have you as an enemy either."

Camy held her hand out so that Malik could shake her hand, ending all beef. Malik, being him, took her hand and pulled her in for a hug.

"We good, Camy."

Even after a good workout, Malik still looked and smelled good. He made it hard to want to be anywhere else but in his arms. Camy liked having his hands around her, so she took her time stepping out of his grip.

"What you doing once you leave here?" he asked.

"The usual—going home, taking a shower, then relaxing. Why?"

Honestly, Camy lost him when she said shower. Now, all he could do was picture her in the shower with him. "You should let me take you out."

"I should?"

"Yeah, I think if we're going to be friends, then we should go out and have some fun."

Camy hesitated to respond, causing him to regret asking.

"My bad if I'm out of line for asking. I should have known that someone as beautiful as you had a man. My bad, shawty."

Malik turned to walk away, but Camy stopped him. "Malik, wait!"

"What's up?"

"I don't have a man, but I did recently just get out of a very toxic relationship. It ended badly, and I guess I have my guard up to protect me."

Malik couldn't help but wonder what dummy let her go. Then, he thought back to something he saw on social media. They said that if a woman looked good as hell and was single, then she just might be crazy. Something in Malik wanted to see if that was a fact.

"I can understand that, but I'm not asking for your hand in marriage. We friends, right? Can't friends go out to eat or something?"

Camy gave him a smile. "You're right. Friends can go out and have a meal together."

Malik was happy that she saw things his way and didn't try to be difficult. She quickly snatched his phone out of his hand to place her number in it. After getting his phone back, he called her so that she would have his number as well.

"Make sure you lock me in. Don't have me call you later and you answer talking about, 'who this?'"

Camy started laughing. "I am."

They separated, Malik going to get freshened up at home, and Camy going back to her place.

As soon as Camy stepped out of the shower, Mona was calling her phone.

"What's up, girl?"

"Nothing much. Just left the gym."

Mona rolled her eyes. Everything that Camy did irritated her soul. Camy already had a nice shape and didn't need to work out for it, in Mona's eyes. She hated a bitch that lived to show out.

"Do you want me to stop by? I got a bottle."

Camy smiled. "Actually, I have a date with a friend. Maybe next time."

"A friend! Damn, so you really said fuck Jason, huh?"

Camy started getting irritated. "Please stop bringing him up. I didn't say fuck him, but I am living my life. Look, I gotta go get ready. I'll call you back later." Before Mona could respond, Camy hung up.

Mona smiled, thinking that it was a good thing she was trying to move on. Maybe if Jason knew she had a new man in her life, he would forget about Camy and let her slide right in. She had only been bringing him up so that once she got Jason to herself, Camy couldn't even get mad because she asked her multiple times if she was sure they were done.

Malik pulled up in front of his mama's house. She was on the porch with Rell.

"What up, bro?"

"What's up? What you doing over here?"

Ms. Patt cut into their conversation. "You don't see me sitting here too, Malik?"

"Hey, Ma. My bad."

Rell laughed. "Anyways, what you up to, bro?"

Malik had a sneaky smirk on his face. "About to take this bad chick out."

"Who? Shay?" Ms. Patt asked, butting in their conversation again.

"Nah, her name is Camy."

Rell gave him a strange look. "Damn, bro, you pulled that already?"

"Hell yeah!"

"My nigga," Rell said, feeling like a proud father as he and Malik gave each other dap.

"What about Shay? Did y'all break up?"

"Ma, I'm ignoring you on purpose. Why I gotta keep telling you that Shay ain't my girlfriend? I'm starting to think you be doing that shit on purpose."

Ms. Patt sat up in her chair. "You gonna get enough of playing with people's hearts. These girls are humans, not toys that you can play with then put them on the shelves when you're done."

"Man, Ma, here you go again, always talking. I'm not in a relationship with anybody. I'm single and having fun out here. That's it."

"Is that what you call it? I know for a fact Shay loves you. Why else would she put up with your bullshit and dealings with other females in her face?"

"She stupid. That's why!" Rell blurted out.

"She not stupid, bro. She loves me 'cause I treat her right, but at the end of the day, we friends, just like any other female I be around."

Ms. Patt shook her head. "You gotta want more to life than friends that you fucking on."

Rell couldn't help but laugh. Their mama was always going off on them, and the shit was funny as fuck to him.

"Hold up," Malik ordered, answering his phone.

Ms. Patt and Rell listened to his conversation, trying to see who he was talking to.

"All right, I'll drive," he said before hanging up. "Y'all can finish this conversation without me. I gotta go."

Ms. Patt watched as Malik walked across the street and met up with her new neighbor. She shook her head, knowing that she was just another girl on Malik's hit list. She just prayed that the young girl could handle the bullshit and heartache that came with dealing with her son.

She talked a lot of shit about his love life, but she had to admit that Malik was letting them know up front that he wasn't trying to cuff them and not to get in their feelings. It was all up to the woman if she wanted to still mess with him. Like Shay. She stood by his side for years. When he decided to mess with other girls, she sat back and waited for him to return to her. Shay was determined to be his woman one day.

"You look good."

Camy blushed. "Thank you, Malik."

Being a gentleman, Malik opened the car door then helped her into his car.

As he drove off and made it to the corner, Shay was turning the block. She stopped the car to stare at Camy and Malik before speeding off.

"What's her problem? That's your woman or something?"

"Hell nah. I don't have a woman. Don't you think if I did, I wouldn't have asked you out?"

"Yeah, my bad," Camy said, feeling foolish.

At the restaurant, Camy and Malik sat at the table, engaged in conversations as they waited for their food.

"So, what do you do besides workout and keeping that body tight?"

"Before moving, I was working in a hair salon," Camy answered.

"Was? What happened to that?" he questioned.

Camy sipped on her drink. "Long, boring story that's gonna lead to other stories."

Malik sipped on his drink. "I got time today. Besides, I'm trying to get to know you better."

Camy paused, debating if she really wanted to go there with him. Although he was fine as hell, she worried that maybe it was too early to be dumping all her business on him.

He reached over the table to hold her hand, and she decided to open up.

"I told you that I had just got out of a bad relationship, right?"

"Yeah."

"Well, after telling him that I was done for real, I sort of ghosted him."

Malik chuckled. "What? You ain't do a nigga like that for real, did you? You out cold with your shit."

"I moved, changed my number, and quit my job. I was tired of giving him chances, and cutting all ties was the only way I could get rid of him. I refuse to allow him any more chances to hurt me again, and I never wanna feel the way he made me feel again."

"And how was that?" Malik asked.

"Alone and worthless," Camy said sadly.

Just as Malik was about to respond, the waitress came over with their food.

Camy smiled. "Damn, everything looks so good."

"Yeah, this is my little spot, so don't be bringing nobody else here either."

Camy giggled. "All right, but if I fall in love with this spot, you gotta bring me here again."

"I got you," he said, stuffing some fries in his mouth.

As the two ate, they continued to talk as if they had known each other for years. The connection was real, and they were both feeling it.

"Now, what did you say was wrong with your car? Why wouldn't it start?"

Camy shrugged her shoulders. "I don't know shit about cars but to drive them and to keep gas in them," she said, laughing.

"I'll stop by in the morning and look at it for you. It might not even be that serious."

"All right, thank you, Malik. I really appreciate your help."

As Camy ate her food, she danced around in her seat. Now, Malik wasn't the dancing type, but this was an opportunity that he couldn't pass up. "You wanna dance, or you good in the chair?"

Camy giggled. "We could hit the floor if that's all right with you."

Malik hesitated at first. Most chicks would have bitched up and stayed in their seat. Camy was more daring, and he liked the fact that she wasn't shy. Malik took her by the hand then led her to the dance floor. As soon as she turned around to dance on him, the DJ switched the music to a slow jam.

Camy smiled as she felt his arms wrap around her waist. As their bodies connected, Malik couldn't control how he was feeling. He slowly placed small, soft kisses on her neck as she grinded her body on his. A mixture of Malik's hands roaming all over her body and his kisses made Camy let out a soft moan. Realizing what was going on, Camy pulled away then tried to walk off, back to the table. It all felt good, but he wasn't about to get it that easy.

Malik thought he had her up until that moment. "Camy!" He called out, grabbing her hand.

"What?"

"What's wrong, baby? Don't be like that. We having a good time, right?"

Truth be told, Malik scared her. She couldn't understand how and why her body craved him so badly when they had just met.

Malik held her in his arms. "I'm not trying to hurt you like the last nigga. I wanna be your friend, Camy."

"I don't feel like myself when I'm around you, and it scares me," she admitted.

Malik didn't understand what she meant by that, but at this point, he was hugging her and praying that she didn't want their date to end so soon. "Don't be like that, baby. When you with me, you don't have nothing to be scared of." Malik lifted her head up so that he could look into her eyes. He then gave her a kiss on her forehead. "You gonna be all right. I got you."

Camy was speechless. Things were moving fast, but it all felt so right.

They went back to their table after that talk.

"You want another drink or something?"

"Nah, I think I've had enough. I'm actually ready to go," Camy responded.

"Okay, cool. I'll get the check, so we can get out of here. I can tell that you're ready to go." Malik didn't want their date to be over, but he didn't want her to feel like he was trying to pressure her into anything.

Malik looked down at his phone again.

"Somebody must be missing you," Camy said.

Malik chuckled. "Nah, not really. Why you say that?"

"I didn't want to bring it up, but you've been getting text messages since we got here."

Malik shook his head. "It ain't shit important. Trust me. Besides, ain't shit I'd rather be doing right now than chilling with you."

Camy couldn't help but to blush. Jason, being a cheater and all, had fucked up Camy's self-esteem, and even after being told that she was beautiful every day, having a man that constantly cheated made her look at herself much differently.

"Don't embarrass me like that," Malik warned, seeing Camy pull out money as the waitress placed the bill on the table.

Camy looked at him, confused. "Huh?"

"Why would I invite you out, just to have you pay for it? Don't let me find out you were dealing with a goofy."

"I'm sorry."

"You ain't gotta be sorry. Just do better." Malik set the bill money on the table, plus a nice tip, before taking her by the hand and walking her out.

Truth be told, Jason never let her pay for shit, but he was her man. Malik was a friend, and she thought that the rules changed.

"You ready to call it a night, or you wanna do something else?" he asked.

Camy was enjoying her time with Malik but decided to call it a night. As far as she could tell, he was perfect for her, but she knew that giving it up on their first date wasn't a good look, and she couldn't go out like that.

"All right, cool. I just gotta make one stop before dropping you off at home."

Malik drove to the gas station to grab some blunts. He wasn't planning on coming back out after he got home.

"Why you so quiet? I thought you enjoyed yourself," he asked as he got back in the car.

"I did have a nice time. The place was nice and drama free, plus the food was great. I also got a chance to chill with a good guy."

Malik smirked. "I guess I did my job?"

"Yes, you did. I hadn't been out in a while, and you made me feel comfortable. We gotta do this again one day."

"Bet. Just be ready when you get that call."

Malik pulled up to Camy's house ten minutes later, but she didn't rush to get out of the car, and he didn't rush her out either. Honestly, they enjoyed chilling with one another.

"Aye, you smoke?" he asked.

"Yeah, a little."

Malik laughed. "You silly as hell. What the hell is a little? Either you do or don't."

Camy giggled. "I guess I do then."

She watched as he pulled out a bag of weed before passing it to her. Camy opened the bag then smelled it.

"Damn, that shit strong as hell. What's that?"

Malik laughed. "That's that cookie dough. I guess you fucking with it?" Not waiting for her answer, Malik pulled out one of the blunts he had just bought from the gas station. Camy watched patiently as he rolled the blunt. Malik hit the blunt a few times before passing it over to Camy. Camy then pulled on the blunt a little too hard and instantly started choking.

"Damn, baby, you gotta hit this shit lightly. You so used to smoking that garbage that you can't handle this hood shit."

Camy playfully hit his arm. "Boy, shut up! But this shit is good."

"I'm glad you like it. Now you know who to go to when you need some more. I don't want you out here copping this shit from them other niggas. Your ass gonna fuck around with some bullshit."

Camy started to laugh. "Man, don't talk to me like I'm a junky and you just supplied me with the best fix of my life."

Malik shook his head while laughing. "Damn, girl, you silly as hell. But for real. I want you to call me, and not just for weed."

"Okay, I got you."

The chemistry was there between them, but both were scared to make the first move, so they kept the conversation on a friendly level.

"Okay, I had a great time today, and I wouldn't mind doing this again," she said.

Malik leaned over, placing a kiss on her lips. "I'm gonna let you get some rest, but I'll see you in the morning to look at your car."

Camy found herself blushing again. Malik had that type of effect on her, and she couldn't help herself. "Thanks again, Malik."

"No problem," Malik said as she jumped out of the car.

He sat there for a minute, watching her get into the house safely. After spending time with Camy, Malik knew that he had to have her. His dick had to have been thinking the same thing because he was ready for her too. Knowing that Camy wasn't about to give him shit that night, Malik drove around the corner to Shay's house.

Hearing her doorbell, Shay climbed out of the bed to see who was interrupting her sleep, but deep down inside, she knew only Malik pulled up to her house unannounced.

"Who is it?" she asked when she got to the door.

"It's me. Open the door."

Shay thought back to how he was just with a bitch earlier that day, then hesitated. "What you want, Malik?" she asked to be petty.

"Man, open the fucking door, Shay!" he demanded.

Shay opened the hard door but left her screen door locked. "I got company. You can't be here."

Malik pulled the door handle, trying to force the door open. "Stop fucking playing with me."

Shay stood there for a few seconds before finally letting him in. "What you want? And make it quick. I got shit to do."

Malik kicked his shoes off. "Stop fucking playing with me, girl."

Shay giggled at him. "I said I got company."

"You know if I feel like you got too many bodies, I can't fuck with you anymore, right? I think you better stop playing with me."

Shay watched as he started putting his shoes back on, and she didn't want him to leave. "Damn, I was just playing, boy. But why the fuck you over here and not with that bitch you were riding around with?"

Malik wasn't about to talk to Shay about Camy, so he kept shit simple. "You want this dick or what?"

Shay was like putty in his hands. As she followed him back to her bedroom, she snatched off her T-shirt. Sometimes, she hated how weak she was for him.

Although he was right around the corner from Camy's house, spending the night over at a chick's house was always a major no-no. Shit like that was breaking all his rules in living a peaceful life.

Malik woke up early to go check out Camy's car. It was no big deal because he got up early every day to hit the gym and the streets. After making a few quick runs, Malik made it to his mom's house.

"Good morning, Ma."

"Good morning. What you doing over here so early? Why you not at the gym?" she questioned, seeing that he wasn't following his daily routine.

"I gotta handle something else."

"How was your date with that girl across the street?"

Malik shook his head, knowing she was about to try to get into his business. "It was all right."

Ms. Patt sat up in her recliner chair. "Shay came around here, snooping around. She said she saw you riding around with some random bitch. She ain't called you and went off yet?"

"Ma, stop entertaining that Shay bullshit. She know what's up."

Malik was too irritated to stick around and have the same conversation they'd been having since he started showing Camy any attention. So, instead of standing around, he walked out of the house to look at Camy's car.

Hearing someone at her door, Camy rushed to the door, thinking that maybe it was Mona, since she was really the only person who knew where she lived.

"Good morning."

With the door halfway open, Camy blushed. "Good morning. What are you doing here so early?"

"I told you I was gonna stop by and look at your car. I need your keys to see what's going on."

Camy tried not to smile too hard, but Malik was doing everything right. "I didn't think that you were serious, but hold on."

Malik watched as she disappeared into the back. As much as he liked to see her beautiful face, watching her ass walk away was just as nice.

Camy came back with her keys in her hands. "Thanks so much. I just hope that you can figure out what's wrong with it."

"My pops and uncle are mechanics, so if I can't, one of them can."

Not wanting to overstay his welcome, Malik walked out, ready to get to work. Camy watched him out the window for a minute. She couldn't help but like him. Not only was he sexy as fuck, but he was also nice and didn't seem like the type to do shit thinking pussy was an award.

Malik played around with her car, trying to figure out why the hell her shit wasn't starting. "Damn," he mumbled, finally putting shit together.

Without saying anything to Camy, Malik jumped into his truck to get what she needed. He shook his head, thinking about how women would drive the hell out of a car and not worry about what was going on under the hood. Malik had no problem buying a new battery for Camy's car. The way he saw it, he was putting in an investment. She was going to be his soon.

Malik replaced her battery and got the car running with no problem. Camy peeked out the door just in time to see Malik walking on the porch.

"It's all good to go," he said.

This time, Camy pushed the door open instead of talking through the door. "Oh my gawd, thank you so much. What was wrong with it?"

"You just needed a new battery, some simple shit."

Camy gave him a look that got Malik's attention.

"What's that look for?"

"I was about to ask you something, but I don't wanna offend you again."

Malik chuckled. "What is it this time? Don't ever be scared to talk to me."

"I was gonna ask you how much I owe you for the battery and your service."

Malik laughed, thinking about how he reacted last time. "Girl, you gonna kill me with that shit. It's some niggas out here just be looking out. Besides, if I told you I was gonna do something, then you got my word."

Camy was embarrassed, and it showed all over her face.

"I see you were about to eat. Fix me a plate and call it even."

Camy giggled. "All right, bet. The bathroom that way. Go wash your hands, and I'll make your plate."

Malik went to wash his hands, then sat at the dining room table. He hadn't had a chick cook for him in a minute and wanted to see what skills she had. Dealing with Shay's ass, he either had to take her out or eat tacos, since that was all that she cooked.

Camy walked into the room with a plate of bacon, eggs, grits, and a bagel.

"Damn, this shit looks good."

"Thank you. Now, go ahead and taste it. It's good."

Malik couldn't help but smirk. His mind stayed in the gutter. He was ready to taste her sexy, thick ass.

Camy was just about to eat when she got back up.

"You good?"

"I forgot something," she said, going back into the kitchen. When she came back, she was holding two bowls that held a variety of fruits. "Can't forget the fruit."

As Malik ate, he watched her eat. He didn't pay too much attention to it the night before, but her little ass could eat. He couldn't believe that she was actually smashing in front of him the way she was. Most chicks played around with their food and played shy in front of a nigga, but not her.

"Damn, you can eat."

Camy burst out laughing. "I tell people all the time that I am supposed to be a fat girl for real. That's why I keep my ass in the gym. I feel like if I miss too many days, the real me would show."

They were both laughing at her now. Malik liked her personality. She was cool.

"I hope I'm not doing too much, but I think you got the perfect shape. You be doing your thing in the gym."

Malik had Camy blushing again. "Thank you, Malik."

After finishing his breakfast, Malik did everything but lick his plate clean. Camy was really good at cooking, and he couldn't deny that.

"I don't drink anything but water and Gatorade. so sorry I don't have any juice, but you can pick from what I have," Camy said.

Malik's dirty mind went far away from the conversation. He laughed to himself before giving her an answer. "I'll take a water. I'm not a big fan of all that sugary shit anyways."

Camy went into the kitchen to get him a bottle of water out of the fridge. Something in her hated that breakfast was over, knowing that he would be leaving her soon. After getting to know him a little better, she couldn't help but enjoy his company. Dealing with one person her whole life, she was starting to believe the old saying that a fresh, new start might be a challenge, but it was good for the soul.

"What you about to get into?" she asked when she brought him his water.

"I gotta turn some corners and see what's up around the way."

Camy laughed. "What all that means?"

Malik didn't answer but couldn't help but laugh.

"Don't even worry about it. Just forget I asked."

"Thanks, 'cause I didn't feel like explaining that shit to you."

"So, what do you do?"

Malik usually didn't lie, but this time, he would have to pass on telling her the truth. "I help my pops and unc with their shop. You see I work on cars."

"Oh, okay," she simply said, knowing he was lying. She wasn't mad or anything. Truth be told, it really wasn't any of her business.

Without warning, Malik pulled Camy in close for a hug. "I'll hit you up later."

"Okay, cool."

With that being said, Malik walked out of the house with a smirk on his face, knowing that it was only a matter of time before he had her.

Chapter 3

Malik and Camy quickly got comfortable around each other and spent almost every day together, whether at the gym, going on dates, or chilling at her house watching TV. When Malik first met Camy, all he could think about was sliding into her, but now, although he would never admit it, he really enjoyed being around her. She didn't ask for much but his attention. Camy had become his peace while Shay became a problem. The more time he spent with Camy, the more Shay called, acting crazy and forgetting the role that she signed up for.

Rell tried to warn him about his feelings, but he wasn't trying to hear all of that. He stood his ground on them just being cool with one another and him being single forever.

"Bro, you sit up in her face whenever you ain't in the streets, and you trying to tell me that you not growing any type of feelings for that girl? You gotta be, nigga, 'cause ain't no way you be sitting over there all day, and y'all not fucking yet."

Malik passed him the blunt. "She cool and easy to talk to."

Rell shook his head. "You lying like a muthafucka, bro. It's okay to settle down, my nigga. Look at me."

Malik looked at Rell and laughed. "See, bro, Tiffany got your ass on lock with all them babies. That will never be me."

"Shut your bitch ass up, nigga. I love my bitch."

The brothers continued to smoke and talk shit to one another like always in their mama's driveway. For some reason, they had always said they couldn't wait to move, but as soon as they moved away, they always wanted to chill at her crib.

"Aye, bro, who is dude walking on her porch?"

Malik damn near jumped out of the car to see what was going on.

"Chill, nigga!" Rell said, getting out of the car right behind him.

If anything was to jump off, he was ready to have his brother's back, right or wrong.

"Who the fuck is that?" Malik questioned.

Rell chucked. "But that ain't your girl?"

"Shut the fuck up, bro!"

Malik watched as Camy let the guy in. Not thinking clearly, he grabbed his gun from the car and then headed across the street.

"Chill, bro. Don't go over there on no bullshit," Rell warned him.

Malik continued to walk. Just as he hit the steps, Camy was letting the guy out.

"I'll be right back with the right piece," the guy said. He walked down the steps but stopped to say, "Excuse me," as he walked past Malik.

Malik mugged him before stepping to the side. Tony didn't respond, seeing Rell standing across the street. He knew they were looking for trouble.

"What's up?" Malik said, going up the steps.

Camy smiled. "Hey, Malik, what's wrong? What's up with the stone face?"

Malik walked into the house, looking around, trying to see if there were any signs of Camy doing something with the guy. He didn't care if they were only alone for a few minutes. He had to make sure.

"What you was doing?" he asked.

"I was doing laundry, but my damn dryer acting crazy. I had to call the landlord ass."

Malik shook his head. "That wasn't the landlord. Who was that nigga?" he asked, trying not to sound too bothered by the nigga.

Camy could tell that his tone was different from what she was used to, but to keep the peace, she kept it real with him. "That's his nephew. Calm down."

"Why you ain't ask me to look at it?"

"Because, Malik, that's their job, not yours."

It wasn't until Malik pulled Camy closer and shared a passionate kiss that he realized that being around her was changing him. He and Shay weren't even kissing like that, just pecks from time to time. He was confused. He liked Camy a lot but wasn't the type to cuff. But at the same time, he didn't want anyone else to cuff her either.

Instead of chilling with Rell like he had planned, Malik decided to chill with Camy. Even when the landlord's nephew, Tony, came back, he made it his business to mean mug the guy again and to pay Camy extra attention just in case the nigga thought he had a chance with her.

"Malik, wait a minute. He's coming back upstairs." Camy announced, pushing him off her. The two had locked lips and hadn't been able to pull away from each other until then. "Damn," Malik mumbled as she stood up from the couch.

He couldn't believe how he was acting with her. He couldn't help but think about what she said the night they went out for the first time. She mentioned how it scared her when she was with him. She also said that she didn't feel like herself when he was around, and now, he was feeling the same way. He peeped the change in him, and it scared him.

Camy thanked Tony for fixing her dryer and sent him on his way. She wanted to get back to entertaining Malik, and the way he kissed and rubbed her body made her want him even more.

Just as Camy shut the door, she felt Malik wrap his arms around her. Camy loved being held in his arms and didn't see the toxic shit unfolding in front of her eyes.

"Don't be mad, but I gotta go."

Camy turned around with an attitude. "What? Why?"

"I gotta go handle something right quick."

Malik didn't bother to get deeper into the conversation. Instead, he walked right out the door.

Camy stood there, feeling foolish. Sometimes, it seemed like he had an on-and-off switch when it came to her.

Malik jumped straight in his truck to go home. After a cold shower, he lay across the couch, thinking about everything that had been going on the past few months. Hearing his phone ring, Malik sat up to grab his phone.

"Yeah, what's up?"

"Don't think I'm stupid, nigga. I see that new bitch got you forgetting all about me," Shay yelled into the phone.

"Fuck you talking about?" Malik responded, getting irritated.

"I be seeing your car parked around there at the bitch house, but you ain't been pulling up on me. What's the deal, Malik?"

Malik shook his head. "Look, don't call my phone with all that shit. I'm single and got the right to do whatever the fuck I wanna do. Now, stop worrying about what I be doing and get the fuck off my line." Malik hung up before she could respond.

"Stupid-ass bitch." He mumbled under his breath before lying back down.

***

Shay was pissed off at Malik. She had let him get away with what she called cheating multiple times, but he had never just downright disrespected her by not showing her any attention. After giving it some thought, she came to the conclusion that he might have real feelings for the little bitch, and she wasn't having it. Shay wished she knew where he lived so that she could pull up, but since she didn't, she did the only thing she could. Jumping in her car, she rolled right around the corner to talk to Ms. Patt.

Since the front door was already open, Shay walked right in.

"Hey, Ma, what you doing?"

"Nothing much. Just sitting here, watching TV. What's wrong with you, girl? Why the hell you storming in like a bat out of hell?"

Shay got comfortable on the couch. "Ma, that damn Malik really been on some bullshit. He ain't been the same since that bitch moved in across the street."

Ms. Patt hated to laugh at another woman's pain, but Malik and Shay's relationship had been a joke from the start. "Girl. don't come around here with that bullshit. You know how he is, so this is nothing new. Whenever that boy sees something he likes, he go get it. End of story."

"Really, Ma? This is different. He hasn't been stopping by or even calling me. I don't like that at all."

"He told you before that you had a choice to either roll with him or roll over for the next one."

"Wow," Shay mumbled.

"Shit, maybe she is the right one for him," Ms. Patt said, shrugging her shoulders.

Shay knew she was right and regretted bringing her ass around there with that mess. She hated that Ms. Patt was no longer on her side, but she had always told it how it was.

"Well, I gotta go. I'll talk to you tomorrow," Shay said, getting up and walking out the door.

Once in the car, she sat there for a minute, just staring at Camy's house. She wished that she would walk out, just so she could see what the new girl was working with and what had Malik's mind gone. Camy never came out, making Shay feel even more foolish, so she decided to just go back home.

Ms. Patt waited until Shay was long gone before calling her son.

"Yeah, Ma?"

"Boy, I don't know what's going on, but that crazy girl Shay came around here in her feelings."

"Ma, she gonna always be in her damn feelings, and that's why I told her not to grow any for me. I don't know why she gotta be hardheaded."

Ms. Patt shook her head. "I think you might need to talk to that girl 'cause she ain't too well in the head. I know you say you're single and can do whatever, but if you're gonna deal with Camy, you need to cut Shay off for good. Ain't no messing with both of them girls. They live too close, and I could see a bunch of bullshit popping off."

Malik chuckled. "Ma, thanks for being concerned, but I got this, and I'm not about to let Shay interrupt what I got going on. Besides, I talked to her earlier and told her ass that she could leave whenever she wanted to."

"Bye, boy," Ms. Patt said, before hanging up the phone. Hearing him talk about him and his women made her dizzy.

***

Being bored, Malik decided to go back out to talk to Shay. He had been pulling away from her because he wasn't feeling her vibe anymore. Truth be told, Camy held his attention for real. Malik knocked on Shay's door, hoping she wasn't about to be on no bullshit.

She opened the door then started going off. "Why do you just pop up over here? Do I just pop up at your shit, nigga?"

"Nah, but I don't let nobody know where I stay, so that's probably why your crazy ass hasn't yet."

Just his laughing irritated her even more.

"I don't see shit funny, Malik. I swear I fucking hate your Black ass," she yelled, pushing him out of the way and then storming off to her bedroom.

Malik followed behind her. As he got close enough, he snatched her then pushed her up against the wall. "Man, why the fuck you acting like that? See, this exactly why I ain't been fucking with you. Why the fuck you trying to switch the game up?"

Shay cried. "Get the hell out my face, Malik. I fucking hate you."

For a moment, Malik felt bad that she was letting her feelings get in the middle of what they had going on. He gave her a kiss on her forehead. "You hate me for real?"

"Yeah, I hate your Black ass. Don't you see what you're doing to me? I hate that you are even here right now."

Trying something different, Malik lifted Shay up on the wall before locking lips with her. Although he had only been doing that with Camy, he wanted to see if it would help their relationship or whatever it was they were doing. Malik pulled back but still carried her to the bed. He didn't like that kissing shit with her but was ready to fuck.

Shay loved the way he was kissing her, so when they went into the room, she was ready for him to stretch her out like always. As they fucked, Shay kept trying to get him to share another kiss with her again, but he wasn't having that. Instead of calling him out, she kept her mouth shut so that he wouldn't leave.

Once they were done, Malik got up to get dressed.

"Baby, can you spend the night with me?"

Malik chuckled. "See, you wanna say I'm acting different and shit, but you acting funny. You know I don't do that shit."

Once Malik left, Shay was back to feeling stupid. She thought telling him that she hated him would help convince her heart that she did, but after getting the best dick that she had ever had, she just couldn't hate him. She loved him even more.

Malik didn't plan on it, but he ended up sitting in front of his mom's house, just watching Camy's house. He wished he would have showered after sex with Shay so that he could go in, but since he didn't, he just sat outside. Up until he saw a car pull up in Camy's driveway, he was fine out there. He put in his mind that if it was a nigga, he was going to cut the fuck up. He then calmed down, seeing that it was just one of her female friends.

Shaking his head on how he was tripping, Malik drove off. He told himself that he was tired and just needed to rest. That had to be the problem.

Camy opened the door for Mona. "Hey, girl, what you doing here so late?"

Mona stepped in. "I was just riding around and decided to check on my best friend. What's been going on with you, girl?" Mona asked, flopping down on the couch.

Camy took a seat on the love seat. "Girl, you just don't know."

Mona was eager for her to fill her in on everything. "What, girl? Tell me."

"So, you know I've been talking to that guy, and I really like him but . . ."

Mona tried to hide her true feelings as she soaked up all the info for Jason. "But what, bitch?"

Camy smiled. "Girl, he is so damn fine, and we chill and talk as if we've known each other for years. He's so cool to be around, but . . ."

"But what? You know what? Forget all that. How is the dick?"

They both started to laugh.

"Come on now, girl. You know me better than that. I haven't given him any yet."

"What the hell are you waiting for? Christmas?" Mona asked with a serious face.

"Mona, you know Jason's the only nigga that I have ever slept with, and although I'm feeling Malik, I can't rush and sleep with him."

Mona shook her head. "Girl, fuck that nigga Jason. Mark your territory."

Camy was cracking up. "You are too much for me."

Mona sat up a little. "When you want a man to yourself, then you gotta be ready to do whatever to get and keep him."

Camy sat there, thinking about what her best friend was teaching her. She then thought about how he had left earlier. Maybe he knew that she wasn't giving anything up.

"So, you think I should just let him hit?"

"Hell yeah, girl!"

Not wanting to look weak in front of a friend, she decided to agree with Mona. "You're right. I'm gonna do it, girl."

The two friends continued to talk with a bottle of wine. After joking around for a little over an hour, Mona got up to leave. "I have to work the rest of the week, but when I stop by again, I better hear that you put it on that nigga."

Camy laughed. "You got it, girl."

Mona couldn't wait to see Jason the next day. She was going to break his heart by telling him that Camy had moved on, and then gladly be the one to pick up the pieces. She was going to get her man no matter what.

Chapter 4

Never wanting to complicate his life dealing with feelings, Malik had tried his best to avoid drama at any cost. Up until now, he had been lucky. Between Shay blowing his phone up, wanting to express her true, deep feelings for him every other hour, and then begging him to stop by, and him trying his best to avoid any contact with Camy, he was going crazy. Camy hadn't done shit to him, but he had been pushing her away, scared to hurt her. For the most part, Camy only left messages, asking if he was all right. She would also tell him that if he felt like it, he could call if he needed someone to talk to.

Since his brother had been MIA for a minute, Rell decided to pull up on his ass. Not only was he Malik's older brother, but Rell had also played the role of his best friend and therapist.

Rell pulled up in front of his house and was surprised to see Malik sitting on the porch. "Aye, bro, what's up?"

"Shit, nigga, what's up?" Malik asked, walking off the porch and to the car.

Rell watched as his brother jumped in. "Why your ass ain't been by Mama house lately?" Rell asked, rolling up a blunt for the two.

"Man, bro, my fucking mental been fucked up. I ain't even been to the gym in two weeks. You know when my soul doesn't feel right, my ass shuts down."

Rell passed him the blunt. "Damn, bro, what's going on? Talk to me, nigga."

"I don't know what to say. It just hit me that I'm really not feeling Shay no more, but I can't stop sliding to her crib. I know she's only good for a quick nut, and that's it. We don't have shit else to talk about."

Rell cut him off. "I've been telling your ass that you were feeling Camy. That's why it's over with Shay," he said, laughing.

"Nah, bro, I've been avoiding her ass too."

"Damn, what she do?"

"Nothing for real. I just hate how I get around her. I feel like I had to push her away so that I don't hurt her and have her all fucked up like Shay. She got a nigga wrapped around her finger. I can't even lie. I ain't even hit yet and be doing shit with her that I never done with Shay."

Rell kept laughing. "Bro, she might be the one."

"Whatever. You know a nigga like me ain't the one for just one chick."

"And that's what's wrong with your stubborn ass now. Your soul trying to tell you something, and you ain't listening."

As the brothers continued to talk, Shay started blowing his phone up, and each time, Malik sent her ass to voicemail.

"Aye, bro, I'm not even gonna lie. You need to figure out what you're gonna do. You can't just ignore both of them. You gotta pick. She knows Camy the one, just like everyone else knows. That's why she acting so pressed. She never acted like that with no other bitch. Think about it."

Malik wasn't trying to hear all that. He shook his head. "I'm good on all that. I ain't never have to pick before. Shay just need to get her shit together and get out her fucking feelings. The same way she sat back and chilled when I fucked with other chicks, she need to show Camy the same respect."

Rell couldn't believe how crazy his little brother's way of thinking was. Yeah, at first it didn't mean shit to him, but after all the time that had passed, Malik had to have seen that he was the problem.

"So, what Camy been up to?" Malik asked with a straight face.

Rell chuckled. "Bro, take your ass over there or call her ass."

Hearing his brother laugh didn't sit right with Malik. "So what? Somebody's been over there? Fuck you laughing for?"

Rell continued to laugh. "You know your ass crazy as fuck? What do you think gonna happen if you ghost a bitch? She's gonna replace your ass with the quickness."

"Stop fucking playing with me. bro. She had a nigga over there?"

Rell wanted to tell him yeah, just to get a good laugh, but then again, he didn't want to have him flipping out and shit for no reason. Malik was a hothead and would fuck around and kill the whole fucking block.

"Nah, nigga, when I be around at Mama's, she be up in the house and shit. I did catch her coming home from the gym one day. She was looking sad. You took that girl's smile away," Rell said, still playing around, teasing.

"Damn, man. I didn't want shit to be like that with her."

"I understand why you dodging Shay crazy ass, but why Camy? What she really do?" he asked again.

Malik paused for a second. "Nothing. We were just getting too close."

Rell shook his head, then snatched his blunt out of his brother's hand. "Yeah, it's time for you to get out of my ride cause yo' ass tripping for real."

Malik snatched the blunt back. "Bye, nigga. See your ass later," he said, jumping out of the car.

Malik went back on the porch to enjoy his peace. The weatherman had predicted a thunderstorm later that night, and the breeze felt too good to be cooped up in the house.

Talking to Rell had only left Malik more confused. Rell wanted him to open his mind to the fact that he was falling for Camy, but Malik didn't believe in that shit. He had lived his life loving the fact that he could fuck a chick without any attachment. Settling down with just one chick wasn't his thing.

Malik looked down at his phone, praying that it wasn't Shay again. He then smirked, seeing that it wasn't her but Camy. As bad as he wanted to hear her beautiful voice, his ego wouldn't let him answer her call. He needed to learn how to control himself around her.

He sat there, feeling crazy as hell and lost in his thoughts, as he let his phone ring for what seemed like a million times. One thing about being stuck in your ways was that when new people came into your life, they could have you acting bipolar as hell, just how he was now.

Malik went into the house to take a shower. "Fuck it. Let me go see what's going on with this girl."

When Malik finally got out of the shower, he saw that Camy had sent him a text. He hesitated to read it at first, knowing that she was about to go off on him like Shay had been doing.

After getting dressed, Malik picked up his keys then walked out the door. It wasn't until he got to his mom's house that he read her message.

Camy: Hey, haven't heard from you in a while. Was just checking on you. Call or text when you're up to it. Hope everything is all right with you.

Malik grinned. That message alone was one of the reasons that he liked her. Camy was a nigga's peace after a storm. She wasn't on all that bullshit like Shay was on.

Malik got out of his truck and then joined his uncle and mama on the porch.

"What's up, nephew?"

"What's up, Unc? How you been, Ma?"

Ms. Patt gave him a crazy look. "I hope you know that you gotta pay my phone bill this month."

"What?"

"I done talked to that girl, Shay, more than anyone. Why the hell is she calling me every day, asking about your Black ass? Why you ain't been calling her?"

Malik shook his head. "Ma, block her ass!"

"All right, but you're still paying my bill," Ms. Patt said, laughing.

Malik found himself looking over at Camy's house. He wondered where she had gone since her car wasn't outside.

"Aye, nephew, you got some of that good shit Rell had on you?" Davon asked.

"Nah, Unc, but I got some new shit, and it tastes better."

"Y'all know the deal. Get the hell off my porch with that shit. And Malik, y'all need to stop smoking with Davon. He slow enough."

"Damn, Ma, you acting like he ain't sitting right here. You don't see it's starting to rain? Don't you see that the storm is coming?"

Davon stood up, not giving her any mouth. "Come on. Let's get in the truck."

They jogged to the truck, trying to avoid getting too wet.

As they smoked, Davon checked in with his nephew. "You good, nephew? Your ass been too quiet for me. You ain't even been over for dinner."

"Unc, you ain't gotta worry about me. Honestly, I've been chilling, getting my mental right. You been all right? Ain't nobody been fucking with you, have they?"

"Only Patt mean ass. Are you sure you good?"

As they continued to talk, Camy's car pulled up. Malik stopped talking mid-conversation to watch her.

"She bad as hell, ain't she?"

"Hell yeah. That's why I pulled her ass already. I couldn't let nobody else get her," Malik warned.

Davon shook his head. "Oh, okay, nephew. I see you. That nigga Tim had tried to holler at her the other day at the store."

"I'll beat that nigga ass! Man, did she talk to him?" Malik asked curiously.

Davon laughed. "Hell nah. She told the nigga that she was good. He was embarrassed like a muthafucka and started talking shit about her not being all that."

"Damn, Unc, for real?"

"Yeah, then when she got in her car, he started talking shit about her not being able to take dick."

Malik didn't like that shit at all.

Davon kept talking. "That nigga was butt hurt behind that. I guess he thought that he could pull her because she was new to the neighborhood and didn't know how he is a bitch-ass nigga."

"Damn, for real, Unc? He said all that? I'm gonna stomp that nigga head in when I see him," Malik said, really paying Camy attention.

Davon didn't respond. He was high now and dozing off. He always tried to control his mouth, but truth be told, he talked too much.

"It's cool, Unc. You did good by telling. Ain't nobody gonna do shit to you no way. I'll kill them all behind you."

Davon smiled.

Malik watched as Camy hesitated to get out of the car. She had told him before that she hated the rain because it always fucked up her hair.

Camy was mad that she didn't make it home before the rain started, but the lines were crazy in the store.

"Fuck!" she yelled, popping the trunk open, then opening up her door. She grabbed a few bags and ran into the house.

Malik passed his uncle the blunt before stepping out of the car. "Here, Unc. You can have the rest. When you get done, make sure you go straight in the house."

Malik grabbed the rest of the bags from the trunk before shutting it. By the time Camy came out of the bathroom and made it to the front door to get the rest of her groceries, Malik was walking in with the bags in his hand.

"Thank you."

Malik went into the kitchen to set the bags down.

Camy stayed in the living room, wondering what to say to him. It had been two weeks since they talked, and she didn't know where to start.

Malik leaned against the wall, watching her. He couldn't lie. He missed her. Then, hearing that other niggas were paying her some attention now didn't sit right with him. He had already put a claim on her. "What's up with you, girl?"

Camy decided to be a smart ass. "Oh, now you can see me? I've been calling and texting your phone, and you've been ignoring me. I don't like to be ignored, Malik."

Malik could hear in her voice that she was really mad about his actions. He walked toward her. "Look, I'm sorry if I hurt you. I just needed a break from life."

Just that fast, Camy had forgotten about her own personal feelings. She walked closer toward Malik, grabbing his hand. "Are you all right? Do you need to talk?"

Malik gave her a peck on the forehead. "Yeah, I think I'm good."

Camy blushed. It was something about his forehead kisses that made her feel loved and weak in the knees.

Malik quickly changed the subject. "What you about to cook?"

"I was about to fry some chicken wings. Why? Are you staying for dinner?"

"Hell yeah. Don't you see how bad it's pouring down out there? I'm not about to play around in that storm."

Camy laughed. "Is that the only reason you are staying?"

Malik chuckled. "Nah, baby. I wanna spend some time with your sexy ass. Seeing your face today made me realize just how much I missed you."

Camy couldn't help but blush extra hard. "I missed you too, Malik."

This time, after kissing her forehead, he slowly placed kisses on her neck. Camy loved his hands rubbing on her body, so she didn't stop him when he grabbed a handful of her ass.

"Damn," Malik mumbled as he finally stepped back.

He could feel his dick getting hard, just off a kiss from her. Not wanting to scare her, he pulled back. Although he wanted her badly, he was trying to move at her pace.

"I'm about to put this food up, so I can start dinner. Why don't you find something good to watch?"

Malik was still staring at her.

"Malik, you heard me?"

Malik shook his head. "Yeah, my bad."

While Camy worked her way around the kitchen, Malik turned on the sports channel. He hadn't had the chance to sit in front of the television lately, and since he knew she was going to be a while in the kitchen, he took that opportunity to play catch-up.

Malik looked on the coffee table as he heard Camy's phone ringing. Being nosy, he saw that whoever it was, their number wasn't saved.

"Aye, your phone is ringing."

"Can you bring it to me?" Camy yelled.

Malik brought it into the kitchen.

"Put it on speaker for me. My hands wet."

Malik was more than happy to hear who the hell was calling her.

"Hello."

Both looked surprised, hating a nigga on the other end.

"Hey, baby. I miss you," Jason said into the phone.

Malik gave her a strange look. Not wanting her to see just how pissed off he was, he set the phone down on the counter and then returned to the other room.

"How did you get my new number?" Camy yelled into the phone. She knew for a fact that she didn't give it to his cheating ass.

Instead of answering her, Jason used that time to confess his love for her. "Baby, I still love you, and I don't wanna be with nobody else but you. What I gotta do to prove to you that I wasn't cheating last time? I need you, baby."

Camy shook her head. "Jason, the bitch left her panties under my damn pillow! Look, I don't even wanna talk about this shit anymore. I don't know who gave you my number, but please don't use it anymore. I'm done."

As Jason started to yell out, "I'm sorry," Camy had just dried her hands and was quick to end the call.

Camy took the last of the chicken out of the grease and then made her way back into the living room with Malik. He sat on the couch, pretending to be so caught up in the TV that he didn't realize that she had walked back into the room. Malik had never been into sharing chicks and wasn't about to start now. If she had another nigga, he wasn't about to deal with her.

Camy straddled his lap, trying to get his attention. "I'm sorry about that, baby."

"That nigga ain't about to be a problem, is he?"

Camy could clearly see that he was bothered by Jason calling her. Camy gave him a sweet kiss on his lips. "No. I don't want anything to do with that guy. I don't even know how he got my new number."

Malik wrapped his hands around her ass. "I'm holding you to your word."

Camy nodded her head to let him know that she understood.

As soon as Malik released her, Camy got up so that she could make his plate. Malik watched as she walked back into the room with his plate and a nice cold bottle of water, just like he liked. "Thanks, baby. You know your ass be hooking shit up in that kitchen."

Camy blushed. Even after hearing him compliment her cooking all the time, she still loved to hear it. "I'll be back."

"You ain't gonna eat with me?" Malik asked.

Camy started to walk off. "Maybe a little later."

Malik could hear the shower water running. Living the way he lived and just being around sneaky-ass people, he got up to see if she had sneaked off to use her phone. Her saying she didn't want to be bothered with a nigga that was hitting her up didn't sit right with him.

To his surprise, she had left her phone in the kitchen.

"Damn, nigga, you gotta stop tripping," he mumbled as he went back into the living room. He didn't want to show it, but he was happy, feeling like he could really trust her.

Malik finished his plate then got back into the TV. He was so glued to the show that he didn't hear her come out of the bathroom.

Camy came out of the back and went into the kitchen to grab her phone. She then went to put it on the charger. Malik watched as she walked back into the living room wearing a T-shirt and some black biker shorts. She then cuddled next to Malik on the couch.

"What are we watching tonight?"

Malik was in a trance. Her fragrance alone had him hypnotized.

"Malik?" Camy called out.

"Yeah, what's up?"

"I asked what we were watching tonight," she repeated, giggling.

"My bad. Why don't you find something this time? You be whining 'cause I always put on something scary."

Camy quickly grabbed the remote from him. "Yeah, I'll pick. It's thundering bad out there, and that doesn't mix well with scary movies."

Although Malik thought it was cute that she was scared, he still laughed at her.

Camy ended up putting on a corny-ass romance movie. It was crazy how she picked the movie out and still fell asleep on it, just as he did. The movie was over when Malik woke up. Somehow, he had ended up laid out on the couch, with Camy's head on his chest. Although he wasn't used to shit like that, he couldn't lie. It felt good. He debated whether to wake her up or enjoy the moment.

Taking his chance, Malik placed a kiss on her forehead as he slowly rubbed on her ass. She had a nice, round ass that any nigga would love to hold on to. Camy started to wake up, which caused Malik to slide his hands out of her shorts.

"What time is it, baby?" she asked, sitting up.

Malik picked his phone up. "Damn, it's 3:17 a.m. I'm about to get out of here."

Camy stood up so Malik could get up, although she didn't want him to leave. She was scared to make her move but knew that she would hate herself if she let him walk out the front door.

Camy walked over to the door with Malik, but once they reached the door, Camy stretched her arms out, preventing him from leaving.

"What's up, girl?"

"I don't want you to go. I want you to stay here with me," she mumbled.

Her confession caught him off guard. "What?"

"I want you to stay the night with me."

Malik grinned as Camy made it her business to pull her shirt off, letting him know just how serious she was. Malik had been waiting for this moment since the first day he saw her and had no problem pulling his shirt off, either. Malik picked Camy up, forcing her to wrap her legs around his waist. As he held her against the wall, their lips locked as they shared a passionate kiss.

"You sure this is what you want?"

Camy could feel his thick, hard dick poking at her through his pants. Instead of backing down, that alone made her want him even more. The feelings that she had for Malik were strong, so in a way, fucking Malik was her way of confirming that she was indeed over Jason.

In between kisses, Camy managed to moan out. "Yes, Malik, I wanna do this. I want you so bad."

Malik carried her into her bedroom. He then gently placed her down on her bed so that he could pull her shorts off. "These tight-ass muthafuckas," he mumbled, trying to pull them down.

Camy giggled as she helped him. She struggled herself to pull them bitches over her ass. Camy was completely naked in bed, waiting for Malik to join her. She watched as he put a condom on before making his next move.

"Bring your ass here," he demanded as he pulled her closer toward the edge of the bed.

Malik wasted no time planting his face in between her legs. All this time, he had imagined that she was sweet as candy, and the more he sucked on her, the more he realized that he was right.

Malik's head game was on point and had Camy going crazy. One minute, she was moaning out loudly, holding the back of his head in place. Then, the next minute, she was trying to close her legs and force him off her.

"Malik. Baby. Oh my gawd." She moaned out, trying to push his head from between her legs.

Malik loosened up the grip that his lips had on her clit just enough for her to calm down a little. "You good?"

Still breathing heavily, Camy nodded her head instead of talking.

"You want me to stop?"

This time, she shook her head.

"Come on, baby. I need you to use your words. You gotta talk to me and tell me what you want," he said, giving her pussy a few small kisses.

After calming down, Camy finally opened her mouth. "Malik, please don't stop."

"That's what the fuck I thought."

Her giving him the green light was all that he needed to hear. Malik gladly got back to working on her body.

Only being familiar with Jason's sex, Camy couldn't hide her true feelings when Malik finally slid into her wetness. "Oh my gawd," she yelled out as she dug into his back.

Seeing that she couldn't handle just the head, Malik slowly fed her pussy. With each stroke, he slid in a little at a time, until every inch was soaked in her juices.

Camy couldn't believe how good he was fucking her. Everything was so different from fucking Jason. Malik, indeed, was blessed.

Over the years, she had gotten so used to Jason's sex that finally fucking someone new, she couldn't handle it. Being with Malik made her feel like she was finally with a grown-ass man. She couldn't lie. Malik knew exactly what he was doing, and he was what her body had been missing.

Malik wanted so badly to fuck the shit out of her, but just his slow strokes were driving her crazy. He started to think about the shit that Tim had said. He was right. She couldn't take dick, but that was something that he'd never find out.

The dick was too good, and knowing she was making the ugliest sex faces, Camy tried to look the other way, but Malik wasn't having that. Malik wanted to see them. That type of shit stroked his ego.

Malik turned Camy's face so that she could look into his eyes. "Look at me," he demanded, giving her a kiss.

Between the kisses and Malik picking his pace up, Camy's moans got louder, and her legs began to shake. "Oh my gawd!"

Malik was feeling himself just a little too much. "That's not God, baby. That's all me. What's my name, baby?"

Camy hesitated to scream out his name. Jason couldn't ever get her to scream out his name, even though he had tried plenty of times. She could never see herself stroking a nigga's ego like that. Camy was going to take the dick like a G, or so she thought.

Malik slid out, then plunged deeper into her wetness, showing no mercy.

"Malik, baby."

"What's my name?" he asked again, fucking her harder.

All that shit that Camy was thinking was now out the window. Malik was serving the best dick that she had ever had, and after he gave her all ten inches of his thick-ass pole, Camy was really going crazy now.

"Malik," she screamed out, loud enough to wake the dead.

Malik laughed to himself. "That's what I thought. Is this my pussy now?"

"Yes, baby, it's yours. It's your pussy," Camy moaned out as Malik started to slow his pace down.

The two locked lips as they continued to fuck each other.

Camy was worn out about the time Malik had finally cum for the last time.

"Damn, girl," Malik mumbled as he rolled off of Camy.

Camy lay there in her thoughts, barely able to move.

She was a little too quiet for Malik, but then again, with anyone else, he would have already been getting dressed and ready to walk out the door.

"Man, bring your li'l ass over here," he ordered, pulling her closer toward him.

Camy rested her head on his chest. She could hear that his heartbeat was racing just as fast as hers.

Malik placed a kiss on her forehead. "You good?"

Camy blushed before nodding her head.

"What I tell you about that shit? Use your words."

"Yeah, Malik, I'm good. Tired, but I'm good."

Malik and Camy shared another kiss before she closed her eyes to fall asleep. He found himself rubbing her booty in a circular motion, just like he had done earlier. He wouldn't have changed that moment for shit in the world.

Instead of falling straight to sleep, Malik lay there, thinking about how difficult shit was with Camy. His people had warned him that some chick was going to come along and make him want to settle down and enjoy love one day. Not wanting to believe in all that, he told himself that shit was different, but only because it was new pussy.

Just as he finally started to doze off, her phone started to go off.

"Man, what the fuck?"

Malik picked the phone up to see who was calling, but the caller had blocked their number.

"Camy, Camy, get up!"

"What's up?" she asked, waking up to him shaking her out of her sleep.

"Who the fuck keep calling you? Is it that nigga from earlier?"

"No, Malik. I told him not to call anymore. I don't even know how he got my new number," she explained again.

Malik wanted to believe her, but it wasn't a damn ghost calling her.

Camy tried to go back to sleep, but Malik was on a hundred.

"Aye, get yo' ass up."

With an attitude, Camy opened her eyes back up. "What now, Malik?"

"I don't want you out here talking to these other niggas," he ordered.

Camy gave him a kiss. "Stop acting so damn jealous," she said, giggling.

Malik pushed her head off his chest. "I ain't acting like shit. Once a chick catches too many bodies, it ain't shit I wanna do with her ass after that. You understand that?"

Camy lay back down on him. "I'm not fucking with nobody else but you, Malik. I don't even pay these other niggas any attention out here. Now, can I go to sleep, baby?"

"And it better stay that way."

Malik then grabbed her face, forcing her to kiss him. Camy didn't see anything wrong with the way he flipped out. She thought it was his way of saying that he loved her and wanted her to himself. Malik held onto her tightly as he drifted off.

Camy was surprised to wake up and see Malik still knocked out. She grinned as she rubbed his chest. After the night they shared and him demanding all of her attention, she felt like she was in love.

"Why you watching me?"

"'Cause I thought you were sleep," Camy said, giggling.

Malik finally opened his eyes and stared at her. "How the hell am I supposed to sleep when you up being weird?"

"Whatever, boy. You want some breakfast?" Camy asked, sitting up.

Malik gave it some thought. "I guess since we already had our early morning workout."

Camy grabbed her robe and then walked out of the room. She wanted to jump in the shower before making her way into the kitchen.

Malik shook his head as he heard the shower going. He took it as his cue to come join her ass. Malik stepped into the shower and instantly grabbed Camy from the back.

"I wasn't invited?"

"Now, you know you're always invited to be with me."

Malik placed a few kisses on her back and then her neck before plunging into her pussy.

"Damn, baby. I'm still sore from last time," she moaned out.

Malik paid her no mind as he slid in and out of her. The louder she moaned and called out his name, the harder and deeper he pushed himself back into her.

"Didn't you say this was my shit?"

Caught up in the dick strokes, Camy couldn't respond.

Malik slipped up and broke another one of his own rules when dealing with these chicks out here. The first one was spending the night, and then, he fucked around and busted in her. This nigga had never even fucked a chick raw until that day. He shook his head as he thought about how her shit was too good to pull out of. As he finished, he told himself he had to be careful next time.

Camy ended up stepping out before him. "I'm about to get this food together," she said, giving him a kiss before getting out.

Malik stayed in a little longer, trying to get his mind together. Camy had his mind all fucked up.

"What time are you talking about stopping by?"

Malik walked into the kitchen to hear Camy on the phone, making plans. He didn't say anything, hoping to hear who she was talking to.

"Okay, I'll be here," she said before hanging up.

"Who was that, your li'l boyfriend?"

Camy didn't like his joke. "Whatever, boy. Stop playing with me, Malik. That was my best friend, Mona. She wanted to stop by and chill for a minute."

"Oh, for real?"

"Yeah," she said, grabbing a plate out of the cabinet.

After eating, Malik sat on the couch, putting on his shoes.

"You leaving?"

"Yeah, you know I have to go turn a few corners."

Malik got up, but Camy stood in front of the door, stretching her arms out.

Malik chuckled. "That shit worked last night, but I can't let it slide this morning."

"Please," she whined.

Malik liked the way she whined. All that spoiled baby shit actually turned him on, but he knew Rell was waiting on him. Malik placed a kiss on her lips. "Baby, I'll be back later. Plus, my phone is on, so you can call me if you need me."

Camy enjoyed the tight hug and the squeezing of her ass.

"Trust me, if I could chill with you all day, I would, but this money calling."

"I understand, baby."

Malik walked out the front door and could instantly feel like someone was watching him. Looking up, he saw his mama and brother sitting on the porch. Not having time for their shit, he called out for Rell.

"Aye, bro, come on. Let's roll out."

"Hey, boy, you know you see me," Ms. Patt yelled out.

Malik looked back up at the porch. "Hey, Ma."

"Come talk to me, boy."

Malik wasn't in the mood and wasn't about to let her mouth ruin his day. "I can't, Ma. I gotta go make some moves."

Ms. Patt rolled her eyes. "All right, Malik."

Rell jumped in the truck. "You know her nosy ass was up all morning, wondering when you were gonna come out of that house. Soon as I pulled up, she was on my head, asking me about yo' ass."

Malik laughed. "Yo' mama something else. She wouldn't be able to mind her own business if someone paid her ass."

"I'm curious to know how ole girl got your ass to spend the night anyways. I thought that was against your rules."

Malik smiled. "She got my head all fucked up, bro. I can't even lie. She be doing something to me. I think she knows voodoo or some shit."

Rell laughed. "What the fuck she be doing, bro? She must have the best head game in the world, huh?"

Malik felt crazy, shaking his head no. "I never let her suck my dick, bro."

"What, nigga?"

"You ever met a bitch so pretty that you didn't want her to be on that nasty shit?"

"Hell nah! I love when a pretty bitch eat this dick up! Yeah, bro, she got your ass open like a muthafucka," Rell teased, shaking his head.

"Whatever, bro. I'm still the same old me."

"So, that ain't your girl?" Rell asked to test his brother's brain.

"Bro, we just some cool-ass friends."

"I heard that nigga Tim was trying to get on. Would you be mad if she gave the boy her number?"

Malik had a serious face but chuckled. "She not my woman and can do whatever she wanna do, but she ain't gonna talk to no other nigga."

Rell shook his head. Just by hearing that, he knew that Camy was tangled in his web, just like Shay.

Rell lit the blunt before Malik drove off. It was money on the table, and they needed to go collect.

Chapter 5

"What's all this, bitch?" Mona asked, walking into Camy's home.

Camy went to take a seat on the couch. "What are you talking about?"

"Don't play with me right now. You glowing, girl. What's new?"

Camy blushed. "This is me after having the best sex of my life. Mona, girl, that man is the truth in the bed."

Mona was all in, soaking up all the tea that her home-girl was about to spill.

"Girl, don't be like that. Tell me all the details."

Camy wasn't usually the type to brag, but Malik's dick was something to scream to the world about. "That man licked and sucked on every inch of my body before fucking me to the point that I could barely move. Then, this morning, we fucked again in the shower. I swear Jason never made me cum the way Malik does. I'm talking about multiple times, back-to-back."

"Damn, bitch. I'm jealous, but you know what they say about them hood niggas? I heard how they got down."

Camy laughed. "I never heard shit, but I guess that's why me and Jason's sex life wasn't popping like that. Jason didn't have a lick of hood in him. Girl, I feel foolish for settling for that bullshit all those years."

Mona gave her a fake giggle. "Girl, shut up. You used to love you some Jason."

"He was my first, bitch. I didn't know any better," Camy reminded her.

Camy got up and then went into her room. When she came back, she was holding a blunt. "Speaking of Jason, did I tell you that he called me yesterday? I don't even know how that nigga got my number:"

"Are you serious? Tell that boy to get lost and that you found some new dick."

Camy laughed. "Girl, he called when Malik was right there, and he didn't like that at all. I told his ass not to call me no more, then hung up. I'm not about to play with that nigga."

Mona wanted to know how he got the number herself. She prayed that wouldn't fuck up her plans. Mona knew that even if Camy told him not to call, he wouldn't stop. He was a silly nigga in love.

"Girl, don't let Jason fuck up what you got going on with your new boo."

Camy passed Mona the blunt. "Girl, I'm not. To be honest, Jason not fucking with Malik on his worst day."

They both laughed and clowned Jason as if Camy had never been in love with him.

"Enough about me. What's been going on with you? Have you found a boo yet?"

Mona smiled. "He ain't mine yet, but I'm working on him."

"Does the nigga have a name?"

Mona laughed. "Let's just call him 'finally mine.'"

Camy was happy for her friend. "Go ahead and get your man, boo. Maybe we could go on a double date or something."

"Sure, I mean, if he is up to it."

After Mona left, Camy tried to have a peaceful afternoon, but with Jason playing on her phone, it wasn't possible.

"Jason, I know it's been you calling me private all afternoon. Can you please stop?"

Little did she know, Jason had worked a double and had just woken up from a nap. "What are you talking about, Camy?"

Camy was beyond irritated. "I wasn't getting these prank calls until you called me last night. I know it's you. How did you get my number anyways?"

Jason shook his head. "I worked a double and just woke up. I haven't been calling your ass."

"And I'm supposed to believe that? This is exactly why I left. Your ass is always lying."

"Baby, you always so quick to go off and never listen to me. I'm trying to win your heart back. Why would I sit up and play on your phone when I can call and talk to you like now?"

Camy thought about what he was saying, but since she couldn't blame anyone else, she had to point her finger at him. "I'm not doing this shit with you, Jason. Whatever we had is over, and I'm not about to double back to be with you."

"I love you, Camy, and I can't just let you go like that. You never gave me closure or anything. How can you just leave me like that?"

Although Jason was the one to hold her heart for years, she had to stand her ground, not letting him play with her anymore. Instead of giving in like she had done in the past, Camy held it together. She thought about all the times he made her cry and beg for him to love her right. This time, she didn't fall for his shit.

"Jason, your side bitch left her panties under my damn pillow. Boy, I can never forget that, or the fact that you would do that shit to me. I can't see myself sticking around, begging you to do right by me anymore when somebody else will."

Jason chuckled but was really butt hurt and in his feelings. "This why you tripping? You got a new man now?"

"And if I do?"

"Look, I'm not even gonna lie to you, baby. Ain't no nigga gonna love and spoil you like I did. I'm your first everything, and you'll never get over me."

Camy held the phone, trying not to cry. She played that hard role, but Jason knew how to break her. Breaking her just to put her back together was what had her stuck with him for so long.

"Camy, I love you, baby, and think you should come back home. If you come back, I won't bring up any of this shit. I still got your ring in the drawer, waiting on you. I know for a fact that you always wanted to be a wife."

Camy shook her head as if Jason could see her. "No, Jason, I don't wanna live like that anymore. I wanna know what real love is, and being with you ain't it. You know I would love to be somebody's wife one day, but I'm not about to settle like I have in the past."

"But I do love you. I bought you whatever you wanted. You never had to ask for shit."

"No, you loved the fact that I loved you, and that made it easy for you to control me. And the gifts were just to get me attached to you."

Camy got up from the couch and heard someone knocking on the door. As she got closer, she saw Malik standing there.

"Look, Jason, I'm not coming back, and I really just want you to stop playing on my phone."

Before Jason could respond, Camy hung up.

At this point, Malik was walking in and wondered what the hell was going on. Camy hurried to wipe her face as she walked back to the couch.

"What's wrong?"

Jason had fucked up her whole mood. "Nothing," she answered dryly.

Malik could tell by the look on her face that she was upset and had been crying. He didn't like the fact that she didn't feel comfortable enough to talk to him. Taking a seat next to her, Malik pulled her into his arms.

"You know you can talk to me about anything. I would rather try to help you out than sit back and watch you be upset."

Camy tried to relax on his chest. "It's nothing, Malik. Can you just hold me?"

Malik held her tighter, the way she liked, but couldn't help but wonder why she wouldn't tell him what was wrong.

The house was quiet as fuck, and they both ended up falling asleep on the couch, inhaling each other's scent. After a while, Malik opened his eyes, looking around, trying to figure out how he fell asleep and how long he had been knocked out.

"Fuck!" he mumbled, trying to get up without waking Camy.

As soon as he stood up, Camy popped her head up. "Are you leaving me?"

"Yeah, I really wasn't trying to fall asleep in the middle of the day like that anyways. I gotta go shoot a few moves, then I'll be back," Malik said, giving her a kiss.

"All right."

Malik stopped himself from walking out the door. "Aye, you all right now?"

Camy gave him a fake smile. "Yeah."

Malik walked out, knowing that she was lying, but since she wouldn't talk about it, he couldn't do anything about it. Since dealing with Camy, Malik tried his best to figure her out and learn what she liked and didn't like. Malik was able to put together that it didn't take much to keep her happy. Camy loved having a nigga's time more than anything else. She liked for a nigga to be in her face all day. Although Malik liked to run the streets, he made it his business to show her some attention when he could.

Camy finally got off the couch to get her life together. She had to learn how to control her emotions, especially dealing with a nigga that clearly didn't care about her feelings.

Camy went into the kitchen. Cooking and eating had always been her go-to when she was upset.

"What's up?"

Shay smiled, happy that he had even answered the phone. "Hey, baby. I miss you."

"Look, Shay, I'm busy, so if that's it, I gotta go."

"Wait, Malik!" she called out.

Malik shook his head. Shay just didn't get that he was over her ass. A nigga was tired of the same shit. "What?"

"What she got that I don't? You think I don't be seeing your car around there all night? You never spent the night with me before, Malik. What is it, Malik? Is that bitch pussy made from gold or something?"

Malik laughed, pissing her off even more. "Shay, stop all that shit, girl. You know how shit is. Why you tripping on me?"

"Because you changed on me. You wanna keep fucking me but falling in love with the next bitch. I want you to love me, Malik. This role I've been playing is getting old."

"Stop playing it then, and stop trying to climb up the ladder. And you can stop all that love talk, too. I love me. I'm not cuffing nobody."

Shay held the phone, crying. She played the role of being his friend for three years, and now, she hated herself for allowing him to toy with her heart. She loved Malik, but at the same time, he really hurt her.

"You know what, Malik? You're right. I did agree to that role at the beginning, and now, I'm over it. It's plenty of niggas that would love to be with me. I'm a good, loyal woman that got caught up with the wrong nigga."

"What the fuck you talking stupid for? You must want me to pull up and fuck you up."

"See, Malik, this is the bullshit I be talking about. You ain't been pulling up, giving me dick or nothing, but when I say I'm gonna be fucking with someone new, you wanna fight and shit. I'm not about to let you keep playing with me like that."

Malik held the phone, listening to the bullshit that she was talking about, and didn't know how he felt about it all. She wasn't his, but at the same time, she was his. All the niggas in the hood knew that his bitches were off-limits.

"Look, Shay, I'm gonna stop by in a minute."

Shay wiped away her tears. "All right, Malik."

Although Malik had just left the hood, he doubled back to pacify Shay's feelings. He didn't want shit to end on a bad note, just to end for good with her. She knew, sooner or later, that whatever they were doing was going to have to come to an end.

Malik knocked on her door, hoping this would be quick and simple. Shay let Malik in with plans of sucking and fucking him straight into a relationship. She might have mentioned moving on, but that wasn't possible. Her love for Malik was irreplaceable.

Shay opened the door, half naked like always. "Hey, baby."

"Come sit down and talk to me."

Shay didn't like the way shit was going already. Before he got there, she told herself that she was in charge, and here he was, taking over.

Shay took a seat like he told her to. "What's up?"

"I'm gonna be honest. I liked what we used to have, but I'm tired of this shit. I'm done."

Shay jumped up. "Don't say that, Malik. We've been through too much to just end like this."

"You want a nigga to be all in love and shit, and clearly, you can see that's not me. Truth be told, we only been fucking for three years, nothing more. I never took you out or nothing. Why would you wanna be with a nigga like me?"

Shay started pacing the floor. "You not about to leave me for that bitch, Malik!"

"This ain't got shit to do with her!" he yelled back.

"Yes, it do! That bitch changed you, and now, she got you saying 'fuck me' like I ain't been the one emptying your balls every night for the last three years. You know what, Malik? Fuck you. I know what I gotta do."

Malik knew what she was saying but wanted her to be woman enough to say the shit to his face. "What's that, Shay? What the fuck you gotta do?" he questioned.

Shay burst out laughing.

"What the fuck so funny?"

Shay continued to pace the floor. "Just playing the process of elimination game. You have so many so-called friends that would love for me to suck them up."

Malik jumped up from the couch. Within a blink of an eye, he had her pinned up on the wall with his hands around her neck. "Bitch, you better stop playing with me before I fuck around and beat your ass."

Shay laughed. "You've been so busy with that bitch, you must have forgotten I love being choked."

Between her laughing at him then sticking her tongue out after talking shit, Malik was fed up. Releasing her, Malik tried to calm down. "I'm done with this shit."

"You can't be done with something that never started, stupid."

"Man, fuck you, Shay, and you better stay the fuck away from me. Don't even call my fucking number, crazy-ass bitch."

Shay didn't back down. "Fuck you, Malik! And don't worry about me calling your Black ass, either. I'm gonna be busy with my new nigga, bitch."

"Go ahead and do what you gotta do then."

Before walking out the door, Shay stopped him one last time. "Malik, you know your slow-ass uncle Davon been checking me out. Maybe I'll give him some pussy, just to see how stupid he really can get."

That was the last straw. Everyone knew that Malik didn't play when it came to his uncle, no matter who it was. Malik snapped and pieced Shay's ass up so quick that she didn't have a chance to run from the ass beating that he was giving her.

"Get the fuck off me, Malik! I fucking hate you!" Shay yelled.

Realizing what he had done, Malik quickly left the house. He wasn't into beating a bitch's ass, but she needed that shit. He had already let her get away with all that shit-talking since he had got there.

Shay looked in the bathroom mirror, crying. She wasn't badly hurt, but her heart was broken into many pieces. After three years, he had finally left her for a new bitch. Shay knew she couldn't beat Malik's ass, so she had plans to reach out to touch Camy. Knowing that Malik would never take her back, she was going to beat Camy's ass every time she thought about him.

Chapter 6

After chilling and explaining what happened with Shay to Rell and Davon, Malik called Camy. Truth be told, after his fucked-up day, he needed a good friend to talk to.

"Hey, you wanna go out for dinner tonight or something?"

"Baby, I already put my dinner on, and it's almost done."

Malik liked how she stayed on her shit. Her soft voice even calmed him a little.

"That's cool. I had a long, fucked-up day and just need some peace. Can I still come see you?"

"Sure, that would be cool. What time are you gonna be here?"

"Give me a minute."

Camy set Malik's plate in the microwave, then cleaned her kitchen. She wasn't sure what time he was going to get there, but she knew she didn't want to have company with a sink full of dishes.

Camy then sent Malik a quick text before getting in the shower.

Camy: Hey, baby, I'm getting into the shower. If you pull up, the door will be unlocked, and your plate is in the microwave.

Malik passed his phone to Rell. "You see this? This is the type of shit that is having me running to her ass."

"That's why you did the right thing by cutting Shay's ass off. It's time for you to follow your fucking heart, bro. Besides, who wants to keep dealing with the same toxic bullshit every day?"

Malik shook his head. "I don't know, bro. All this shit so different for me. I can't say I don't like it, but it's really not my thing. I feel funny."

"I've been told yo' ass that this shit was coming, bro. You growing on your grown-man shit, nigga. If you stop playing around, you'll see exactly what I'm talking about."

Malik told his brother that he would hook up with him later. He wanted to go see Camy's sexy ass before she got out of the shower.

Just like she said, the door was unlocked, and she was in the shower. He wasn't thinking about the food because she had what he wanted to eat. Malik undressed, then went into the bathroom, catching Camy off guard when he opened the shower curtain. She jumped.

"Fuck, Malik! You scared me, boy."

Malik stepped in the shower. "Sorry for scaring you. Let me make it up to you," Malik said, wrapping his arms around her.

Camy felt like her skin was melting into his as he held her from the back and placed kisses on her shoulders and neck. "You make me feel so good, Malik."

"That's my job, baby."

The two ended up making love all night and into the early morning. They had both had a stressful day but found peace in each other.

Camy ended up waking up first, just like last time. Grabbing her phone off the nightstand, she turned her phone off Do Not Disturb. She didn't want all those prank calls fucking up her night with her man. Camy relaxed her head back on his chest. Without giving it any thought, she snapped a picture of them in bed together. Being silly, Camy thought about placing a smiley face emoji over him with the caption "no face, no case" but went against it at the last minute. She wanted to show off her man. Besides, they looked good together.

The sound of Malik's phone going off had him jumping up from his sleep. "What the fuck?" he mumbled as he saw that Rell, Shay, and a handful of other muthafuckas had started blowing his shit up at once.

"Everything all right?" Camy asked.

Malik climbed out the bed. "I'm about to find out."

Malik went into the bathroom to see what was up. "What's up, bro? What's good? Everyone all right?"

"Bro, you see what the fuck your girl posted online?"

"Who? What girl?"

"Camy, nigga. Go look at what she tagged you in," Rell ordered.

Malik went to his page and saw that Camy had posted their picture. In just a few minutes, it already had over fifty comments and a whole lot of reactions.

Malik shook his head. "Man, bro, this girl bugging the fuck out. Let me call you back."

Malik didn't bother to call anyone else because he already knew what tip they were on. They only wanted to be nosy, asking a million questions and talking shit. He walked back into the room, unsure how to handle the situation. If he flipped out, he would hurt her feelings, but if he didn't say shit, she would have thought it was all right.

"Good morning. Is everything all right, Malik?"

Malik took a seat on the edge of the bed. "Aye, why you post that picture of us on social media?"

Camy could tell that he was upset but really didn't understand what she did wrong. "I thought it was cute. Was that a problem?"

Malik hesitated to answer, which told her exactly what she needed to know. Camy picked up her phone and deleted the picture. "I took it down. I hope you're happy now."

"What the fuck you take it down for? Shit, the damage already done."

His words hit her hard. "Malik, really? The damage? And what does that supposed to mean?"

Malik stood there for a minute, not saying anything, which made Camy storm off.

Trying to explain himself, Malik went after Camy. "Camy, come here, baby. I didn't mean to say that shit," he yelled, grabbing her by the wrist.

"Malik, let me go. You said exactly what you meant. So, what do you think? I'm supposed to be some fucking secret or something? Your friends online can't see us together? Or is it somebody else that you're trying to hide me from?"

Malik looked at how she was tearing up and felt bad. Through everything, he never wanted to hurt her feelings. "Baby, stop saying stupid shit like that. I'm sorry for tripping like that. You know you're my baby."

Camy smiled as Malik gave her a kiss. "I'm your baby, Malik?"

"Yeah, you are. I just don't like all my business on social media like that, but I'm sorry for flipping out on you. Matter of fact, you can put it back up there if you want to."

Camy's smile got bigger. "Okay, Malik."

Malik held onto Camy, trying to make her feel better. He didn't lie. She was his baby, and he wasn't telling anybody else shit like that. "We good now?" he questioned.

"Yeah, Malik, we're good. But for real, I should have asked first."

"You good, baby."

Just like that, Camy had forgiven him for tripping and wanted nothing more than him holding her. "You want me to make some breakfast, or you gotta go?"

"I gotta go handle something right now, but I should be back in about two hours. I got something planned for us when I get back."

"What?" Camy asked with a huge smile on her face.

"Just be ready."

After getting dressed, Malik left out, ready to deal with all the bullshit everybody was about to be on. Shay's crazy ass had already called and texted him over a hundred times, wanting to know how Camy was able to post that picture when she was never able to even take a picture of him. Malik tossed his phone into the passenger seat, wishing he could go MIA until the shit died down.

Malik started heading toward his house. He needed to shower before meeting up with Rell. Twenty minutes later, Rell was walking into his brother's home.

"What's up, nigga? I see you and your girl broke the internet this morning," he teased.

Malik shook his head. "Man, I don't know why she did that shit. Her ass caught me when I was knocked out this morning," Malik informed him.

"Bro, didn't you say that was the main reason why you didn't spend the night at these bitches' houses? You said you knew that they be snapping pictures and shit, trying to get a nigga caught up in shit."

Malik shook his head in agreement. "Hell yeah. That girl be having me slipping on my own shit. I even slid in her ass raw a few times like I wanted all the problems that come along with that bullshit."

Rell shook his head. At this point, he didn't know what to say to his bro. Malik could act crazy if he wanted to, but Camy was going to be the one to change his whole life around.

"Okay, enough of this bullshit. Let's go get this money."

The brothers left, driving off in Malik's truck.

"I saw that picture with you and that nigga. So, that's your new man?"

With a huge smile on her face, Camy happily answered. "Yes. Yes, he's the one that's keeping me happy all while fixing a broken heart that you broke."

Jason was jealous and didn't care if it showed. "You ain't even been knowing that nigga long enough to be acting like you in love. Besides, I know you still love me because if you didn't, you wouldn't have answered my call."

Camy laughed. "Boy, I only answered your call to prevent you from making so many prank calls during the day when I'm chilling with my man. Now that you know where I stand, don't bother to call me no more."

Before Camy could hang up, Jason called out to her. "Baby, I still love you and wanna be a part of your life. Why you act like another nigga gonna love you the way I did?"

"Jason, I'm tired of hearing that stupid-ass lie. You did it, nigga. And how you did me, I pray no other nigga love me the way you did. Now, get the fuck off my line."

"I hope that nigga dog yo' ass and have you running back to me!"

Camy set the phone down on the counter, in her feelings. When she turned around, Malik was standing right there.

"Who was that?"

Camy jumped, not expecting him to be there. She forgot that she had left the door unlocked. "Nobody," she mumbled, walking out of the kitchen.

Jason had fucked up her whole attitude. In the past, he knew telling her that he was the only one that would love her used to have her stuck dealing with his shit. Even though Malik was proving him wrong, his words still hit her hard. Jason had always had a way of making her feel at her lowest.

Malik followed her to the bedroom. "Is there something we need to talk about?"

"Not really, Malik. I just need to clear my head."

"You want me to leave?" he questioned.

Camy shook her head. "Malik, I don't want you to leave. Just give me a minute. Please."

Malik went into the living room to give her the little space she asked for. But really, he needed to calm himself down. This was the second time he had to ask her about that nigga after she told him that he wasn't going to be a problem. The fact that another nigga could have her all in her feelings didn't sit right with him.

Malik thought letting her get her shit together was the best thing to do, but hearing her cry over some dumb shit her ex said bothered him. The fact that she was crying over a nigga while he sat there, waiting to take her out and blow some bread on her, pissed him off. Instead of sticking around any longer, Malik got up to leave. He didn't play second to anyone, and that was something that was never going to change about him.

Camy heard the door slam shut and then jumped up. She was an emotional wreck and had let the fact that Malik was even there slip her mind.

Malik!" Camy said, racing toward the door, but when she opened the front door, he was pulling off.

Malik ended up sitting in front of Shay's house. Yeah, they had just gone through their bullshit, and he had to put his hands on her, but he never had to worry about her dealing nor crying over another nigga. She might talk her shit when she needed some extra attention, but that was as far as it ever went. Camy's behavior had him questioning everything he thought he had been feeling lately.

Shay's front door was shut, so Malik called her.

"What you want, Malik? Yo' ass been ignoring me all morning, and I know you saw all my texts."

"You wanna sit on the phone and bitch, or you gonna come open the door for me?"

Shay hung up with an attitude but made her way to unlock the door. Malik had her mind so gone that she forgave and forgot about him beating her ass just the day before.

"Hey, baby."

"What's up? What you got up?" he asked, taking a seat on the couch.

"Wondering why the fuck a bitch posting a picture with the nigga I'm in love with. What you got up?"

Malik laughed. "Why the fuck you on that bullshit? Can we just chill?"

Shay had more to say, but the look of irritation was all over his face. So, to keep him from leaving, she decided to chill. "Let's go to the room. I want some dick."

Shay had always been so forward about what she wanted, which was always dick. Malik wasn't in the mood for all that. Truth be told, Camy was on his mind heavy.

Not thinking clearly, Malik tried to get Shay to play Camy's role. "Why don't you put on a movie or something? Let's just chill."

"A movie? Now, you know I'm not into shit like that. We can make a movie, nigga."

Malik shook his head. "Man, put a damn movie on."

After searching, Shay finally put something on. Malik let her cuddle up under him, just as he did with Camy. Although it didn't feel right because Shay kept trying to pull his dick out, he tried to be cool.

"Come on, girl, watch the movie."

"Malik, stop trying to turn me into that other bitch. Give me some dick."

Malik didn't respond, so Shay laid her head back down on his chest. Shay tried to chill out, but toward the middle of the movie, she had his dick in her mouth. Just because he was acting like he didn't want her, she decided to make it extra sloppy.

"Damn, Shay. Fuck!"

Shay released his dick. "I know for a fact that bitch ain't sucking it like this."

Camy had never had the chance to suck his dick, so he answered honestly. "Nah, she ain't."

Shay then climbed on his lap to ride his dick. She missed him so much and felt like she had something to prove. Instead of taking him to the room, Shay fucked him like there was no tomorrow on the couch. She was trying her best to win him back.

"Baby, you know I love you so much?"

"Yeah, I know," Malik responded.

Shay rolled her eyes, expecting him to finally say it back.

Malik held Shay in place as he picked his pace up to release.

Shay smiled as she climbed off of him. "Damn, baby, that shit be hitting each and every time."

As Shay got up to bring him a warm washcloth, Malik's phone went off. He debated whether he wanted to answer for Camy. Then, because Shay was taking forever, he decided to make it quick.

"Hello."

"You just left without saying anything."

"Yeah, you was on some other shit, and I didn't wanna sit around while you handled that."

Shay walked in, carrying the washcloth. Malik quickly held up one finger, hoping her dumb ass didn't say shit.

"So, are you coming back?"

"You done playing with that other nigga?"

Camy hung up the phone. It was childish, but he was being childish, too. Plus, the fact that he was acting so insensitive to her feelings bothered her.

"Trouble in paradise?"

Malik snatched the washcloth from her. "Mind your fucking business." Malik then fixed his clothes so that he could leave.

"Let me get this straight. She pisses you off, and you run over here. Now, that bitch calling, and you go running back to her. What the fuck, Malik? What part of the game is this?"

Malik threw the nut rag at her face. "Shut the fuck up. I gave you dick. Ain't that what you wanted?"

"Fuck you, Malik. I don't even know why I let you come back over here."

"You know why," he said, grabbing his dick.

Shay stood there with her arms folded, feeling stupid as fuck. Again. "From now on, ain't no more running back and forth, nigga. Stay around there."

Before walking out the door, Malik went into his pocket and tossed some money at her. "Shut all that bullshit up."

Malik went back around the corner to see what was up with Camy. All this going back and forth was really getting on his damn nerves.

"I'm outside."

Camy went to the front door and then just stood there. She was still upset that he was insensitive to her feelings but still wanted him around. Malik got out, seeing that she wasn't about to come to him. Instead of talking on the porch, he followed Camy back into the house.

"What the fuck you hang up on me for?" he asked.

"'Cause you was asking me stupid questions about another nigga."

Malik took a seat on the couch, trying to calm down. "I asked you before if that nigga was gonna be a problem, and you told me no. Why the fuck I walk in, and you on the phone, crying and shit to that nigga?"

Camy shook her head. "I wasn't crying to him. He said some shit that made me upset. And I'm still telling you that he ain't gonna be a problem."

Malik was jealous, which caused him to get in his feelings. "What you even on the phone with him for anyways? You told me that the nigga hurt you, but you still be on the phone talking to him."

"Malik, he called about that picture of us. I was just telling him not to call me anymore because it was over between me and him. He won't be a problem anymore."

Malik sat there, trying not to say all the mean shit that was on his mind. Having real feelings for her past the bedroom had him biting his tongue and sparing her feelings.

Malik stood up and then went over to where she was standing. "Get your number changed if you can't stop that nigga from calling," he said before placing a kiss on her lips.

"All right," she mumbled in between kisses.

Once they separated, Camy took a seat on the couch. She thought about what he said, and he was right. She should have blocked Jason's ass when he first started calling.

"Malik, I swear I didn't give him my number, but I was wrong for talking to him. He's gonna keep calling, so I'm just gonna block him. He not worth fucking up what we got going on."

"I'm glad you recognize that. Now, if we're done with this shit, can I still take you out today? It's still kind of early."

Camy had gotten over Jason's shit already, and as long as Malik was all right, then she was good. "That sounds like a plan." Camy got up and then went back into her room. She was already dressed and only needed to fix her hair and grab some lipgloss.

Malik wanted nothing more than to have a good time with Camy, so he rolled a fat blunt they could smoke on their drive and calm their nerves.

"Malik, this is too much. You know you don't have to do all this, right?"

Malik sat in the chair, watching her spin around in a new fit with matching shoes and accessories. "Chill, baby. I told you today was all about keeping that smile on your face."

Malik had no problem cashing out on whatever Camy picked up in any store that they went into that day. He was trying to show her that he could make her happy with more than just dick.

"You're gonna have me spoiled if you keep doing shit like this, Malik," Camy said as they waited for their food to be served.

"I guess you can say this is my way of apologizing for tripping earlier. You're too fucking beautiful to be crying or to be sitting around upset over anything, and I was wrong for not being there for you. I let my own personal feelings get in the way, and I should have just been there to make sure you were all right."

The waitress set their plates on the table and then left.

"It's all right, baby. I just need to not let people's words get the best of me."

The two shared a meal before making their way back to her house.

Ms. Patt watched her son and his new play toy carry in a bunch of shopping bags from her front window. Seeing that made her think that her son had finally caught feelings and was tired of playing games. She knew he gave Shay money, but that boy had never taken her shopping. He never took her out of the house.

Malik followed Camy into her bedroom.

"Damn, baby. I don't think I have enough room in here for all my new clothes."

Malik didn't say anything. Instead, he stood there, enjoying the look on her face. Camy was happy, and if he had to spend every dime in his pocket to keep that smile on her face, he wouldn't mind. He was willing to do anything to keep her from crying again.

Camy straddled Malik's lap. "Now, how am I supposed to pay you back for buying me all this stuff?"

Malik kissed her lips. "Be my date for my birthday dinner. You already got something nice to wear."

Camy giggled. "I sure do, thanks to you. But yes, I would love to be your date for your birthday."

Climbing off his lap, Camy started leaving the bedroom door. "You going home, or do you want to join me in the shower?"

"What the fuck you think?" he asked, standing up, snatching off his shirt.

Camy loved the way their bodies became one whenever they hooked up. Malik didn't fuck her as if he was only looking for a nut. He had this thing where he took his time pleasing every inch of her body, making sure she came multiple times before he would finally cum. Just how he handled her body made her feel like he loved her.

That night, just like any other time, Malik was hitting it right, and Camy couldn't control herself. "Malik, I love you," she moaned out.

"I love you too, baby."

Malik was so caught up in his lovemaking with Camy that he didn't even notice that she got him to say those words. "Fuck! Shit, man! I done fucked up!"That was when he realized that he wasn't just thinking that shit. He had actually said that shit out loud.

As Malik rolled off Camy, she sat up. "What's wrong, baby? What the fuck you talking about?"

Malik was still out of breath as he climbed out of bed and tried to get dressed. His thoughts were everywhere, and he didn't know how to explain how he was feeling, but he knew that he needed to get away from Camy.

"Man, Camy, what the fuck you do to me, girl? I swear, since I've been fucking with you, shit has been different. What the fuck you do?"

Camy started climbing out of the bed. "What are you talking about, baby? Why don't you sit down and tell me what's wrong?"

Malik put his hands up, preventing her from coming any closer toward him. "Keep your ass over there. Don't fucking touch me. You gotta be doing that voodoo shit on a nigga."

Camy stopped in her tracks. "Boy, you're tripping. Are you high on something?"

Malik headed toward the door. "I gotta go figure some shit out."

Camy was dumbfounded by what the hell had just taken place. She had never in her life dealt with or heard of a nigga running out while making love before. The whole thing was weird to her.

Peeking out of her window, she saw that he was still sitting in front of her house. Picking up her phone, she dialed his number. She then watched as he looked at his phone before tossing it on the passenger seat.

Camy stormed back into her room, finally not thinking about his feelings, but her own. She sat on the bed and cried. She had told Malik that she loved him, and he happily said the shit back, just to run out on her like he was on drugs. Then, the whole voodoo shit still confused her.

Staying up, trying to figure out what had gone wrong, had given her a headache. Popping two Tylenols, Camy finally dozed off.

Malik pulled up in front of Rell's house. Being his brother and best friend, Rell had always been Malik's go-to person. Malik knew it was late, but he wasn't about to drive all the way home without figuring out what was wrong with him. He knew Camy was also confused.

He ended up calling Rell four times before he finally answered.

"Bro, I swear you better be somewhere dying. What the fuck up?"

"I'm outside. I need you, bro," Malik said before hanging up.

Rell gave Tiffany a kiss. "Sorry, baby. I'm gonna make this shit quick."

Tiffany smacked her lips. "I swear that boy act like everyone works on his time."

"Man, don't start that shit. He barely come over here."

Tiffany was pissed, but she didn't bother to go in because she knew how those two were. Couldn't shit come in between them.

Rell got dressed, trying not to make so much noise. "Baby, I'm gonna be right outside. I'm not pulling off with him or nothing."

"Still be careful, Rell."

Rell gave his girl another kiss before leaving.

They sat there in silence for ten minutes. Rell had grown irritated. He gave his brother the stare of death. "Bro, you come over here late as fuck, waking up Tiffany, almost waking up my kids, get me cussed out, and now, you ain't saying shit. What's up, nigga?"

"I think that girl put some type of voodoo on me, bro. I'm all the way fucked up."

"You woke me up cause yo' bitch ass in yo' feelings, nigga?"

Malik passed his brother the blunt. "Camy pissed me off today, so I went to chill with Shay. For the first time in three years, I slid in her raw. I slipped up and wanted Camy so bad I fucked Shay, picturing it was Camy. Then, tonight, I was fucking Camy and told her that I loved her. Aye, bro, what the fuck I'm supposed to do?"

Rell hated being the older brother when it came to bullshit like this. Malik wanted him to have all the answers, and he didn't. Sometimes, shit just came to him as they talked. "Bro, I've been telling yo' ass the same shit for a minute now. Yo' ass need to learn how to fucking listen. Ain't nobody doing no fucking voodoo on you. Nigga, you love that girl, and that's it."

"I kind of told her I did, then told her to stay the fuck away from me while leaving out the front door."

Rell tried to hold it in, but he couldn't help but laugh at his brother's goofy ass. "So, you ran away from her like a bitch. Yeah, you might as well pass her down."

"Man, stop playing with me. Nigga, I'm not letting nobody touch that."

Rell continued to laugh at his brother. "You probably scared the damn girl away. She already looking for your fucking replacement. Bro, you are weird for that shit."

Malik had to laugh himself. He wasn't sure how he was going to explain shit to Camy. At this point, he couldn't do shit but pray that she would continue fucking with him.

"This shit feels funny, but at the same time, it felt like something was lifted off my chest when I told her."

"So, you mean to tell me that you never felt this way with Shay?'

"Nah, nigga. With Shay, all we do is fuck, but with Camy, we take our time and actually make love to one another. How did I let this shit happen?"

Rell laughed harder. "Bro, stop questioning shit like this. Ain't nothing wrong with being in love. Don't you understand how your body has been giving you warnings? Learn to listen, my nigga."

As they sat in the truck, smoking, Malik finally decided to listen to his brother's advice.

After they had been talking for two hours, Tiffany came to the door, looking for her man.

"Aye, bro, let me get my ass back in the house before she comes out, going off on the both of us."

Malik got out right along with Rell. "Hey, Tiffany, I'm sorry for disturbing y'all sleep. Aye, don't be mad at bro. I just really needed him."

"Umm hmm, it's all right, Malik."

After getting back in the truck, Malik drove straight home. He heard everything that his brother said, but he still didn't know how he was going to approach Camy after running out like a bitch. This was definitely going down in the books.

Chapter 7

"Hey, Jason, what are you doing here?"

"Can I come in and talk? It won't be long. I just need a listening ear real quick."

Mona stepped to the side so that he could walk in. They both then took a seat on the couch.

"What's up, Jason? What's going on?"

"Mona, we've been cool for years now, and I know I'm no longer with your girl, but can you be completely honest with me?"

"Yeah, what's up?"

Jason gathered his words. "Is Camy really happy with that nigga she fucking with now?"

Mona kept a straight face, but her insides were celebrating. She had him exactly where she wanted him. He was a step away from being hers.

"I can't lie. That girl is splurging on him. I'm actually surprised at how quick she let him smash and now calling it love. That's my girl and all, but you can do so much better."

Jason shook his head, thinking that maybe she was right. The girls had been besties for years, and Mona wouldn't have shown any concern if it wasn't true. It was going to be hard, but he was going to have to move on.

"How the fuck am I supposed to move on? I might have been on some bullshit, but I loved her."

"I hate to break it down like this, but she doesn't love you, Jason. You gotta let it go."

Jason held his head down low, and Mona could tell that he wanted to cry over Camy's funky ass.

Mona left to go get them a drink from the kitchen.

"Here, Jason. You are still my boy, and I hate to see you like this."

Jason grabbed the cup and killed it. Mona was more than happy to pour him another one. Shit was going to be too easy.

It had been two weeks since Camy had last heard from Malik, and after so many calls and texts, she had started telling herself that maybe shit was over between them. There was no way in the world a man could love a woman and just ignore her the way that he did. She was once told that all good things must come to an end, and maybe this was the end for them.

Camy picked up her phone to call Mona again. She was another muthafucka that had been MIA. After she got no answer, Camy set her phone down, realizing that she really didn't have anyone in her corner. Everybody was moving funny.

"Damn, everyone must have forgotten about me. Jason ain't even been calling private, playing on my phone," she mumbled to herself.

Trying to shake the feeling of being alone, Camy got up so that she could go to the store. When everyone else failed, she still had food. In the store, Camy looked over the cucumbers for her salad. As she was minding her business, a chick stood next to her.

"Decisions, decisions, decisions. I think that one is the thicker one, like Malik. That is what you're looking for, right?"

"Excuse me?"

The girl then sat her purse down in her basket. "Bitch, don't think that you're the only one eating that dick up. Bitch, you ain't special."

"What? I don't know what you're talking about, but bitch, you better get the fuck out my face."

Since Shay was a little bigger and thought she could beat Camy, she stepped closer in her face. "Bitch, move me."

Camy wasn't scared of any bitch, but she also wasn't into all that fighting shit unless she had to. "Look, I'm not about to fight you over a nigga I'm not even dealing with right now. Go fight yourself, big goofy-ass ho."

Camy tried to walk away, but Shay wasn't backing down.

"Scary-ass ho," she yelled, pushing Camy.

Camy quickly turned around, connecting the first three hits to Shay's face. She wasn't about to let no bitch bully her or stop her from getting her food. Their fight didn't last because it broke up soon after Camy started swinging on Shay, and they were sent on their way.

It just so happened that Tim was in the store that day and was close by to stop Camy from beating Shay's ass. He used this as his opportunity to shoot his shot again as he walked her outside to her car. "It's crazy how you couldn't even get your food because of that stupid-ass girl."

"Yeah, it is. Damn, all I wanted was a damn chicken salad, and bitches forcing me to lay hands on them. Then, that owner in there wouldn't even let me pay for my shit. That's the real bullshit."

Tim laughed at how she was more worried about her food than some bitch that wanted to fight her. "Why were y'all fighting anyways?"

"I was trying to shop. She wanted to fight over a nigga."

"Oh, damn. So, do that mean you got a man?" he asked, knowing what it was when a bitch fucked with Malik.

"Aye, thanks for walking me to my car, but I'm not too worried about that girl."

Tim chuckled. "I see, Baby Tyson. She wasn't able to touch you after she pushed you first." Tim held her door open as Camy jumped into the car. "I'm gonna follow you to make sure you make it home all right."

"You don't have to do all that. I'm not scared."

Tim jogged over to his ride. He wasn't trying to hear shit she was talking about. Plus, he needed the block to see him with her.

Camy wasn't sure why, but she waited for Tim to get behind her before going home. She wasn't scared at all, but since he wanted to help out, she allowed him to.

Camy pulled up into her driveway while Tim parked in front of the house. She got out, then walked over toward his car. "Thanks again, Tim."

"No problem. You be good now," he said before looking over at Rell on his mama's porch. He then sped off, knowing his job was done.

Ms. Patt and Rell watched as Camy went into the house, not knowing the hell that she was about to bring to the block.

"When the last time you talked to your brother?" Ms. Patt asked.

"It's been like two days. He going through some shit."

"Well, I think it's time for you to call him up."

Rell wanted to call him as soon as he saw them pull up, but Malik would kill Camy and Tim's ass with no questions asked.

Davon walked outside, holding his phone.

"Nephew, it's time for you to come out and play. That nigga, Tim, on the block with Camy."

Rell quickly grabbed the phone from him. "Man, go sit the fuck down somewhere."

"What up, bro?" he said into the phone.

"What the fuck Unc talking about?"

"Shit, bro. Go back to chilling until your birthday, nigga."

Playing the role of a dummy, Malik hung up the phone and jumped up to see what was happening on the block. He knew Davon couldn't hold shit in but would never lie, either. Malik was on his way to be the storm to fuck up everyone's picnic.

Tim knew he had an audience, so to take it even further, he went to pick up chicken salad from Coney. Acting like he wasn't in the wrong, Tim pulled up in front of her house, hopping out with her food in his hand.

Hearing someone bang on her door, Camy opened the door and was surprised to see Tim standing there.

"What's up? Why are you here?"

He noticed how her attitude was different now, and she was back to being a bitch.

"Damn, shawty, I was just bringing you your salad."

Being home with nothing to eat had made her grumpy, and Tim's uninvited knock on her door made him the target. "I'm sorry for snapping, but thank you so much. You really didn't have to do this. I was gonna head to another store."

"But now you don't have to."

Camy took the bag from him. "Thanks again."

Tim tried to push his luck since she was being nice again. "You want some company? Maybe we could talk over a meal."

Camy burst out laughing. "Is that what the fuck y'all niggas over here think about me? Do you really think a bitch-ass meal gonna get y'all some pussy? Get your bitch ass off my porch before shit gets ugly."

Tim looked around and saw that he still had the same audience he had earlier. Feeling embarrassed because she had gotten loud, he got loud right back. "Fuck you then, bitch! I was only trying to fuck anyway. Who the fuck you think you is? Walking around this bitch acting like you too good to talk to a nigga."

Camy laughed. "See, I'm not acting like shit. I'm just not the type to fuck any and everybody. Now get the fuck off my porch."

"Nah, bitch, you owe me twelve fifty for that," he said, talking about the salad.

"Oh, wow," Camy teased, laughing at him.

"I'm not leaving until I get some pussy or my money."

Camy went to grab the money from her purse. At about the time she came back outside, Malik was outside beating Tim's ass. Camy ran over toward the crowd, trying to pull Malik off of Tim. She didn't like Tim at all, but she could tell that he couldn't take any more hits.

"Malik, stop! He had enough!"

Malik snatched away from Camy. "Take yo' ass in the house!" he barked.

Camy backed up. "You bring your ass in the house too. Why the fuck are y'all fighting anyways?"

Malik let Tim go, then stepped back. "Don't bring your bitch ass back on this block, nigga."

"Fuck you, nigga, and that stuck-up-ass bitch!" Tim barked, racing to get back into his car.

"You good, bro?" Rell asked Malik.

"For sure, nigga. Let me go deal with this girl."

Camy went into the house with Malik on her ass.

"What the fuck you think you doing?" he asked.

Camy gave him a crazy-ass look. "I'm about to eat this salad."

Malik shook his head and laughed a little. "You still gonna eat that shit after I just beat that nigga ass?"

"Yeah, I paid for it," she said, laughing, thinking about how she threw the money at him when he was trying to get off the ground.

Malik stood there, watching her, and couldn't believe how she was still going to eat the food that nigga brought to her house. "You disrespectful as fuck. You know that, right?"

Camy swallowed the food that was in her mouth. "Let's talk about what's disrespectful. You walk out on me and disappear for weeks. Today, I had to beat a bitch ass for calling herself checking me over you. What's disrespectful is you making me fall for you when you have somebody."

"What the fuck you talking about? Who was you fighting?"

"Your bitch!"

"I don't have a bitch. Stop acting stupid, Camy."

"Then who was the bitch I had to lay hands on then, Malik? You having a bitch would explain a lot, like you going MIA on me and shit."

Malik repeated himself. "I don't have a bitch, Camy."

Malik didn't want to argue with her about Shay, but he did want to get to her and Tim. "That nigga Tim your new man? What the fuck was he doing over here, bringing you food and shit?"

Camy laughed, pissing him off even more. "Why are you asking about a nigga I don't even know?"

"Why the fuck was he here and bringing you food then?"

Camy grabbed her food and walked away from him. Malik followed her into the living room.

"You don't fucking hear me?" Malik asked, knocking her food out of her hand.

"Boy, what the fuck is wrong with you? Why would you do that?" she yelled.

"Oh, now I got your attention? It took for me to knock that bullshit down for you to see that I'm not playing around with you. Now, why the fuck was that nigga over here?"

Camy rolled her eyes as she started picking the food off the floor.

Malik snatched her up from the floor. "Man, get the fuck up and talk to me."

"Malik, let me go! You're hurting my arm," she whined.

Thinking about what he was doing and who he was doing it to, he let her go. "Camy, can you please just come sit down and talk to me? Please?"

"Where have you been, Malik? I need answers just like you want some."

Malik gently grabbed her hand and placed her on his lap. "Can we talk now, please?"

Camy went first. She started by explaining what happened when she went to the market and how Tim got into the picture.

"That nigga only did that to get my attention. He know that I fuck with you," Malik said.

"Do he? Because according to the bitch in the market, you hers. That's your bitch, Malik?"

"No, I ain't got no bitch. Now, can we stop talking about that shit?"

"You still ain't tell me where you were at."

Malik didn't want to talk about it, so he kept it simple. "I was at home."

Camy broke loose from his grip around her. "That's not good enough, Malik. The last time I saw you, we were in bed, making love, telling each other that we loved one another. You then ran out on me. Now, today, you over here fighting a nigga because you thought I was with him. I don't like what's going on here."

Malik tried to keep her from walking away from him. "I'm here now. Damn, Camy, chill."

"Chill? Really, Malik? You not about to play with me like that. I explained my day and everything, and you can't even tell me why you ran out on me?"

Malik held her in his arms, trying to calm her down. He hated when she was mad at him, and he wasn't man enough to tell her the truth. The real question was, how was he going to explain to her why shit was the way that it was?

"You said you fucked up. Were you admitting that this between us was all a mistake?"

At this point, Malik could see the tears forming in her eyes and felt bad. "Was what a mistake?"

"You telling me that you loved me. I can handle the truth, Malik. You know that, right?"

Malik didn't respond, causing Camy to go into her room with a face full of tears. She lied. She couldn't handle his truth, but it was something that she needed to know.

Malik felt like a weak-ass pussy. He was leaning against the wall, hearing her in the back room, crying because he was too stubborn to admit his feelings. He didn't know how he was going to fix shit with her. Camy wasn't like Shay at all. It was going to take more than dick to get shit back in order.

Finally getting his thoughts together, Malik went to her bedroom. Standing in the doorway, seeing her cry her eyes out, killed him. Malik climbed into the bed with her. As he tried to pull her closer toward him, she fought against him.

"Leave me alone, Malik. Just leave me alone. You promised that you wasn't gonna hurt me like the last nigga," she cried.

"I'm sorry, baby. I'm sorry if I hurt you. That's something that I never wanted to do. I do love you, and I ain't never been in love before. I was scared. Damn."

Hearing this calmed Camy. She could tell by the lost look in his eyes that he was telling the truth, which would explain most of his weird behavior.

Face to face, the couple looked into each other's eyes, trying to read each other's souls.

Malik placed a single kiss on her lips. "Camy, baby, I do love you."

"I love you too, Malik."

The couple started to lock lips. Getting hot and bothered, Malik climbed on top of Camy.

"Aht aht, Malik."

"What?" he asked, confused.

Camy giggled. "I just had to tell a nigga earlier today that I wasn't about to fuck him for a meal, but you owe me some food for this, boy."

Malik laughed at her silly ass. "Let's get dressed and go eat then. I wanna do everything right to prove that I do love you."

Not being with each other for the last few weeks only made the sex ten times better while in the shower.

Malik looked through her closet for the clothes that he had left over her house. "Damn, Camy, what you do, burn my shit?"

"No, crazy. I told you I didn't have enough room in my closet for all my stuff, so your clothes and some of my stuff are in the other room," she explained.

Malik walked into the second bedroom. Up until that day, he didn't even know she used it. "What's up with all this hair shit?"

Camy stepped into the room. "I told you I used to do hair before I moved over here."

Malik pulled out the outfit that he was looking for then headed back to her room. "Man, from the looks of things, you were about your business. I think you need to get back on that shit. Hoes always want they head combed."

"I thought about it, but I'm not sure yet."

Outside, Ms. Patt watched as Malik helped Camy into his truck. She smiled, seeing that they had worked out their problems.

"Where you wanna go, or do it matter?"

"I wanna go to your favorite place," she said, giggling.

"All right, I got you, baby."

Malik drove them to his favorite spot. He had warned her from jump that she was going to fall in love with that spot. Helping Camy out, Malik grabbed her ass under her dress.

"Malik!"

"My bad, baby. I couldn't help it:"

She might have stopped him, but that smile on her face told him that she loved the attention that he gave her.

"What's going on, Malik?" Camy asked, noticing that his phone kept blowing up.

"Nothing, baby. I'm about to just cut this bitch off, so we can focus on us."

"You don't have to cut your phone off. What if it's an emergency or something?"

Malik looked at his phone again. Shaking his head, he laughed.

"What?"

"People are crazy. They keep tagging me in that damn fight with you and Shay at the market."

"So, you do know the bitch?"

"I never said I didn't know her. I told you she wasn't my bitch, and that was the end of that conversation."

Camy's attitude was back. "I'm ready to go."

"Don't start that shit. The food just got here, baby. Go ahead and eat."

Camy picked over her food, wondering if she had been too quick to forgive him. Malik was a mystery. He told people what he wanted to tell them and when. You had to stay five steps ahead of him to understand him. Camy tried to enjoy her food since he wasn't about to take her home. It was good, but she wasn't ready to be in a happy mood when he was on bullshit.

"My last boyfriend was a liar and cheater. Not only did I have to fight bitches, I also found a bitch funky-ass panties under my pillow. I was so disgusted that I vomited all over his bed."

"You gonna eat or talk about panties and vomit?"

His nonchalant ways pissed her off even more. "What the hell are we doing, Malik?"

"I'm trying to eat, and you're sitting here, letting your food get cold. Ain't that what it looks like?"

"I'm talking about with us. I know that girl was the same girl that was staring me down the first time you took me out. I asked you if she was your bitch—"

Malik cut her off. "And I told you no. Look, I'm telling you this now for the last time. I don't have a bitch. Now, can we please enjoy our evening?"

As they continued to eat, Malik noticed that she had started dancing in her seat again. He used this as an opportunity to completely get back on her good side.

"You wanna go dance?"

"No, especially not with you."

Malik chuckled. "Why you acting so mean to me, baby?"

"Can I trust you with my heart, Malik?"

"Hell yeah," he answered, looking into her eyes.

"Completely?"

"Most definitely."

Camy picked her fork back up so that she could finish her food. He answered her questions, and there wasn't shit else to bitch about. Soon after, the couple was on the dance floor, grinding on one another. The DJ played two fast songs followed by a slow jam. This time, when the slow jam came on, Camy didn't run away when he began to place kisses on her and rub her body down. She loved the way their bodies craved for one another.

"I love you," Malik whispered in her ear as they danced.

"I love you too, baby."

The two barely made it out of the parking lot without taking each other's clothes off. Making love was heavy on their minds that night.

They were so busy trying to rush into the house that they didn't see the trouble that was waiting for them. As soon as they walked in, they started to undress. That was when the rounds of shots went off.

"Get the fuck down!" Malik yelled, forcing her to the floor. Malik covered her as she lay there, balled up, screaming. Soon after, he could hear the tires screeching off.

"Man, what the fuck!" Malik tried to get up, but Camy grabbed him tighter.

"Baby, please don't leave me."

"I'm gonna be good, baby. They gone." Malik gave her a peck on the lips before jumping up and going over to the window. He could see people peeking out their doors and windows. That was when he saw his mama and uncle racing over to Camy's house.

"Ma, y'all go back over there."

"Are y'all okay?" Ms. Patt asked, stopping in her tracks.

"Yeah, Ma, we good."

Malik went outside to talk to his mama and uncle. If nobody else saw shit, he knew they did.

"You know that was that nigga, Tim, right?" Ms. Patt said.

"Yeah, Ma, I know."

Davon butted in. "What you gonna do, nephew? What you want me to do?"

Malik smiled. His uncle stayed with the shits. "Just keep your eyes and ears open, Unc."

Rell soon pulled up, hopping out of his car. "Bro, y'all good? Ain't nobody get hit, did they?"

"Hell nah, but I'm about to take her to my crib. I gotta get somebody to replace these windows tomorrow," Malik said, looking over the damage.

It wasn't the right time to joke, but Rell couldn't help it. "You taking a chick to your house? Okay, li'l bro. I see you."

"I gotta protect her."

Malik walked back into the house to get Camy. "Baby, grab some clothes so we can go."

Camy was terrified and still hiding on the floor.

"Come on, baby. We gotta go."

"I'm scared, Malik," she admitted.

He helped her off the floor. "I got you, baby, and I'm not gonna let nothing happen to you."

Camy allowed him to lead her into her room to grab some clothes. "Where are we going?"

"My crib."

"Your crib?" she asked, giggling.

He was confused. "I do have a house, girl. What the fuck you thought? I was homeless or something?"

Camy laughed harder. "No, not homeless, but I have never even heard you talk about your house. That's it."

"Oh, okay, silly ass."

As they rode to Malik's house, Camy started to get worried. She had tried joking around back at her house to keep from crying, but she was scared. She didn't want to get shot over a nigga's bruised ego.

"Do you know who did this, and are they gonna come back? Are we gonna be okay?"

Malik ignored her and continued to drive home.

"Malik, do you hear me?"

Camy sat back, rolling her eyes, seeing that he wasn't paying her any mind.

Malik pulled into his garage and then hopped out. When he got over to Camy's side, she sat there with her arms folded.

"You not getting out?"

Camy allowed him to help her out, but her attitude was clear as day. Malik held her hand as they walked into the house. He knew that she was scared, and that was why she was acting out.

Camy looked around and could admit that he had a nice place. "Nice place."

"Thanks. Follow me."

Camy followed Malik into his bedroom. "Look, we both had a long night. The bathroom right up the hall. I can run you some bath water, so you can relax and get some sleep."

"What about you? Where are you going?"

Malik headed out of the room, leaving her standing there with her unanswered questions. He went to run her bath water like he said he would. He wasn't in the mood to answer her questions because she had to have known that he wasn't about to let that shit that Tim did slide.

When Malik came back into the room, Camy was no longer with an attitude. She was now standing there, crying.

Malik wrapped her up in his arms. "Baby, don't cry. I'm gonna handle this shit."

"It's not that, Malik."

"Then what is it?"

"I'm scared. I'm really scared, and I'm not used to feeling like this."

Malik held her and noticed how her body trembled in his arms. He was really ready to put hands on Tim for scaring his baby like that.

It took some convincing, but Malik finally got Camy to relax in the tub. He used this time to hit Rell up.

"What's up, bro? Where you at?"

"Aye, bro, Camy tripping. Let me get her together, then I'll be that way."

Rell shook his head. "I'll go handle this shit by myself while you take care of the wife."

Malik chuckled. "Bro, chill out. I'll hit you up when I'm ready to meet up."

"All right, my nigga."

The brothers got off the phone just in time for Camy to walk in.

"You good now, baby?" Malik asked.

Camy smiled. "That did feel good. Your tub is so much bigger than mine, and your water gets hotter."

Malik watched as she went through her bag to grab something to sleep in.

"You can't wear clothes in my bed."

"Shut up, boy," Camy said, laughing at him.

Camy put on a T-shirt and then climbed into bed. "Come join me, baby."

"I can't. I gotta go meet bro and handle some shit."

Camy sat up. "Malik, I'm not stupid, and I know what you are thinking."

"Camy, chill. You don't know shit."

"Well, come to bed with me."

Malik shook his head. "Why the fuck you gotta do this shit? Why can't you just take your ass to bed?"

Camy pulled the cover off. "Malik, I'm telling you now. I don't like this shit. If you leave, I'm leaving!"

Malik buried his face in his hands. "Why the hell you gotta be like this? Do you really think I'm supposed to just sit back and let this shit slide?"

Camy was now back crying. "I'm sorry. I just can't imagine how I would feel if anything happened to you. Just leave the shit alone please."

Malik tried not to let her tears stop the way he was feeling for real. He wanted Tim's head on a stick, but she was acting like she was going to run off if he left the damn house.

"Don't I keep telling you that ain't shit gonna happen to me? Look, go to sleep and I'll be right back."

Camy tried to listen to him, but her tears kept falling. She hadn't felt so scared in her life. Malik hadn't been in her life for a long time, but he had come into her life and loved her. She loved him enough not to want anything bad to happen to him.

Malik could see that she wasn't calming down, so he climbed into bed with her. She didn't even need dick to make her feel better. Malik held her in his arms and rubbed her until she had cried herself to sleep.

Twenty minutes later, Malik grabbed his phone off the nightstand. "Aye, bro, shit got crazy, but give me about ten, and I'll be there."

"All right," Rell said, trying not to laugh. He could see now that Camy was going to change his brother, and it just might be for the best.

Malik slid out of the bed, praying that she wouldn't pop her ass up like she would normally do.

While driving, Malik could only think about making it back home to Camy. She was going to fucking kill him if he had let a nigga take him away from her.

Their love story was new, but they were locked in.

Chapter 8

Camy awoke in Malik's arms, which felt like the softest place on Earth.

"Don't start all that weird shit, staring at me."

Camy giggled. "Now, you know if I didn't do that, then my day wouldn't be on the right track."

Malik gave her a kiss on the forehead before climbing out of bed. "I'm about to go get breakfast."

Camy sat up. "Malik, I hate eating out all the time. I think I wanna cook today."

"Ain't no food in that kitchen. That's why I been getting takeout."

Camy was confused. "Are you serious? So, you don't be cooking or nothing?"

"Nah, I really don't know how, but I know how to place an order," he answered.

"Damn, that explains a lot," she said, giggling.

Camy finally climbed out of bed. "How about you go get something from the market, and then I'll cook? If I eat out of a foam container again, I'm gonna go crazy. Then, I haven't been to the gym in about a week. Look at me," she said, spinning around so he could get a good look at her.

Malik smirked. "I don't see shit wrong with you. I like that thickness. Spin around again for me."

Camy blushed. "Thanks, baby, but I'm off my workout schedule, and it's starting to show."

Malik went to get food, and Camy had no problem keeping her promise by cooking it.

"Baby, can I go home today?"

Malik continued to eat, acting as if he hadn't heard her.

"Malik, why do you do that shit? I hate when you go deaf when I ask you certain questions. I know for a fact if I asked you if you wanted to fuck me on this table, I would have got an answer."

Malik had Camy staying at his place for the last four days, and although Camy didn't know the reason, she was very curious to know. "Malik, why am I still here?"

"These eggs good as fuck. I love your cooking, baby."

"Malik, stop playing with me. I wanna go home," she demanded.

Malik got up from the dining room table and took his plate into the kitchen. He then went into the living room and completely ignored her.

Camy followed him into the living room. "Since you're ignoring me, I'll just get my stuff and catch an Uber home."

Malik watched as she stormed back to his room. "Fuck!" he yelled, making his way into the room. "Why the fuck you can't just sit yo' ass down somewhere and chill out?"

"Malik, I can't do that because you can't even answer simple questions. How hard is it to tell me why I can't go home?"

Malik walked toward Camy. "Baby, I swear the best thing right now is for you to be here with me."

"Why? Can you at least tell me that?"

Malik hesitated to respond at first.

"See, Malik, you can't even talk to me. I ask questions, and you become a mute."

Camy started grabbing her belongings and stuffing them into her bag. "Fine, don't say shit. I'm going home," she yelled.

Malik snatched her bag and then tossed it across the room.

"What the fuck, Malik?"

"Damn, listen to me, Camy. I can't let you go home yet. Just sit the fuck down somewhere," he yelled, giving her a little shake.

Camy was tired and scared, which caused her to start crying. "Why?"

"'Cause I can't fucking protect you if you at home in the middle of all this shit. I need you here with me until this shit dies down. Can you please do me a favor and give it a few more days? I promise I'll make it up to you."

Camy had never asked what happened the night he sneaked out after her house was shot up, but now, she felt like she needed to know. "What happened, Malik? What the hell happened?"

"What you think happened?"

Camy could only imagine the worst. "Oh my gawd, Malik."

"I told you I wasn't gonna let shit happen to you, and if that means keeping you locked up over here, then that's what we gotta do. I know you wanna go home, but just give it a few more days."

"He dead?"

Malik smirked but ignored her question, like always. "Breakfast was good as hell. I might need a nap off that shit."

Camy now had a clearer understanding of everything and used the information she had learned to calm her nerves, but she still had questions. "Was this all because of me?"

"Nah, baby. My beef with this nigga go back, a few years back, to be exact. It was only a matter of time before I got at that nigga. I honestly think he was trying to get at you because he saw us together."

"Oh, can we cuddle now and watch a movie, baby?" Camy asked, finally trying to change the subject.

Malik chuckled, thinking that she was crazy as hell, just like him.

"Damn, Mona, if I would have known you were this freaky, I would have been fucked you."

Mona brought her head up from under the covers. "When you were with Camy, did you ever think about it?"

"Nah. To be honest, you were the best friend and always been off limits. I did my dirt, but there were certain lines that I wouldn't cross."

Mona rubbed Jason's chest as she rested her head on his it. After lying up with Jason for a couple of days, she was completely satisfied with all the work that she had put in to finally get her man.

"Baby, I was just thinking—"

Jason cut her off. "What's up?"

"I was just thinking that since we both like what's been going on between us, maybe it's time for us to break the news to Camy. We owe her an explanation." She smiled, knowing that it would kill Camy if she found out that they were together now.

Jason sat up, pushing her head off his chest. "Bitch, is you stupid? We ain't got no love story to tell. We fucked, end of story," he barked.

"What?"

At this point, Jason was putting his clothes on. It was clear that Mona had lost her damn mind. Camy was still the top pick on his list.

"Jason, you really about to play me like that? You been at my house for the past few days, fucking me and calling me baby, making me feel special, and now, you're tripping. You still love that bitch?"

Jason put his shirt on. "Play you like what? What you really thought was going on here? Just because a nigga fuck you while looking deep into your eyes and call you baby don't mean that you're more than just a nut. If you ask me, you played yourself. You know who got my heart."

Mona cried, feeling stupid as Jason walked out. She never saw this coming. The crazy thing about getting played by your best friend's ex is that you always want to run to her to tell her how you got played. Mona did all that planning to get Jason, and he turned out not to be shit, just like Camy had been saying for the longest.

"Happy birthday, baby!" Camy yelled, waking Malik up.

Malik had stayed in his house for a few years and never had a woman over, and now, he had a chick over, jumping on his bed as if she had lost her damn mind.

"Damn, Camy, you knew I put my phone on Do Not Disturb for this exact reason, and yo' crazy ass still woke me up."

Camy continued to jump on the bed. "I'm sorry, old man. Did you need some extra sleep this morning?" she teased jokingly.

Malik pulled the cover off his face, trying to ignore the fact that she was irritating as hell.

Camy eventually got tired of jumping and flopped down. "Are you ready to eat? Your birthday breakfast is ready, baby."

Malik sat up enough to grab Camy. "Let's just eat some sleep for breakfast. I'm tired as hell this morning, baby."

"I'm not sleepy."

Malik's grip got tighter around her. He was determined to get some rest.

Camy might have said she wasn't sleepy, but she soon found herself drifting off. This wasn't the first time he put her to sleep just by holding her.

When Camy woke up, she was surprised that Malik was now out of bed. Walking around, she found him at the table, eating.

"Eww, baby. Why are you eating that old food?"

Malik was confused. "How is this old? You just cooked this shit this morning."

"It's twelve now. Who warms up breakfast food? That's like eating leftovers."

"Every day, you show me just how crazy your ass is for real," he teased.

Camy giggled. "It's your birthday. You at least deserve a hot meal."

"I put this shit in the microwave. It was hot and good."

They looked at each other across the table, each thinking the other was crazy and had issues.

"Hold up, let me get this."

Malik answered his phone while she made herself a bowl of cereal. She was serious about not eating the food that she had cooked earlier that day.

"So, everything good?" Malik paused while on the phone, listening to what the caller had to say. "Yeah, all right. See you later." Malik hung up with a smirk on his face. Everything was falling into play for that evening.

"Baby, my clothes at my house for the party tonight," Camy announced as he walked back into the dining room.

"Yeah, I know. I'm gonna stop by and grab it."

"Can I go too? I need other items too. It only make sense that I get ready there. It would be too much to have you go over there then come back here then go back over there."

"Yeah, I guess, but we coming back here after the dinner."

"All right."

Truth be told, Camy could have gone home by now, but Malik had become selfish with her time and craved to be around her all day. He was still trying to figure this whole love thing out too.

Camy had left his gifts at her house and wanted him to have them, especially since he didn't think she got him anything. On top of that, she missed her home. She couldn't wait for all this bullshit to be over so that she could stay home for good.

Malik got up from the table. "I'm about to step in there. Everybody and their mama calling, and I don't wanna disturb your breakfast," he said, laughing.

"Whatever, boy. The only reason you don't like cereal is because fast food places don't deliver it," she teased.

Malik disappeared into the other room to tell everyone thank you for all the birthday love.

On his birthday, he could do anything in the world that he wanted to, but he made it a tradition to have a family/ friend dinner at his mom's house. Every year, she would cook, and everyone would sit around and just enjoy themselves.

The only difference this year was that he was coming with a date. He knew his mama had already told anyone who would listen that he had a friend coming.

After breakfast, Malik drove Camy to her house. "Baby, please don't take all day. I want you to meet everybody before they get too drunk."

Camy was all smiles as they pulled up to her house. It felt like it had been too long since she was there. "Stop acting like you know me. I only have to get dressed and touch up my hair."

Before going into the house, Camy ran back to the car. "Thank you, baby."

"For what?"

Camy had a big smile on her face. "For getting my shit fixed."

"That's nothing. Now, go get ready."

Camy raced into the house. "Home sweet home," she said, breaking out in a little dance.

Malik walked into the kitchen. "Hey, Ma, everything smells so good."

"Thanks, birthday boy. Your Uncle Jimmy got that grill going for your special day."

"Yeah, I know. I already went to the backyard and saw him."

"So, where that girl at? You did invite her, didn't you?"

Malik smiled at his mama mentioning Camy. "She is across the street, getting ready. I think everything is gonna work out just fine tonight."

"All right, boy. Get out of my kitchen, and I'll see you later."

"Thanks again, Ma," Malik said, giving his mama a peck on her cheek.

"You know I got your back, son. Now, gone."

Malik went across the street, feeling good about the night. The food was smelling good, and he and Camy were about to walk in looking good. What could possibly go wrong?

Malik waited patiently on the couch for Camy to walk out. Although he had picked her outfit, he still couldn't wait to see just how fine she was going to look with it on.

"Malik, I can't wear this!" she yelled from the bedroom.

"Camy, stop playing with me. Come on out here, girl."

Camy slowly walked out of the room. "This dress doesn't fit right anymore. You think it shrunk?"

Malik didn't mean to, but he laughed. "Did it shrink, or did you grow?" he asked, noticing that she had put on some weight.

Camy stuck her middle finger up before storming off. "I'm really not going now," she yelled.

Malik laughed as he walked back into the room to calm her spoiled ass down. "Come on, baby. You look good as fuck. Ain't shit wrong with that dress."

"I'm not going, Malik," she said, stepping out of the dress.

"Don't do me like that, baby. You gonna fuck up my birthday like that?"

Camy took a seat on the bed, folding her arms. "You think I'm big?"

"No, baby, but I do think you spoiled as shit," he said, trying to hold his laugh in.

"Malik!"

Malik went over to the bed and grabbed her hand. "Baby, I swear you are perfect in my eyes, and it would mean so much to me if you would get dressed and help me enjoy my birthday."

Camy smiled. "Baby, you sure that dress doesn't look bad on me?"

"Positive, my love."

Camy stood up to redress. Once the dress was on, she stared at herself in the mirror. She had to admit that she had gained some weight. "Baby, I gotta start going back to the gym. I got too comfortable laying up under you."

"We getting fucked up tonight, so we can start back in about three days."

They both laughed.

Malik watched as Camy continued to get ready. He hadn't noticed before that day, but she had put on a little weight.

Malik eventually went back into the front room while she got ready. His phone was blowing up, and he didn't want to distract her from getting ready.

Camy walked out into the living room again, wearing the dress that he had picked out for his special day. "Let's try this again. How do I look?"

"Good as hell. Come give me a kiss."

Camy happily gave her man a kiss. "You ready?"

"Do you see all those cars out there, waiting on me? Hell yeah."

Malik wasn't a tad bit surprised by how his family had welcomed Camy with open arms. He had told a few that she was cool and easy to talk to before.

"Aye, cuz, happy birthday."

"Thank you, Toya."

Toya looked around to make sure no one was listening. "Cuz, I like her. You better keep her around, or I'll snatch her ass up."

"Yeah, she a cool friend."

Toya was the first but wasn't the last who approached him about Camy. His mama even mentioned how she liked her because she wasn't scared to eat.

"Aye, Camy, come be my partner and beat these mutha-fuckas' ass in this spades game," Malik called out.

"I can't."

"Stop playing and come on, girl!"

Camy went over to the table, but instead of having a seat, she whispered in his ear. "Baby, I don't know how to play this."

Malik looked at her with a strange face before cracking up, laughing. "Are you fucking serious?"

"What's going on? She playing or not?" Ms. Patt asked.

Camy gave Malik a look, begging him not to say anything, but it was too funny not to share. "Aye, don't judge my baby, but she don't know how to play spades."

Everyone that was around the table laughed.

"Aye, where the hell did you grow up at?" someone else yelled out.

Camy wasn't too embarrassed. She had heard all these jokes before. She even had to laugh because they took that shit so seriously.

Malik got up from the table. "Y'all can stop clowning her. Spades probably wasn't her thing."

"Get the hell up so me and Tiffany can play then, bro," Rell said, coming to the table.

When their family played cards, they always made it a habit to have couples going against each other. Malik had never brought a date, but in prior years, Shay had popped up and had been his partner.

Malik and Camy went to the other room to talk and to have a drink.

"Are you enjoying yourself?"

"It's your birthday. I should be asking you that."

"Yeah, but whenever me and my people get together, it's never nothing but love and a good time."

Camy looked around. "I see. But yes, I'm having a great time with you guys."

Malik gave Camy a kiss.

"Get a damn room!" Ms. Patt yelled.

Camy giggled. "Damn, I'll be back. I forgot your present at home."

"My present? I didn't know you got me something."

"Yeah, boy, it was a surprise," she said, walking out the door.

Malik watched her cross the street. She might have been bitching about that dress, but that muthafucka was doing exactly what he liked.

"Aye, boy, don't let that girl drink too much."

Malik turned around to see his mama standing there.

"What's up, Ma?"

"That girl is pregnant."

Malik had a dumb look on his face. "Fuck you talking about?"

"I've been watching that girl all night. She ain't just greedy like you said. She pregnant."

"Ma, chill on that. Ain't shit like that going on."

"You know I ain't never lied to you or that brother of yours. I'm the one that told him about Tiffany each and every time. You better listen to what I'm telling you."

Malik was having a good night up until that moment. He sat on the couch, thinking about what she said, while everyone continued to party. She didn't know it, but she had low-key fucked up his night.

Camy walked back into the house, carrying three gift bags with a bunch of balloons connected to them. She had a huge smile on her face as she handed him the bags. "Happy birthday, baby."

"Yes, happy birthday, baby!"

Everyone turned their attention toward the door.

"Shay, what the fuck you doing here?" Malik asked, surprised that she had the nerve to show up.

"Nephew, I told you that bitch crazy," Davon yelled out, eating a plate of ribs.

Malik didn't want any drama, so he quickly tried to handle the situation. "Aye, Shay, you gotta go. I really don't know why the fuck you here anyways."

She started to laugh. "It's your birthday, baby. Why wouldn't I be here? I'm the bitch that's been here for the last three years," she said, giving Camy a strange look.

Camy fixed her mouth to say something, but Malik started talking over her. "Look, you wasn't invited. You gotta go."

Camy was irritated and ready to fight if she had to. At this point, he had asked Shay to go a few times, and she was fucking up the vibe.

"Oh, so I'm not invited this year because you got a new bitch on your arms?"

"Who the fuck you calling a bitch? Didn't I just beat your ass?" Camy yelled.

Shay kept laughing at Camy. It tickled her how she was at that party, thinking she was special when she wasn't. "Aye, new bitch, I suggest you calm the fuck down. See, I didn't want to bust your bubble like this, but bitch, you ain't special. Truth be told, you're just another bitch he fucking. We all gotta play our role. No one bitch above the other."

Malik grabbed Shay. "Man, get the fuck from out here with that shit."

Shay wasn't about to let him just toss her out like trash without outing him. "Malik, tell her! Tell her how we was fucking for three years, and we was just fucking a month ago. Fucking you ain't make him stop fucking me, girl."

Now, Shay had Camy's attention. "What?" Camy asked, trying not to get in her feelings.

"That's right, bitch. Malik ain't shit but a good fuck. You ain't learned your place yet?"

Camy turned Malik's way. She could tell that he was pissed, but fuck all that. She was pissed too. "What is she talking about?"

"We can talk later," he snapped.

"No. What is she talking about? I asked you multiple times if that was your bitch."

"And I told you multiple times that I didn't have a bitch. Now, can we talk later?"

Camy wasn't about to let the shit die down. "So, the whole time we been together, you been fucking her."

"He been fucking both of us, bitch. He is both of our dick, silly bitch."

Instead of addressing Shay, Camy focused on Malik. "Really, Malik?"

Malik had had enough and finally snapped. "Look, y'all not about to fuck up my night. I'm grown as fuck and can do what the fuck I want. I'm not in a fucking relationship with nobody, so can't nobody question me about shit I do," he yelled.

Camy's whole face dropped, listening to him crush her soul. "What the fuck you mean you not in a relationship with nobody? What the fuck was we doing all these months?"

Malik could hear the pain in her voice, but that was the reason he wanted to talk to her in private. Malik tried to grab her hand, but she snatched it away.

"No, Malik! You ain't shit! You don't tell people that you're just fucking that you love them. How could you be so fucking heartless and do me like this?" Camy wiped away her tears before storming out of the house.

"Damn, Malik, she crying and shit," Shay teased.

"Get the fuck out, stupid-ass bitch! Why the fuck would you do that?"

"I told you I wasn't about to let you play with me no more."

Ms. Patt finally spoke up. "Shay, it's time for you to go, and please, don't come back around here."

Shay knew not to give her any mouth, so she finally left, proud of the damage she had created.

Camy went straight home and dropped to the floor, crying. Malik had made everything feel so real, and it was hard for her to wrap her mind around the fact that he was playing her the whole time.

Malik tried to chill out after they left, but after sitting there for twenty minutes, he got up to leave. He didn't even bother to say shit to anyone.

Camy was hurt and, usually, she wouldn't have wanted to be bothered, but she had to call Mona to tell her what had been going on with her. She needed to catch her up with everything since they hadn't spoken in a few weeks. After dialing her number three times, and each time no answer, Camy finally set her phone down.

Camy didn't bother to move, hearing the banging on her door. She knew that it was only Malik.

"Camy, open the door, baby."

Not paying him any mind, Camy got up from the floor and then went into her bedroom. A hot shower and her bed were about to be her only friends.

Malik had come up with the idea that he would just sit on her porch until she came out or eventually let him in. After a while, as he chilled on her porch, he started to see his people slowly leaving his party.

Finally remembering that he had a copy of her house keys, Malik let himself in. The house was quiet, but as he reached her bedroom, he could hear her crying. Malik wasn't coldhearted like she had called him, and her crying actually made him feel worse than he had before. Hurting her feelings was never in his plans.

"Baby, can we please talk?"

Camy jumped up, scared. She hadn't heard him come in over her crying. "Get out my house, you fucking liar."

"Camy, I never lied to you about shit. Stop saying that shit."

Camy climbed out of the bed. "I'm not about to do this with you. I need you to leave."

"So, you not gonna hear a nigga out? How the fuck you just gonna react off what that bitch said and don't hear me out?"

"Hear you out? Not only did I hear you, but a house full of people heard you clearly say that you were single. I also heard it out of your own mouth when you said you weren't in a relationship with anybody."

"Cause I'm not!"

Camy punched Malik in his chest, but her hit had no effect on him.

"Aye, keep your hands to yourself."

"'Cause you not? Did you really just say that shit again? What the fuck were we doing then, Malik? What was all this love shit then?"

Malik answered her questions. "We were friends, right? Friends can't love each other?"

Camy gave him a strange look. "Are you fucking re-tarded? I don't just give my body or my heart away to just someone that's a fucking friend."

Malik watched as she paced the floor while crying. He stood there, thinking of a way to calm her down, but every time he reached out to touch her, she swung on him.

Camy felt crazy. Never in a million years would she have thought that Malik would hurt her the way that he did. He made everything feel so good while they were together, just to say it all happened while they were just friends. There was no way around it. He played her.

"Camy," Malik called out.

Camy stopped pacing. "Just leave me alone please, Malik. I told you I didn't like being played with, and I hate for people to play with my feelings."

"You need to stop tripping. I still love you. We just not in a relationship. We doing us. Ain't that good enough? What more do you want from a nigga? Didn't I still treat you right?"

Camy shook her head. Thinking about everything, it was fucked up, but he was right. When they first started talking, he did mention him trying to be her friend. Yeah, they started fucking around and falling for each other, but not once did they ever make shit official.

Now that shit was clearer, it didn't make Camy feel better. Knowing the truth and having to face the truth hurt her even more.

Camy started crying even harder. Malik didn't care if she was fighting. He still pulled her closer toward him to hold her. "I'm sorry. I'm sorry if I hurt you. I promise I never wanted to hurt you."

Camy hated how she was hurt to the core but still allowed him to hold her. She didn't want to love him, but she did. Finally getting herself together, she pulled away. "I think you need to leave."

"I thought we were going back to my place after my party?" he asked as if she wasn't in the mood to kill his ass.

"Bye, Malik."

"You know I still love you, right?"

Camy shook her head. "Get the fuck away from me."

Malik placed a kiss on her forehead. "I'll call you in the morning."

Malik left, giving her a chance to process everything. He hoped that by the morning, she'd be right back to being his baby.

Camy woke up the next morning feeling cranky. Once Malik had left, she thought she could get some sleep, but her stalker was back playing on her phone.

Staring at her face in the bathroom mirror, she noticed a change in her image. She was hurt, and it showed. Malik had hurt her soul and broken her spirit. Camy walked away from the mirror, hating herself for being a fool in love again.

"See, Camy, that's what you get, moving too fast with these niggas" she told herself over a bowl of cereal.

Halfway into the bowl, she started to feel sick. She then got up and tossed the bowl in the sink. Lying down on the couch, she figured the milk upset her stomach because she had been drinking the night before.

It wasn't long before she dozed back off.

"Aye, bro, Tiffany said I can't hang around yo' ass no more," Rell said, joking into the phone.

"Ask her what I do."

"Bro, I'm not asking her that shit. For real, though, you know you ain't shit, right?"

Malik shook his head. "Bro, you sound like Mama. You know she woke up, blowing my phone up, talking that same bullshit you on now. I don't know why y'all tripping. I ain't do shit wrong."

Rell was now shaking his head. His brother didn't see the bullshit that he had been on with Camy. Rell honestly thought he would have changed his ways after admitting that he had fallen in love with her. "You talked to Camy this morning? How she doing?"

"Man, bro, she ain't even answering my calls. I know she mad, but I never lied to her about shit. It ain't my fault that she assumed some shit and never bothered to confirm."

Malik could hear Tiffany yell out to Rell, "Get the hell off the phone with his ass!"

Rell laughed. "See, bro, that bullshit you pulled last night at your party wasn't cool. You got my baby mad at me just for being your brother."

Malik still didn't see anything wrong with what he did. "Man, females be tripping and stay in they feelings. That's the damn problem, not me."

"Rell, hang up now!" Tiffany yelled again.

"Aye, bro, I gotta go, but I'll hit you later."

"All right," Malik said before hanging up.

Malik then tried to call Camy again, and once again, he didn't get an answer.

Since he had not given her back her house keys, Malik decided to get dressed and then stop by her house. Walking in, Malik didn't hear anything, but since her car was outside, he knew that she was there.

"Hey, baby, you good?"

Camy opened her eyes and was shocked to see Malik standing over her. "What the hell you doing here? How did you get in?"

Malik held the keys up.

"I'm gonna need those back."

"Damn, can I have a good morning or something?"

"Fuck you, Malik," she said, sitting up.

Instead of getting mad, Malik took a seat next to her. "I see you ain't make no breakfast. You wanna go out and grab some food?"

She hated him so much that not even the trapped fat girl in her fell for his food trap. "No, Malik, and I think you need to leave."

"Damn, baby. How you trying to put me out when all I did was come over and check on you?"

"If you think that's all you did, you really are slow."

"Stop talking to me like that. You all in your feelings when I did nothing wrong. I never lied to you. You are my baby, and I do love you. You actually the first female that I can say that I actually loved, but ain't no titles on shit. Think about it. I never gave out a title, but I did treat you right. We were friends. You were the one that threw the pussy at me."

Camy wanted to beat his ass because she knew he was right. It hurt knowing that she played herself. "Malik, I just don't want you around me. This wasn't a game that I wanted to play. You made sure I wasn't fucking with no other nigga when you had another bitch. How does that work?"

"So, what you saying is we can't chill no more? I know you loved us hanging out and shit. I don't understand why we need to switch shit up. Didn't I always show you a good time? And as far as me making sure you were all mine was simple. I don't share pussy."

Camy couldn't even respond. Even through her pain, he was right, and his smooth-talking ass almost had her giving in. Jumping up from the couch, Camy pulled herself together. "I'm done with this shit. At this point, I don't want no friends."

Malik stood up, grabbing her into a hug. "You really wanna end this shit?" he asked between sweet kisses on her neck. He knew he was her weakness and that her neck was her spot.

Feeling herself giving in and ready to give him all of her, Camy pushed him off of her. With tears in her eyes, Camy repeated herself. "I need you to leave."

After Malik finally got the point and walked away, Camy put him on the same block list as Jason. She was so sick of niggas.

Malik sat in front of Camy's house, debating his next move. He wasn't used to his female friends cutting him off like that. Shit, Shay still wanted him and knew everything. He wished Camy would at least agree to do the same.

Looking at his phone, Malik could see that Shay was still blowing his phone up. He really wasn't in the mood to deal with her, but since he needed to curse her ass out, he drove around to her house.

Shay had heard Malik banging on her door, but she was scared to open it. Although she had been blowing his phone up, she only wanted to talk over the phone.

"Shay, open the door. I know yo' big-headed ass in there."

"What you want, Malik?"

"You already know what I want. Open the fucking door!" he ordered.

Shay was scared. He was a little too aggressive for her. "I don't want to fight, Malik."

"I came to give you some dick. Ain't that why you been tripping? You miss Daddy?"

With a smirk on his face, Malik could hear her unlocking the door. She allowed him to step in, thinking that now that Camy was out of the picture, things could go back to normal.

Malik moved fast, choking her ass up on the wall. "Why the fuck you do that to that girl? What would make you do some stupid shit like that?"

"Let me go, nigga! Don't come around here trying to put the blame on me when you the one who was on all bullshit."

Malik banged Shay's head up against the wall. "Bitch, shut the fuck up! You fucked shit up with her."

Shay stared at Malik like he was crazy. He really didn't see how he was the problem in all this bullshit, stringing bitches along the way. "Malik, you know I love you, but I'm done with this shit. I don't wanna be a part of your game anymore."

"Fuck you talking about?"

"I thought with that bitch being out the way, you would be all mine, but I don't even want that position anymore."

Malik stood there, looking confused. His mind couldn't wrap around the fact that both of his bitches were on some bullshit. "I can understand why Camy on some bullshit, but what did I do to yo' punk ass?"

Shay couldn't help but laugh. "You are fucking delusional."

"How? What the fuck have I ever done wrong to you? I pay all your bills and your fucking rent. On top of that, I keep your pockets right. Ask yourself this—when was the last time you worked?"

Shay was speechless. He was making a point. Besides his not wanting to commit, he did take good care of her, but at the end of the day, her heart needed to be taken care of.

Malik was pissed but tried to keep his cool. He knew beating her ass wasn't going to help their situation, so he didn't bother to knock her upside her head. "Listen here. Camy not fucking with me no more because of the shit you did, and now, you trying to cut me off. What the fuck really going on? You gotta owe me."

Malik planted soft kisses on her neck while rubbing on her booty, hoping to get his way.

Shay could feel herself giving in and knew that after they fucked, he was going to be out in the streets, looking for a new bitch. "Stop, Malik. I said I'm not doing this shit anymore."

Grabbing her by the neck, Malik gave her one last kiss. "Fuck you then. Your dumb ass bet not call me back over here for shit. For now on, figure it out yourself."

Shay knew what she was doing was right, but she couldn't understand why she was crying when he walked out the door.

Malik couldn't believe the day he was having. If it weren't for bad luck, he wouldn't have had any.

Chapter 9

"I still love yo' ass," Malik said, grateful that Camy had even allowed him to come over so they could talk things out.

Malik waited for a response from Camy, but she remained quiet.

"You hear me talking to you, girl?" he asked, pushing her head off him.

"Dang, I hear you," she said, lying back down.

"When somebody tells you they love you, you're supposed to say something back with your rude ass. Now, let's try this shit again. I love you."

"I wish you'd stop telling me that."

"Why?"

"Because I hate you."

Malik pushed her back off of him. "Why the fuck you playing so much? You really hate me for real?"

"Yes, Malik, I really hate you."

Malik sat up. "Stop saying that shit before I start believing it."

"I never lied to you before, have I?" she asked.

Malik gave Camy a strange look. He couldn't believe how she was acting after giving her some good dick.

"Why are you looking at me like that, Malik? You can't possibly think that dick was gonna make me forget about all the games that you've been playing."

"Games? Really? What about the bullshit you been on lately?"

"What the fuck you talking about?"

"Stop acting crazy, girl. My mama already put me on game a month ago, and you still ain't said shit yet."

Camy was dumbfounded. She really had no clue what he was talking about. She knew his mama stayed in the window or on that porch, watching her, but she hadn't been doing shit to talk about. "What the hell are you talking about, Malik?"

"You ain't got shit to tell me?"

"No," Camy said, lying back down.

Malik sat there, watching her act like there wasn't shit going on. He shook his head as he thought about choking her ass up. "Since you wanna act like ain't shit going on, I'm gonna act the same way. I guess we'll talk when you ready to stop acting stupid."

"Malik, I don't know what you talking about."

Malik lay back down, and then Camy moved back over to lay on him. Malik couldn't help but wonder if she was playing with him, or if she was serious about not knowing she was pregnant. His mama was never wrong before with Rell and Tiffany, so he didn't have any reason to believe that she had made that shit up.

Camy was knocked out, while Malik stayed up with his mind on a hundred. Instead of rubbing on her booty like he would usually do, Malik found himself rubbing on her belly. She wasn't big or anything, but there was a small pudge. She was growing. Malik had also noticed that when they were fucking, her pussy was super wet. She always had some wet, good pussy, but it was different this time.

Malik placed a kiss on Camy. "I don't give a fuck what you say. I know you love me. We gonna do good at this parenting shit, too."

Camy lay there, pretending to be asleep, but she heard everything that he said. Instead of asking him what the fuck he was talking about, she thought back to everything. It made sense now. She had been so busy with Malik and getting fucked good that she hadn't noticed that she wasn't having a period. Then, when they broke up, she thought it was all the stress that had her fucked up.

Knowing what he was talking about now, instead of sticking around to talk to him, Camy left before he woke up. Camy walked into her house, rushing straight into the bathroom. She had picked up a home pregnancy test and needed to know if there was any truth to what Ms. Patt was telling her son. Camy wasn't feeling like herself as she paced the floor, waiting for the results to show. Those couple of minutes felt like hours to her.

"Fuck!" she yelled, holding the test in her hand. She still loved Malik, but having a nigga's baby wasn't a part of the plan. She couldn't believe that she slipped up and let his ass trap her.

Sitting on the couch, Camy pulled her phone out to call Mona. Camy knew that Mona had been in this situation twice before and could help her out, or at least be a listening ear.

"What's up, girl?"

"Mona, I fucked up for real. I need someone to talk to."

Mona was all for hearing how the perfect Camy fucked up. Hearing her on the verge of crying only excited her.

Mona quickly got off the phone to race to Camy's house.

"Hey, boo. I got the wine this time."

Camy took a seat on the couch while Mona went into the kitchen to get them some wine glasses. When Mona returned, she poured them both a glass.

"Here, girl. I can see the stress all over your face."

"I can't drink that."

"Girl, you know wine is our go-to when we are stressed."

Camy got up to go into the bathroom. When she returned, she was carrying the home pregnancy test in her hand. "I can't even drink, and I'm stressed the fuck out."

Mona jumped up. "Damn, girl, you pregnant for real?"

"Yes, Mona, and I don't know what to do. You know, for the most part, my dad still take care of me, so if I go to him with this shit, he gonna flip the fuck out. I don't see him being too happy about a baby."

Mona shook her head. "Girl, I say do what I do each time I get pregnant. Get rid of it. You are still young and have a full life to live. Then, to keep it real, you not even with the baby daddy. How is that gonna work? Do he even know? Do he even want this baby? And what about his other bitches? You can't be out here pregnant and fighting all his bitches."

Earlier that day, when Malik woke up and saw that Camy was gone, he was pissed. After showering, he raced to her house. They still needed quality time together. Using the key that he refused to return to Camy, Malik let himself in. He walked in just in time to hear all the bullshit that Mona was saying to Camy about them.

"What the fuck?" he barked, causing both girls to jump and look toward the door.

"Malik, what are you doing here?"

All of Malik's attention was on Mona. "Aye, bitch, you gotta get up outta here. You running your mouth about shit you don't even know about."

"Malik, calm down and stop talking to her like that."

Malik was now walking toward Camy. "Shut yo' lying ass up. I thought you didn't know shit. Now, get this bitch outta here before I beat both y'all asses."

Camy had never really seen him upset like that before, especially toward her. She was scared to say anything else. Instead, she just looked at Mona. In a way, she wanted Mona to stay and help her, just in case he tried to fight or hit her, but she also wanted her to leave and not get beat up too.

"I'm out of here, Camy. Just remember what I said."

Malik picked up one of the glasses and threw it at her as she walked out the door. "Get the fuck outta here, ole funky bitch."

Once Mona left, Malik continued to go off. "You hate me so much that you would lie about knowing you were pregnant? Then, you sitting yo' ass up in here with that bitch, drinking wine and talking about killing my baby like it was a fucking sport. I really should fuck you up," he barked, jumping in her face.

"I didn't know until this morning, and I wasn't drinking," Camy cried.

Malik grabbed Camy by the neck, giving it a squeeze. "Let me smell your breath." His choking her caused her mouth to open a little. He then gave her a kiss because he didn't smell wine on her breath. "Thank you," he said, letting her go.

"I asked her to come over because I needed someone to talk to after finding out. I didn't agree to shit she was talking about. You gotta calm down," she said as he paced the floor and mumbled about killing her.

Malik stopped for a second. "I don't like that bitch, and she ain't your real friend."

"What? I've known her for years."

Malik helped Camy sit back down on the couch as he calmed down. "That bitch ain't your friend. The way she called herself giving you all that bad advice, I can tell she is really jealous of you. And just to respond to all that bullshit she was talking, yeah, we ain't together, but I'm not a ho-ass nigga. You know I do love you and my baby. I ain't never been no daddy before, but I know I'll be there for both of y'all every step of the way. You got my word on that."

Camy started to cry.

"What's wrong? You don't believe me?"

"I do believe you. I believe everything that you said. I'm just scared."

"You ain't got shit to be scared of. I got you."

Camy moved closer toward Malik so that she could straddle his lap. She then rested her head on him. Malik held her in silence while rubbing her back so that she could calm herself down.

"Why the hell did you leave out like that this morning? You ain't even leave the forty dollars on the dresser."

Camy started to laugh. "Shut the hell up, boy. Anyways, I needed to come home and get my head together."

"You know, if you ever need someone to talk to, you always got me. Fuck that bitch you call your friend. I'll listen to you, even if it's about me."

Camy continued to laugh. Malik always made her laugh, no matter what the situation was.

Malik held Camy, thinking about their situation. He was about to be a first-time dad, and although he was scared as hell himself, he was also happy.

"Malik, is having a baby gonna mess up your life with your bitches?"

"You goofy as hell. I don't have no bitches. I told you that shit before. You about to be the mother of my child. Worry about that shit. My baby better be your top priority from here on out. I don't need him stressing over shit. Do you hear me, Camy?"

"Yes, Malik, I hear you. But also, you better not give me a reason to be stressed out. You need to be on your shit, too."

Malik gave Camy a kiss. "You know I love you, right?"

"Yeah, I know."

"You really ain't gonna say the shit back? You a mutha-fucka with your shit, girl. I'm giving you one of the best gifts in the world, and you treat me like I ain't shit," he said, rubbing her belly.

Camy giggled. "Shut up, boy. Besides, we just friends. I don't have to tell you that every time we together."

Malik didn't like the way she said that "friends" shit, but she had only repeated the shit that he had been saying.

Camy got up so that she could get her phone.

"Who the fuck is that texting you?"

Camy quickly said, "Nobody," as she read the text.

Mona: Gurl, that nigga is crazy. This is exactly why you don't need no baby with his ass. Is he still there? He ain't over there beating your ass, is he?

Camy set the phone down, shaking her head.

Since she was acting weird to him, Malik grabbed her phone and then read the message. "I talk a lot of shit, but I ain't never beat yo' ass or nothing. Tell that bitch to stop speaking ill on my name before I really give her something to talk about."

"Malik, calm down. That is my best friend. She is only looking out for me."

"Tell her you good. You are good, ain't you?"

"No, I'm not good."

Malik sat up. "What's wrong with you? What you need?"

"I'm hungry."

Malik laughed. "Girl, if you don't get the fuck on. Don't start all that whining shit for some damn food."

Camy was cracking up. "Baby, we are hungry for real."

"You want me to go pick something up, or you wanna go out?"

"Go out. I need to get out of this house."

"Go get dressed then."

Camy got up, but before going into the bathroom, she told him to clean up the wine and glass that he had spilled on her floor.

As soon as Malik heard the shower water running, he picked up her phone to respond to Mona's bitch ass.

Camy: You don't have to worry about me. I'm good.

Mona quickly responded.

Mona: Are you sure? He seems like a wild one.

Malik responded as if he was still Camy.

Camy: We good, bitch. Matter of fact, he balls deep in me right now. You need to mind your fucking business.

Mona could tell that she had pissed Camy off, and it was clear that Malik really had her mind gone. Instead of responding, Mona went to visit Jason. She knew that he would do exactly what she needed him to do.

"I'm surprised to see you here. What's up, Mona?" Jason asked, letting her in.

Mona sat on the couch with fake tears in her eyes. "I just left Camy's house, and it's a lot going on. I'm so scared for my best friend."

Jason was concerned. "What's going on with her? She got a nigga blocked, so I haven't talked to her in a minute."

"She dating this guy, and he beating on her."

Jason jumped up from the couch. "What? I know you lying. She too smart for that shit."

"I was just over there, and the nigga kicked me out. He told me that if I didn't leave, he was gonna beat my ass and hers."

"Man, you gotta give me her address. I can't let that shit slide."

"Jason, Camy would never forgive me if I did that. Besides, this guy is not your average nigga. He crazy and be having guns and shit. He might be a little too hood for you."

"Damn, you saying that like I'm a bitch or something."

Mona laughed. "Nah, not like that, but this nigga don't fight nobody but Camy. He shoot niggas. She even told me that he had shot her house up not too long ago because he thought she was talking to a nigga at the market," she lied.

Jason shook his head. "Man, are you serious?"

"Yes. I think we need to figure out how to save her from him before it's too late."

Mona had planted a seed in Jason's head, and he was going to make sure he found a way to save Camy.

It only took Jason twenty minutes to pull up to Camy's father's house.

Camy had gotten used to being back under Malik again. He made sure she was good and ate every day. He even tried to cook a few times. She was loving all the attention and not just because of the gifts.

"Malik, I'm about to go by myself. You're gonna make me late."

"Shut yo' ass up. I'm pulling up now."

That morning, Camy had her first doctor's appointment. Instead of Malik spending the night like he had been doing, he had gone home for whatever reason. Now, Camy was worried about being late.

Camy walked out the door just as Malik was pulling up. He jumped out of the car to help her get in.

"Malik, I'm not disabled. I got it."

"I wasn't helping yo' ass. I was helping my baby. And here is some food for him. Yo' ass bet not enjoy it."

Camy pulled out her hash brown, cracking up laughing at him. "Thanks, baby. Why do you keep saying 'him'? What if we later find out it's a girl?"

Malik placed a kiss on her lips before driving off. "'Cause I just know."

Camy was surprised that Malik acted as if he had some sense at her appointment. Instead of cracking jokes, he was serious and asked questions to make sure she was doing everything right to keep the baby safe. Camy knew he was going to be the perfect father.

On the way home, Camy's phone started to blow up.

"Who that?"

"Damn, friend, get out my business," she teased jokingly.

Once again, Malik didn't like her saying that shit. For some reason, he was okay when he said it, but her saying it made him get into his feelings.

"Hey, I'm gonna call you back when I get into the house."

Malik listened, trying to figure out who she was talking to.

"All right, I'll make sure I call you back, and I love you too." Camy put her phone back into her bag.

"Man, who the fuck is that?"

"Why you so nosy? Stay out my phone conversation," Camy snapped back.

Malik continued to drive, but his mind couldn't get off her telling somebody that she loved them when she hadn't been telling him.

Malik helped Camy into the house. "You need anything while I'm out?"

"No, I'm about to take a nap."

Malik followed her into the bedroom. Camy didn't know what his problem was, but he was quiet, and his watching her made her nervous.

"What's wrong, Malik?"

"Nothing, man."

Camy undressed and then put on a long T-shirt before climbing into the bed. She knew something was bothering him, but since he didn't want to talk about it, she wasn't going to press the issue.

"All right, I guess I'll see you later."

"Okay, Malik."

Malik then kissed her while rubbing her stomach. "You know I love you, right?"

"Yeah, baby. I know. I love you, too," she mumbled as she closed her eyes.

That was all that Malik wanted to hear from her. Lately, he had been feeling like she was serious about not loving him anymore.

Malik gave her one last kiss before walking out. He went straight across the street to tell his mama the news. It was hard keeping it a secret, but he had decided to wait until the doctor confirmed that she was pregnant.

"Aye, Ma, what you cooking?"

"I got some spaghetti, chicken, and garlic bread in there. You want a plate?"

"Yeah."

Ms. Patt stared at her son, wondering what was going on with his ass. "I see you and Camy back hanging out. How has she been?"

Malik's face lit up as if he had been waiting for her to ask. "Ma, we went to the doctor today. Her ass is pregnant. I'm about to be a daddy."

Ms. Patt smiled at how happy he was. "I told your ass a month ago that girl was pregnant. How she taking the news?"

"She's happy. I'm happy. We good. I'm praying for a heathy-ass little boy."

Ms. Patt wasn't trying to start shit, but it wouldn't be her if she didn't run her mouth. "So, is she okay with having a baby by a nigga with commitment issues?"

"Damn, Ma, I just told you we was good. Why you bothering me with that bullshit?"

"Because I don't wanna see her crying and hurt over your ass again. Then, to bring a baby in this world with a guy like you don't make no fucking sense. You can't commit to her, so I don't see you committing to a baby."

Malik stood up. "So, what you trying to say?"

Ms. Patt stood up, accepting his challenge. "I'm saying she don't need to have that baby. You still a boy and have a lot of growing up to do. You are not ready to do shit that real men do."

Ms. Patt hurt his feelings, and as bad as he wanted to snap, he had to remember that she was his mama. "Ma, that's some fucked-up shit to say. You want her to abort my baby? You should know better than anybody that I'll do right by mine. You know how hard it was for me not to have a daddy growing up and always running to Rell for everything. How the fuck you gonna try to play me like that?"

"I'm just saying, why put that girl and that baby through all your bullshit?"

"You know what, Ma? Don't say shit else to me."

"I'm just making sure you ain't about to fuck that girl life up!" she yelled, not caring if he was mad.

Malik stormed out of the house, making sure to slam the door. He was beyond pissed off, and his feelings were hurt. He did act like his daddy with that whole "scared of commitment" shit, but he would never run out on his baby. Growing up without a daddy taught him just how much a child needs a daddy, especially a little boy.

Malik did want to chill with his mama, but after she pissed him off, he went back across the street to be with Camy.

Malik undressed, then climbed in bed with her. Just like a magnet, she moved over to be close to him.

When Camy finally woke up, Malik was up, just lying there.

"How was your nap?"

"I ain't been to sleep yet," he answered dryly.

"You all right, baby?"

"Not really. We need to talk about something."

"What's up?" she asked nervously. She could hear the seriousness in his voice.

"When you found out you were pregnant, I told you that you were keeping my seed. I never asked you how you felt about having my baby, knowing how things are between us. How do you really feel? Do you think having my baby will fuck up your life?"

"Malik, where is all this coming from? Are you still thinking about all that shit Mona said? I told you I wasn't listening to that shit."

"Hell nah, I ain't talking about that shit, but somebody else just said the same shit, and it hit me that I never asked you how you really felt about everything."

"Malik, I want my baby. We might not be together, but that doesn't stop the fact that this baby was made out of love. You do love us, right?"

"Hell yeah. I told you that you were the first girl that I ever loved, and I ain't never lied to you about shit before. The baby ain't even fully developed yet, and I love him, too. I want this baby more than anything in the world."

After talking to Camy about everything, Malik felt a little better. He couldn't imagine telling Camy to have an abortion. That shit didn't even sit right with him. He also couldn't believe that his mama would fix her mouth to say some shit like that to him.

"You hungry?" he asked.

"Yeah, I haven't ate since this morning."

"What you got a taste for?" he asked, sitting up.

"Malik, you ain't been to sleep yet. I want you to relax now. I'm gonna go into the kitchen and make something while you sleep."

"You sure, baby? You know it ain't shit to go pick something up. Is it even safe for you to be on your feet like that?"

Camy giggled. "I'm good, baby. Thanks for being concerned." Camy walked out of the room before he could ask any more questions. She could see that he was going to be very overprotective of her and their baby.

While Camy worked her way around the kitchen, Malik still couldn't sleep, especially with her phone going off back-to-back. He wanted to answer it, but seeing that it was her dad, he decided not to.

"Here, baby, it's your daddy," he said, handing her the phone.

Because she was cooking, she put the phone on speaker. "Hey, Daddy. I know I was supposed to call you back from earlier, but I came in and went straight to bed. What's up?"

"That boy, Jason, called me and told me that you were in trouble. Why the hell you ain't call me yourself?"

Camy giggled. "What? I haven't talked to him in months, Dad. I don't know why he won't leave me alone."

"He said you got a boyfriend, and the muthafucka be hitting on you. You know I don't play that shit, and if you need me, I'll drop everything and come handle that shit."

Camy shook her head. "Daddy, that boy is probably telling you that because he can't handle the fact that I'm talking to someone else. Dad, do me a favor and block that fool."

"Yeah, I'm gonna go ahead and do that soon as I get off the phone with you."

"Dad, before you hang up, I need to tell you something."

Malik gave her a strange look. He prayed that the news didn't make her dad want to kill him before even meeting him.

"What's up, baby girl?"

"Dad, I'm having a baby."

David held the phone in silence, trying to process the news that his little girl had just told him.

"Daddy, are you still there?"

"Yes, baby, I'm still here. I'm so happy for you, Camy, and I know if your mom was still here, she would be so proud of you, too. Now, when can I meet this guy? I need to see who knocked my daughter up."

"Dad, maybe we could stop by on Sunday for dinner?"

"Yes, that sounds like a plan. I'm gonna go over the plans with Sarah so that she can make enough food. I'm so happy for you, Camy, but I gotta go. I wanna tell everybody the good news."

Camy got off the phone with a huge smile on her face. She always pictured her dad going off if she ever got pregnant, but he took the news better than she thought.

"Malik, we're having dinner with my dad and his wife Sunday."

"So I heard."

Camy peeped his tone. "I'm sorry. I should have asked you before I just jumped into his plans. I'm sorry, baby."

"Ain't shit to be sorry about. It's cool. I'm just wondering why the fuck that nigga, Jason, speaking ill on my name."

"Right. I wonder what the fuck was he thinking. Why the fuck is he even talking to my dad anyways?"

"Aye, calm down. Let me worry about this bullshit. Just make sure you don't burn the food."

"Shit!" Camy yelled, racing back over toward the stove to check on the food.

Malik went back into the living room to replay everything that had just taken place. There was no way that nigga had just made that shit up. Camy hadn't talked to him in months, and he knew Camy wasn't lying about that shit. Malik had looked through her phone enough to know who she had been talking to.

"That funky bitch," he mumbled as he put everything together in his head. "Aye, Camy, come here for a minute," he called out.

Camy walked into the living room. "Yes, baby? What is it?"

Malik patted his lap for her to come take a seat. "Do you trust me?"

"Umm, I guess I do."

"Don't just guess. I need you to know for sure."

Camy gave it some thought. Even though he did hurt her, and she often told him that she hated him, she couldn't lie. She did trust him. He had already proven to her that he wouldn't let anybody hurt her.

"I trust you, but where is this going?"

"I don't want you hanging out with that Mona bitch. She moving funny as hell. You gotta watch her."

"Malik, she has been my friend since we were like ten years old. She's like a sister to me."

"Cut that bitch off. And she ain't gonna be our baby godmama either."

Camy jumped up off his lap. "Malik, you're tripping. You ready to eat?" she asked, trying to change the subject.

"Yeah, fix me a plate."

The couple sat at the table, eating in silence. Her mind was on trying to figure out why Malik hated Mona so much, and he was thinking about meeting her daddy in a few days.

"You're not gonna answer your phone?" Camy asked.

Malik snapped out of his daydream. "My bad," he said.

Camy watched as he picked up the phone.

"Aye, I'm eating right now, but I'll be out in a minute."

"You gotta go?" Camy asked as soon as he put the phone down on the table.

"Yeah, I gotta go meet up with bro. You know how shit be."

"Yeah, I know, but will shit be different when the baby get here?"

Malik paused. For once, he didn't have an answer for her, but he didn't want to lie and tell her what she wanted to hear. He decided not to say shit.

"Let me go see what's up with bro," he finally said, getting up from the table.

Camy took that to mean he didn't plan to stop doing whatever he was doing in the streets.

Camy finished her food before putting their plates in the sink. Just by the conversation that they didn't have, it made Camy wonder if they were doing the right thing.

Malik jumped into his brother's ride. "Bro, I need your advice on some shit."

"Don't you always? I'm gonna start charging your ass," Rell teased.

"I'm serious, bro. Camy pregnant."

"Damn, for real?" Rell asked, trying to sound surprised.

"Hell yeah, bro. We went to the doctor today to confirm that shit."

Rell passed his brother the blunt. "Congratulations, bro. How you feel about having a baby? You ready to get on your grown-man shit?"

"Hell yeah, bro. I'm really happy about this shit, and she's happy too," Malik said, passing the blunt back to Rell.

"I'm not gonna lie. Mama called me and told me what happened earlier."

Malik cut him off. "Oh, yeah, that bullshit."

"Bro, I swear I told her that she was wrong as hell for saying Camy needed to abort that baby. That shit pissed me off. I would had said fuck her too if she would had said that shit about one of mine. I hope you ain't listen to that bullshit."

"Hell nah. I want my baby. I really think Mama is scared I'm gonna run out on my baby like my daddy did me since we both got those commitment issues she loves talking about."

The car was silent for a minute while they smoked.

"Aye, bro, Camy dad wants to meet me Sunday for dinner. I'm not gonna lie. I'm scared as fuck. He sound cool with her being pregnant over the phone, but what if I get there and he tries to kill my Black ass or something?"

Rell was cracking up. "Malik, you crazy as hell. That man ain't gonna kill you and have his daughter and grandchild out here all fucked up and shit. Go meet the man and be yourself. Let that nigga know how much you love Camy and ready for the baby to get here."

Malik was all smiles, just thinking about his little family. "Aye, bro, you think if I ask her to marry me, she would do it?"

"Bro, let's be real right now. Do you love that girl enough to want her to be your wife, or are you just saying this shit because she is about to have your baby?"

Malik shrugged his shoulders.

"What happened to all that 'just friends' talking you've been doing? Are you trying to marry her for love, or are you just trying to lock her in because you don't want another nigga to have her or be around your baby?"

Malik shook his head. "We are just friends, but since we started back hanging out, she's been saying that shit like it's cool, and I don't like the way it's been making me feel. I be ready to punch her ass dead in her shit. It's like I can hear her saying some ho shit like 'I can fuck whoever because we just friends,' and that shit don't sit right with me. She already know I bet not catch her talking to another nigga, especially carrying my baby."

"You now know why you saying that shit to her hurt her so bad. You need to stop playing with her and make her your girl, nigga. And another thing, you need to get your mind together on whether you gonna be with her for real or not. Stop playing with that girl."

"What I gotta do? Walk in the house and tell her she is my woman now?"

Rell was cracking up. "You really is slow as fuck like Davon."

"Shut the fuck up, bro."

"Nah, but for real, you can't demand shit. You can ask her if she is ready to make shit official. Then, as time goes by, if you still feel like she is the right one, ask her to marry you. You can't ask her to marry your ass just because she is saying y'all friends now."

"All right, I'm gonna do that."

After their talk, the brothers drove off. It was time for them to turn some corners.

Chapter 10

Camy paced the floor as she repeatedly called and texted Malik. It was Sunday, and they were supposed to ride together to meet her dad for dinner.

"Malik, where the fuck are you? Please be on your way," she left on his voicemail.

Being desperate, Camy walked across the street to ask Ms. Patt if she knew where Malik was at. Since she was already looking out her window, Ms. Patt met Camy at the door.

"What's up, girl? Come on in."

Camy walked in, saying hello to Ms. Patt and Davon.

"You all right, Camy? You hungry?"

"No, I'm actually about to meet up with my daddy for dinner."

"What can I help you with? Because I know you ain't came over here to just chill with me and Davon."

Camy giggled. "I was wondering if you knew where Malik was, or if you heard from him today."

"Nah, I don't know where he at, and that boy ain't talked to me in almost a week now."

"Damn, we were supposed to go to my dad's, and he been ignoring me all day."

"Camy, I hope I'm not outta line for saying this, but you need to get rid of that baby before it's too late."

"What?" Camy asked, thinking that this lady had lost her fucking mind.

"I'm just saying. Malik is so much like his dad. He will never love you enough, and he'll forever play this game with you as long as you let him. He probably got you pregnant on purpose to lock you in. Malik ain't gonna never be shit. Just watch what I tell you. He's gonna claim your bed but never your heart. My son fucked up in the head like that."

Camy couldn't believe what she was hearing. She rushed out of the house, crying, but couldn't help but wonder if Ms. Patt was right about her son. That was his mother. She would know him better than anyone.

Davon was the slow one, but he was smart enough to know that what his sister did was wrong, and Camy was hurt. If Malik didn't answer for anyone, Davon knew Malik would always answer for him and Rell. He sent a text.

Hey, nephew. Yo' mama tripping on Camy, and she crying.

"I know your ass over there texting my son. All you do is sit around and soak up everyone's business, so you can have something to talk about. I don't give a fuck. Malik don't need no damn baby. Shit, he just as slow as you."

"Fuck you, fat bitch!" Davon yelled, getting up to walk outside.

"Spell it, slow bastard!" she yelled back.

Those two had been living together their whole life, and these little arguments were nothing new.

Camy tried calling Malik a few more times and still got no answer. She didn't have a key to his house, but she drove over there just to see if he was there. Her mind started thinking that something bad had happened to him because she felt like he wouldn't just ghost her, knowing how important that day was.

Feeling too embarrassed to go through with dinner with her dad, Camy called him to cancel, claiming that she wasn't feeling too good. Camy took her clothes off, then climbed back into the bed. She ended up crying herself to sleep.

Hearing loud banging on her door woke her up from her sleep. Camy rushed to the door, thinking that maybe Malik had lost his key or something. Camy quickly opened the door.

"Daddy!"

"Hey, baby girl. Since you couldn't make it to dinner, I brought dinner to you," David said, walking in.

"Thanks, Daddy. You're the best," Camy replied with a huge smile on her face.

Camy and her dad took a seat on the couch to talk for a while before he had to go.

"Soon as I get back in town, we can try this family dinner again," he said.

"Yeah, that would be nice."

David looked around, trying to get his thoughts together. "If you're not feeling well, why is that guy not here, making sure you and his baby are all right?"

"Come on, Daddy. Please don't start. I don't need him in my face all day," she lied.

David stood up. "I'm gonna get up outta here. I can see that you all in your feelings, and I'm not trying to upset you or my grandbaby."

Camy stood up to walk him to the door. "All right, Daddy. I'll call you in the morning."

Before walking away, David stopped in his tracks. "You know, no matter what, I'm here for you. You don't gotta take shit from no nigga."

Camy secretly wanted to cry. She knew that from that day, her daddy would never respect Malik.

Across the street, Davon shook his head as he watched some man hugging Camy before getting in his car and driving off.

Camy couldn't believe two weeks had passed and she still hadn't talked to Malik. She went through different emotions during his disappearance. At first, she was worried that maybe something bad had happened to him, or maybe he had gotten himself locked up. She then became angry, thinking that his mom was right about him getting her pregnant just to trap her. She cried and prayed hard for answers.

Going against what Malik wanted her to do, Camy called Mona. She believed that Mona was the only one that she could talk to. Malik had once told her that if she needed to talk, he would be there for her, but since he was on some dumb shit, Camy had to turn to her friend.

Mona hesitated to answer her call. She knew Camy only hit her up when her head wasn't stuck in Malik's ass. She was surprised to hear from Camy, especially since the last time they talked was the day Camy texted her, telling her to mind her own business. Now, she was calling, wanting to tell more of her business. Being messy was the only reason she answered.

"Hey, Mona, what are you doing?"

Mona rolled her eyes. "Nothing. Why? What's up?"

"Can we meet for lunch? I need some food and some-body that really cares about me to cheer me up."

"What's wrong, friend?"

"It might just be this pregnancy that has me in my emotions, but I just need a friend right now."

For a second, Mona felt bad for her. "Where do you wanna meet up at?"

Camy texted her the address to Malik's favorite spot, which was now her favorite spot.

Camy got there first and got them a table. She was going over the menu when Mona finally arrived.

"Bitch, what you know about this place? I've drove past it a few times but never stopped in to get food from them."

"Malik put me on to this place, and I absolutely love it here. Let's order."

The girls quickly went over the menu before placing their order.

After they ordered, Mona wanted to jump straight into the tea. "So, girl, what's been going on? What got you so down?"

Camy sipped on her lemonade. "I'm having some issues with that nigga, Malik."

"Even carrying his baby, he still don't want to be in a relationship?"

"It's not that. To be honest, I'm learning to deal with that mess. I'm pissed because two weeks ago, we were supposed to go to my dad's for dinner, but he didn't show up."

"Damn, girl."

"That's not the killing part. I haven't talked to him in those two weeks. I asked his mom about his whereabouts, and she basically told me that her son was still a little boy, and I didn't need to have his baby." Camy started to cry.

"Aww, boo, don't cry. Being your best friend, I told you the same thing because, apparently, me and his mama see something is wrong with him, and because you're in love with him, you just can't see it. Don't let that nigga bring you down, girl. You better than this."

Camy wiped her eyes. "I just always pictured me having a baby by a man that loves me and my baby without all the bullshit and games behind it. I thought Malik could at least be half of that, but I guess I was wrong."

Mona sipped her wine. "So, what are you gonna do?"

"I don't know. I keep thinking about this shit. I don't know what to do about Malik, but I want my baby. I might have to do this shit by myself. I want my baby to have a dad, not a guy that's gonna disappear or run in and out of its life."

Mona got up to give her a hug. "It's okay, baby. Auntie Mona gonna be here to help every step of the way."

Camy began to cry harder, just thinking back to when Malik said the same shit to her.

"Stop crying, Camy. Fuck that nigga. You better than that."

Camy excused herself to go to the restroom. "I'll be right back," she said, grabbing her purse.

Camy went into the restroom and stared into the mirror. "Come on, girl. You gotta shake this shit, " she mumbled to herself. After cleaning her face, Camy walked out of the restroom with her head hanging low.

"Excuse me," she said after bumping into someone.

"Camy!"

Camy finally looked up to see Jason standing there with a huge smile on his face. "Damn, girl, you looking good as hell."

"Get the fuck away from me. And why are you calling my daddy, telling him that I'm fucking with a nigga that's beating my ass?"

"Damn, Camy, calm down, baby. I was just trying to help your ass. Your daddy needed to know what you left me for."

Camy tried to walk away, but he blocked her.

"Move out my damn way."

"I love you, Camy. Ain't shit gonna change that. We need to just leave and go somewhere and talk in private."

Gamy shook her head. "No, Jason. I can't do that. Now, can you move out of my way? My food is getting cold."

Jason chuckled. "You still love your food, girl? I see ain't shit changed."

Camy wasn't trying to be his friend and spare his feelings. Knowing it would cause him to leave her alone for good, Camy rubbed her stomach. With a smirk on her face, she teased him. "Yes, me and my baby love food."

The sight of her rubbing her belly and the bullshit damn near made Jason pass out. "The fuck! A baby? You let that nigga get you pregnant?"

Camy pushed Jason out of her way. "Please leave me and my family alone."

Mona gave Camy a strange look when she got back to the table. "You all right? What took so long, girl?"

"Yeah, I'm good. Just ran into that fool, Jason. He on some bullshit."

Mona wasn't in the mood to see Jason, so she jumped into play. "Hey, I think we need to get out of here before he makes a scene. He is on his way over here."

Camy looked up and saw Jason storming their way. "Go away, Jason. We don't want to be bothered."

"Man, I'm just saying. You about to have that nigga baby? What about all those years I begged you for a baby?"

"Jason, you're embarrassing me. Please leave me alone."

Mona tried not to even look his way. She hated seeing how he was on the verge of crying over a bitch who threw him away like he was garbage.

"So, you really don't love me anymore?"

Camy grabbed her purse. "Mona, I'm sorry, but I need to get out of here."

Mona had to think quickly on her feet. "Jason, please get away from our table. She not feeling too well."

Mona then helped Camy sit back down. "You looking funny, girl. Sit down and drink this," she said, handing her the glass of lemonade.

"Camy, are you all right?" Jason asked, showing his concern.

"Just get the fuck away from our table! She don't need you," Mona yelled.

"She don't need you either, fake-ass bitch," Jason yelled, walking away.

Camy drank her lemonade, trying to calm down and not let Jason stress her the fuck out. "I think I'm just gonna go home and lay down."

"Do you need me to follow you?" Mona asked, pretending to be concerned.

"Nah, I'm good. Maybe we can do this another day."

"Sure."

Camy was upset because of Jason and really wanted to lock herself away from everyone, but as she started to drive, she really started feeling funny. Trying to make it home, she began to speed up a little.

Jason was behind her. He had seen her come out of the restaurant, and he was desperate to talk to her. Knowing she would be going home, he started following her. Jason felt like he needed to talk to Camy about her having another nigga's baby. Just thinking about the shit was driving him crazy, and at that point, he would do anything to talk to her.

Once Camy noticed Jason was following her, she got scared. Not wanting him to know where she lived, she thought about letting him follow her ass straight to Malik's house. She knew that if he was there, he would handle Jason.

Picking up her phone, she called Malik. Once again, he didn't answer. Instead of hanging up, she left a voicemail. "Malik, I've been leaving you messages, and since your voicemail isn't full yet, I know you've been listening. Look, I'm scared. Jason is following me. I went past your house for help, but your car wasn't there. If you're in the neighborhood, please get to my house. I don't know what tip this nigga on, but he mad I'm pregnant. Something's wrong. I'm feeling real diz—"

The beep went off before she could finish. Camy prayed that if he loved her the way he said he did, he would at least show up at that moment.

Malik listened to the message she sent him and then jumped up.

"What's wrong?"

"I gotta go," he barked, putting his shoes back on.

Shay jumped up, furious. "No, that wasn't part of the fucking plan, Malik. You said you were gonna be here for me if I got rid of the baby."

"Look, I know what I said, but something came up, and I gotta go handle this before somebody ends up hurt."

"Somebody? You talking about that bitch Camy?"

"Man, watch yo' fucking mouth."

Shay began to cry. "I do whatever for you, and this bitch snaps her fingers, and yo' dog ass go running. What the fuck, Malik?"

"I appreciate what you did, and I've been here for you, right?"

"Fuck you, Malik. I wanted my baby," Shay said, sitting back down on the bed, crying.

"You know it wasn't the right time. I got other shit going on right now."

"Other things like what, Malik?"

Malik knew that if he told her the truth, she might have killed him and then herself.

"I'll be back, all right?"

"Whatever!"

Malik gave her a kiss on her forehead. "Lay down and get you some rest."

While Malik was driving to Camy's, Camy was trying to get away from someone herself. She was feeling dizzy and could barely keep her eyes open as she turned on her block. Just as Malik turned the block coming from the opposite way, she was getting ready to pull into her driveway and passed out, hitting Malik's car.

Ms. Patt, along with Rell and Davon, witnessed what they thought was everything. They all rushed to the cars, thinking that Malik and Camy were on bullshit and hit each other in some toxic relationship shit.

Rell ran over to his brother's car first. "Aye, bro, you good?"

Malik turned his head to face Rell. "Yeah, check on Camy! Is she all right?"

"Mama over there with her. She on the phone with the ambulance now."

Malik stumbled as he got out of the car. "Where the fuck you think you going, nigga?" he yelled, racing over to Jason's car.

Jason tried to ride right past them, but Malik was on his ass. Snatching Jason out of the car window, Malik tossed his ass on the ground. "Bitch-ass nigga! What the fuck you following her for?" he asked while stomping Jason in the face.

"Aye, bro, chill. The police and shit on the way!" Rell yelled, giving his brother a warning.

Knowing that Camy was hurt pissed Malik off, but he didn't need to be getting locked up. Malik walked away like shit hadn't just happened.

Jason thought about lying there, playing dead until the police came, but he was so embarrassed that he dragged himself off the ground and into the car. He then backed his car up to turn around and leave.

At about the time that Malik finally made it over to Camy, the ambulance was pulling up. "Ma, move. Let me see her."

Ms. Patt let him get closer. "Malik, she won't wake up. I done tried everything."

"What?" He tried to shake her up, but nothing. "Camy, baby, stop playing and get yo' ass up," he yelled, shaking her even more.

"Sir, I'm gonna need you to move."

Malik turned around to see an EMT standing behind him. Not wanting to give them a hard time and wanting them to help Camy and the baby, Malik moved without having to be told twice.

Rell and Davon stood by Malik as they put her in the back of the ambulance.

"You gonna ride with her?"

Malik was scared as hell but jumped in the back. He wouldn't know what to do if anything happened to Camy and his baby. "Have Unc come get this shit together."

Rell nodded his head.

Malik waited in the waiting room as the doctors worked on her. He wasn't a religious man, but he silently prayed for them to be all right.

David soon showed up after getting the emergency call. He, too, was told to wait in the waiting area until the doctors came to speak to him about Camy. David was a nervous wreck as he paced the floor. All he knew was that she had been in a car accident, and when she was brought in, she was unconscious.

"Family of Camilla Thompson."

Malik jumped out of his seat, racing to the doctor. At the same time, David stopped pacing to meet with the doctor.They both looked at each other strangely before giving the doctor their attention. They listened as the doctor explained that they had found GHB in Camy's system. They believed that the drugs caused her to become unconscious before causing the car accident.

"Is my daughter gonna be all right?"

Malik wanted to know the same thing, but he also had his own questions. "Aye, Doc, what about my baby?"

The doctor's pause told Malik all that he needed to know. He shed a tear before he even heard the doctor tell them that he was sorry, but she, in fact, did lose the baby. Malik was pissed and wanted to walk right out the doors to find Jason, but he knew that Camy was going to need him at this time.

"Can we see her?" Malik asked.

"Not yet, but I'll send someone out when it's time."

With that being said, the doctor walked away.

David turned his attention toward Malik. "Hey, Malik, I'm David. I'm Camy's dad. I'm so sorry about the baby."

Malik accepted his handshake. "Thanks, man. I really just wanna be back there with her. She really wanted this baby. I need to hold her and let her know that everything's gonna be all right."

David thought he wasn't going to like him, but after listening to him talk about his love for Camy and how worried he was about how her mental state would be different after losing the baby, David could tell that the young man really cared for his baby girl. The two sat and talked, trying to prepare each other for dealing with Camy afterward.

"I'm sitting here worried about how the hell she got that shit in her system. I know for a fact that she was happy about becoming a mom. She wouldn't have taken any drugs," David said.

Malik wanted to tell him about Jason and the phone call he received from Camy right before the accident but decided against it. Malik knew that David would have gone after Jason, and he couldn't let that happen. He wanted that nigga for himself.

"We're gonna have to wait until she's ready to talk about it," Malik said, looking toward the doctor who was walking their way.

"She's awake, but still not completely up."

"Can we see her?" Malik asked, cutting him off.

"Yes, but one at a time."

Malik wanted to jump up but knew it was only right for her dad to go in first to check on his baby girl. David stood up to follow the doctor to the back. His heart hurt, knowing that someone purposely hurt Camy, and she was one of the sweetest girls in the world.

David walked in, grabbing her hand. "Hey, baby girl. You scared me for a minute, but I know everything's gonna be all right."

"Daddy," she said, just above a whisper.

"You still weak, baby. Don't try to do too much."

Camy started to cry again. She hated everything about that day. She could have lost her life, and her baby was gone.

"It's all right. Everything is gonna be all right."

"I didn't do this," Camy cried.

"I know, baby girl. I know. That boy out there gonna get to the bottom of this. I can see it in his eyes."

Camy gave him a strange look, wondering what he was talking about, but she didn't have it in her to ask.

David stayed with Camy for a while, trying to comfort her, until he remembered that Malik also needed to see her. "I gotta get on out of here, baby girl. That young man out there waiting to see you. I love you," he said, giving her a hug.

"I love you too, Daddy."

David walked back out to the waiting room and saw that Malik had gone downstairs to buy Camy some flowers and balloons from the gift shop.

"She's waiting for you. Once she's up to it, we're gonna try that dinner thing again."

"All right, bet," Malik said before walking toward the back.

Hitting Camy's room, Malik stood in the doorway, watching her. Knowing how fragile she was at that moment, he was scared. She was looking toward the windows, so she didn't even know that he was watching her for a minute. Malik finally walked in and set her flowers on her table. She stared at him but didn't say anything.

Malik sat at the edge of her bed, holding her hand. "Baby, I'm so sorry."

Camy started to cry harder. "I'm sorry, Malik."

"You ain't got shit to be sorry about, baby. I should have been there with you."

Camy wanted to ask him where he was, but it wasn't the time or place. They had both just taken a loss and needed time to heal.

Camy cried in Malik's arms. She was beyond hurt. "Malik, I don't know what happened. I didn't do anything. I wouldn't take anything knowing I was pregnant. I wanted my baby," Camy cried.

"I know, baby. I know you wouldn't do this shit. Listen, baby, I don't want you to worry about that shit right now. Just try to heal and relax. I got you."

"How do you got me, Malik, when you keep running away from me?"

Malik shook his head. "Not now, Camy. Don't do that shit here."

"Just leave. Go back to wherever you were at."

Malik didn't move. He wasn't trying to go there with her ass. "I know you hurting, but don't take that shit out on me. You know I wanted this baby more than anything in the world myself. Let's not do this here. We just need to try to be here for each other so we can deal with this situation."

Camy had so much to say to him, but her tears overpowered her words.

Chapter 11

Camy was ready to go to bed, but Malik's mind was racing, and he was ready to kill a muthafucka like always.

"Aye, Camy, wake yo' ass up, girl."

"I'm tired," she whined.

"Listen, I gotta ask you something."

"Yes, Malik," she said, smacking her lips.

"How was you feeling before you got up to go to the restroom?"

Camy gave it some thought before answering. "You promise you won't get mad?"

Malik gave her a look, basically telling her that she better get to talking.

"I was telling Mona how I loved you but hated your ass. And how I was scared to have the baby and have to raise it on my own."

"You tripping. You know that would have never been the case. Anyways, you went to the restroom for how long?"

"I was in there for about ten, twelve minutes. When I came out, I bumped into Jason, then we argued for like five, six minutes before I went back to the table."

Malik thought over everything that she said. He couldn't put his hands on it, but shit wasn't sitting right with him. "Baby, now, you said you were trying to leave when yo' li'l friend told you to drink yo' lemonade?"

"Yes, Malik. I drank it, then left. Please don't make me repeat the rest."

"So, that bitch was alone with your food and drink for almost twenty minutes? She talked you into drinking whatever she put in yo' shit."

Camy sat up a little. "What? Malik, don't do that because you already don't like her."

Malik grabbed Camy's face, forcing her to look into his eyes. "That bitch did that shit, and when I see her, I'm gonna kill that bitch."

Camy pulled away from him. "Malik, she wouldn't do that to me."

"I been told you that bitch wasn't your friend. And I peeped some shit not too long ago. Remember the day I walked in, and she was talking all that shit about you getting an abortion? That night, she texted you, asking if I was beating on you, right?"

"Yeah."

"Right after that, yo' daddy called, talking about that nigga Jason called him, saying he heard you was fucking with a nigga that was beating yo' ass. Where the fuck you think he got that shit from, Camy? You been blocked that nigga. How the fuck he even know about me?"

Camy sat there, dumbfounded. It was hard at first, but she had to wrap her mind around the fact that her bestie was her number one enemy.

"Baby, wipe them tears away. Don't sit in my face crying over that bitch. Fuck her fake ass."

Although she was crying, Malik had made her laugh.

"That's my crazy-ass baby right there," he said, placing a kiss on her lips.

"I'm ready to fight her now."

"All right, Tyson," Malik said, laughing.

Camy lay back on Malik, trying to calm down, but the disloyalty and betrayal hurt her to the core. "I swear I never saw this shit coming. That bitch really had me fooled. Now that I've replayed everything from that day, I wonder why Jason called her a fake bitch too."

"But that bitch is fake as hell. You were in the hospital for a few days and been home for like two days already, and that bitch ain't called, texted, or visited yet. That's that fake bullshit. Jason even called your daddy to see how you were doing since you still have him blocked and yo' daddy never blocked him. I know he wasn't the reason for the accident, but I still wanna fuck him up, and I'll let you do Mona ass in."

"I never did anything wrong to that girl, and she killed my baby. Why? I was just telling her how much I wanted my baby. Why would she do that?"

Malik held her a little tighter. He hated that she was going through all this bullshit. "It's okay, baby. I'll give you another one whenever you ready."

Camy gave him a strange look before giggling. "Why you so damn crazy?"

"I'm not. I'm just willing to do whatever to make you happy again. I love you, girl."

"I love you too, Malik."

Malik smirked. It had been a minute since she told him that.

Ms. Patt felt so bad for Camy and Malik. She had told them both that they needed to get rid of that baby, but she didn't want her to have a miscarriage. Camy had been home from the hospital, and she noticed that Malik had been going out to get them food. So, she decided to cook them dinner as her way of saying she was sorry.

Ms. Patt had been blowing Malik's phone up, but since he called himself not talking to her, she took that as why he wasn't answering any of her calls. Giving up on calling, she finally decided to walk the food over to Camy's house.

Malik and Camy had just started to doze off when they heard someone ringing the doorbell.

"Who the hell is that?" Camy jumped up. She knew it wasn't her dad because he had just stopped by the day before and was leaving to go out of town. Because Mona was the only other person that knew where she lived, she raced to the door, ready to knock a bitch out.

"Ms. Patt, hey."

"Hey, Camy. I hope you don't mind, but I brought over dinner."

Camy's face lit up. "Thank you so much. It smells so good."

"I was calling Malik's phone all day and couldn't get an answer, so I just brought it over," she explained.

Malik walked up from the back room.

"Baby, your mama brought us some dinner."

Malik wouldn't even look her way. "Give her that shit back."

"No, Malik. I'm hungry."

Malik started putting on his shoes. "I'll go get you something to eat. Give her that shit back."

"Malik, that's mean. You don't have to go get anything. We can eat this."

"Fuck that shit! You know I'm not fucking with her ass. Shit, what she said was mean."

"Li'l boy, when the fuck you gonna get over that shit?" Ms. Patt asked.

Malik was really pissed now. "I'm not no li'l-ass boy. I'm a grown-ass man. Now, get the fuck out and take that bullshit with you," he barked.

Ms. Patt looked at Camy. "Girl, you can keep the food, but you need to watch the company that you keep."

"Give her that shit back!"

Camy held the food out for Ms. Patt to grab. "Sorry, I can't take this."

Malik snapped. "What the fuck you sorry for? She is the same one that wanted you to kill my baby. She ain't apologize for saying that bullshit."

"I was trying to be nice because I felt bad about what happened, but fuck you, Malik. I'm not sorry for what I said and will never be. You a little-ass boy, trying to run around fucking up these girls' minds and playing with their feelings. You wasn't ready for a damn baby with nobody." Ms. Patt gave Malik a look, daring him to say something else. She had been itching to let his secret out.

Malik smirked. A part of him didn't give a fuck what she knew, but the part of him that did care didn't want to crush Camy, so he calmed down a little. "Ma, just leave," he calmly ordered.

Ms. Patt walked out, leaving Camy holding the food. As Camy locked the door, she could hear Malik slamming the bedroom door.

Since she still had the food, Camy went straight into the dining room to eat. So caught up in her dinner, Camy didn't hear Malik sneak up behind her.

"So, you still gonna eat that shit?"

Camy looked up from her plate. "Malik, I said I was hungry. Besides, she left it here for me. Camy whined.

Still being pissed off, Malik started grabbing the food and throwing it away in the trash can.

"Malik, please stop!"

Malik didn't stop until it was all in the trash. "That's what's wrong with yo' ass. You let muthafuckas do and say whatever to yo' ass and be too fucking quick to forgive. She told you to kill my baby, then bring her ass over here waving food in your face, and you jump to forgive her. You gotta do better in this world, Camy. It's a dog-eat-dog world, and you gonna be ate, acting too fucking nice."

Camy stormed off, back into the room, crying. It wasn't even all about what he said. She really was hungry, and that food was good as hell.

Malik took the garbage out, hoping his mama saw him get rid of her food. He loved her, but until she apologized for talking crazy, he wasn't fucking with her.

Malik sat on the porch, trying to calm down before going back into the house. He didn't want to fight with Camy, especially about some damn food.

Before he could go back in, Camy came out and took a seat. "I need a new car."

"I know, baby. I'm working on it. My shit got fucked up too, remember?"

"Do you think I should just go to my daddy?"

The last thing Malik wanted was for her daddy to think that he wasn't man enough to take care of her. "Nah, I told you I got you. You ain't gotta call nobody for shit."

Camy took his word for it.

"I know you hungry, so I'm about to go get you some food now. I'm sorry for tripping, but my mama know how to push my buttons, and once she starts, I can't calm down."

Camy went over to his chair, then sat on his lap. "It's all right, baby. I understand."

"I love you. I swear, for the most part, you a nigga peace."

Camy smiled. "I love you too."

The couple had begun to kiss when they heard someone yell out.

"Ain't that cute. Malik, come here."

They looked up and saw Shay parked in front of Camy's house.

"What the fuck she doing over here, Malik?"

"Chill out. Let me go see what's up."

Camy jumped up. "You and that bitch got me fucked up!"

"I said chill out," he barked, walking to Shay's car.

Camy wanted to cry, but she wasn't about to look weak in front of a weak bitch like Shay. She faked being cool until Malik jumped in the car and they drove off. Camy went into the house, crying, feeling like shit. She couldn't handle the disrespect. It hurt that he left, knowing what she had just been through.

"So, you just left me to go sit up with that bitch. You ain't even been answering the phone," Shay said.

"Look, I just asked for a ride since you wanted to be funny and stop by."

Shay kept driving but was pissed. She promised that he was going to hear everything that she had to say before she took him back to Camy's house. "Malik, you a fucking liar, and I hate you, dawg. You begged me to get an abortion, promising me that you'll be there for me while I recover, and then, you run out my fucking house to lay up with that bitch. Why the fuck you keep playing with me like that?"

Malik was already irritated, and she was making shit worse. "Shay, shut the fuck up with all that shit. I told you before that I don't have to answer to nobody, including yo' ass. I do what the fuck I please. You ain't the only one that needed me."

"I was the mother of your child. Don't that mean I should have came first?" she asked, pulling up to the restaurant.

He didn't want to go there with her, but she pushed it out of him. "She was carrying my seed too. Do you really think a nigga can be at both places at the same time?"

Shay had a stupid look on her face. "What? You got that bitch pregnant too?"

"You knew you wasn't the only one that I've been fucking. What the fuck you crying for?"

Something came over Shay, and she started attacking Malik. Just thinking about him also getting Camy pregnant and trying to play house when all he did for her was pay for an abortion hurt her to the core.

Malik wasn't even trying to fight her back. All he did was try to hold her hands. "Stop with yo' crazy ass!"

"I fucking hate you! I hate you! I hate you!" she yelled, still trying to swing on him.

Malik was finally able to jump out of the car. "You a crazy-ass bitch!" he yelled, walking into the restaurant to get Camy's food.

Malik wasn't surprised when he saw her driving off. He shook his head. This was exactly why he was happy to be going to pick up his car the next day. This was exactly why it paid to know people with gifted hands.

Malik caught an Uber back to Camy's house. He knew she was going to be pissed and even want to argue, but since he bought food, he thought that maybe she would be all right.

Malik knocked on the door.

Camy peeked out the window. "Leave the food on the porch, but you gotta go."

"Fuck you talking about? Stop playing and open the fucking door, girl."

"No, Malik. Just leave me alone. Take yo' ass back to that wack-ass bitch."

Malik shook his head. "That wasn't about shit. I didn't even know she was stopping by. I just asked her for a ride. Can you open the door?"

"Fuck you, Malik!" Camy yelled, shutting her window and then walking to her room in the back.

Malik set the food down and then pulled out his key to her house. He always forgot he carried it around with him. Malik walked in, put the food on the dining room table, then went into the bedroom.

"Why the fuck you on that bullshit?"

"Why the fuck your girlfriend pulling up to my fucking house and your Black ass jumping in the car with her stupid ass?"

A smirk crossed Malik's face. "I don't have a fucking girlfriend. I got friends."

"Oh, you think shit funny? Why are you in my face playing? Just leave me the fuck alone."

"Yo' food on the table. You need to eat and chill the fuck out. You ain't yo'self when you hungry."

"No, I haven't been myself since I started fucking around with you."

"Damn, straight up?" Malik asked, taking a seat next to her on the bed.

"People kept saying I didn't need a baby by you, and I wasn't trying to listen to that shit, but maybe that accident happened for a reason. Maybe God was giving me a chance to move on from you."

Malik was speechless. He never looked at things that way until she said that shit. Honestly, his feelings were hurt behind her words. "I'm sorry for hurting you in any way that I did. I was only trying to learn how to love you right."

Camy was crying, not because she wanted someone new but because she wanted him to be the right one for her, but he just didn't know how to be her person.

Malik gave her a kiss on her forehead before getting up. Without any words, he walked out. Camy then heard her front door shut.

Camy lay back in the bed, crying. She loved him, but he had been the one that just told her that she needed to stop taking people's shit. He just forgot to say it included his.

***

The knocking on the door woke Camy up from her sleep. "Who is it?"

"It's Jimmy. I'm Malik's uncle."

Camy opened the door. "Malik's not here right now."

"Yeah, I know. I was dropping your car off. Here's your keys."

Camy smiled, taking the keys out of his hand. "Wow, that was fast. Thank you so much."

"No problem. My nephew paid good money to make sure your car got done before my other jobs."

"Oh, okay. That sounds like him."

Jimmy walked away and then began to take her car off the tow truck.

Camy shut the door and then went into the back to grab her phone.

"Hello."

"Good morning. Thanks for taking care of my car. How much do I owe you?"

"It's ten in the fucking morning. Why the fuck are you calling me with that bullshit? I know you hate me. I got that out of our conversation last night, but you not about to call me fucking with me and shit. I did that shit out of love, dumb ass."

Camy heard the phone hang up but was stuck holding it. She couldn't believe how he went off on her like that.

Malik didn't want to hurt her, but she called him on some bullshit, and he was tired of everybody at that point.

For the next couple of days, the two didn't call or text each other, and both were going crazy without one another. Malik didn't know what to do to make her happy, and Camy couldn't understand how he held her heart the way that he did, all while using that "friend" word.

That morning, Malik had planned on getting back right with everyone. His mental was all off, and for once, he admitted that maybe he was half the problem. His mama was first on his list. He pulled up to her house with his truck full of groceries. He was dead-ass wrong for throwing her food away, especially when the prices were as high as they were.

"Why you banging on my door, boy? You came to go off on me again?"

"Nah, but I got something for you."

Ms. Patt took a seat back on her couch and watched him run in and out, bringing bags of food in.

"Thank you, Malik."

"No problem, Ma. You know I be tripping sometimes, but I got you."

"I'm sorry if I hurt your feelings. I was wrong for trying to tell y'all what to do. I just want you to be careful."

"Thanks, Ma. I needed to hear that shit for real. Look, I gotta go handle some shit. I'll be back later." Malik placed a kiss on her cheek before walking out.

As he was walking on Camy's porch, she was coming out of the house.

"Can we talk?"

"No, I actually got somewhere I need to be," Camy said, still walking away.

"Camy, baby, please. I need to talk to you. I'm sorry."

"For what, Malik? You ain't do shit but be yourself."

"Okay, well, I'm sorry for that. I'm trying to change for you, but I don't know what to do when it comes to you. I tried to be your Mr. Right, but I've been fucking up. Give me another chance to get this shit right, please."

Camy could hear how sincere he was in his voice, but all this back-and-forth shit was draining, and she was tired. "I have a lunch date. I need to go."

"The fuck? A date? For real, Camy? With who?"

He watched as she drove off. He could actually feel his heart breaking into pieces, thinking he might have lost her for real this time.

Malik jumped in his car, then drove off. He went home, not wanting to be bothered at all. He really wanted to go home and cry. He was far from being a bitch, but being a young man that was never taught how to handle all the different emotions that came with dealing with life, he was confused.

Camy knew she hurt his feelings, but she didn't lie. In fact, she was meeting up for lunch with an old classmate who owned her own shop. Camy was trying to get back into doing hair and getting her life in order. The love that she had for Malik's Black ass had her not wanting to do anything but lay up under him. Her day was never complete if she didn't smell his cologne. It was time for her to do something else with her time in order to get over Malik.

"Hey, Camy. I'm so happy that you could join me," Krystal said with a huge smile.

"Hey, boo. Sorry I'm a little late, but I'm here now, so let's get down to business."

As they ate lunch, they discussed the details of Krystal's shop and the fees she charged for the booth Camy would be renting.

"I know you were out of the game for a minute, so I hope that you understood everything that we spoke about."

Camy sipped on her drink. "Yes, I understand, and it all sounds great."

"So, when can we make everything official and welcome you to the team?"

Camy wanted to join right away, but she had to get everything she needed to jump back into the hair game and have her rent for her booth. She couldn't dare have her daddy pay for it. He had recently stopped paying her rent when Malik started. Once she got in good and would no longer be considered the new girl, she knew she would be making money and could cover it herself, but she was going to need help for the first few months.

"I'll hit you up at the end of the week," she lied.

"All right," Krystal said, getting up from the table and leaving.

Camy was happy that it was over. She needed to pee, and she'd be damned if she let another bitch drug her.

Afterward, Camy went straight home. That food had her sleepy, and her bed was calling her. Camy walked in and was surprised to see her dining room table filled with flowers and a bunch of balloons floating around.

Although he had Camy smiling, she told herself that she needed to stop whatever was going on between her and Malik and get her house key back from him. He had been holding on to that key since he had to run back and forth when she was staying at his house.

Thinking back to some shit, Malik had always left Camy money in her drawer to spend, but since he stayed buying her shit and she stayed in the house for the most part, she never had a chance to spend it. Looking in the closet for the shoe box he started stashing it in, Camy was surprised that when she told him that she was done for good, he didn't take it all back. She then shook her head at herself for even thinking like that. Deep down inside, she knew he would never take shit back that he gave her. She also felt like he would still look out for her if she were to call him. Camy now had the money to improve her life and couldn't help but smile.

"What's up with you, bro? I heard you and Mama made up."

Malik sat back in his brother's car. "Yeah, she was wrong for saying that shit, but at the end of the day, she is my mama. Y'all know that's my muthafuckin' dawg."

"I feel that, bro," Rell said, rolling up. "I ain't seen you with your girl lately. What's up with that?"

Malik shook his head. "I think I fucked that up for good, bro. It's like the harder I try to get her back, the more I fuck up, but I can't walk away from her. I don't know what to do at this point."

Rell passed him the blunt. "That girl loves your ass. Shit gonna work out. Just give her some time. Don't keep stressing over the shit. She'll be back."

"You think so?"

"Hell yeah, nigga. As long as you stay the hell away from Shay. Speaking of Shay, whatever happened to her? Her ass been real quiet lately."

"I really ain't been fucking with her. Once I made her get that abortion, she knew it was a wrap for her ass."

Rell chuckled. "Dawg, the way she acts about you, I still can't believe she really went through with that shit."

"I paid for it and paid her to do it. Plus, I stayed at her place for like two weeks, and she was loving that shit. She had to get rid of that baby. I wasn't trying to fuck shit up with my baby Camy."

"You really love that girl, don't you?"

"Hell yeah, more than she knows. I just need her to be patient with me."

"Li'l bro, to be honest, she has been patient with your ass. All that girl wanted was your love and time. Completely. You the one that was doing all that running back-and-forth with Shay."

Malik hit the blunt, nodding his head. He knew that Rell was right. He was the one that fucked everything up. It hurt his heart not having Camy around. "Rell, I can't live like this anymore. I don't want to. I just want my girl back and not on no 'just friends' shit. I want her as my one and only."

Rell smiled. "What the fuck you telling me this shit for? You need to be telling her this shit. She would love to hear all this shit. She only been begging you to say this and mean it."

When the brothers separated and went their own way, Malik sat in front of Camy's house, trying to come up with a master plan to get her back.

"Why are you stalking me?" Camy asked, walking off her porch.

"'Cause you so fucking beautiful and 'cause you mine," Malik yelled with his head hanging out the window.

"I don't think so. Now, can you move out my way? You're blocking my driveway."

Instead of moving, Malik stepped out of the car. "Where you going?"

"Do it matter? Why you in my business anyways?"

Malik tried to hug her, but she stepped back.

"Damn, why you gotta be like that? You hate me now?"

"Come on now, Malik. You're gonna make me late for work."

"Damn, where you working at? Maybe I can bring you lunch or something."

"I'm gonna have to work through my lunch break if I'm late."

Malik kindly released her hand. Rell had warned him about being too demanding when dealing with her.

"I'm gonna let you go, but call me so I can bring you lunch or something."

"Okay, I'll think about it," she said, getting into her car.

Malik watched as she drove off. He wanted to follow her ass, but that would have been another reason to push her away. Malik drove around, handling his business while waiting for her to call. Once nighttime rolled around and his mama called, letting him know that she had just pulled up, he knew that he was losing his grip on her.

Malik waited a few days before contacting her again. This time, he decided to go about things his way. He followed her to work, just to see what she was up to.

Malik was proud of his baby. Camy had finally gone back to doing hair, and from the little that he could see, she was good at it. Sitting in his car, he ordered her some roses and a few balloons to be sent to her, just so that she knew how proud he was of her.

"Camy, you have a delivery!" Stacy yelled with a smile on her face.

Camy went over to the door to sign for her items. She knew that it could only have come from Malik.

About the time she stepped outside, he was pulling off.

"Damn, girl, I didn't know you had a man," KeKe said, smelling the flowers.

"Because I don't," Camy said, taking her gifts to her station.

Once on her lunch break, Camy called Malik.

"Hello."

"Hey, I was just calling to say thank you for the balloons, flowers, teddy bear, and the money. Malik, I really appreciate all of it."

Malik smiled, knowing that his job was done. Seeing her face light up earlier that day and then hearing how happy she sounded over the phone really made him happy.

"I saw you driving off. I wish you could have waited for me to say thank you to your face."

"I can always come see you later. Would that be all right?"

Camy gave it some thought. Since leaving him alone, it had been hard for her to sleep at night, but she had to stand her ground. She knew that if she allowed him to stop by, she would have been butt naked, telling him how much she loved him.

Camy shook her head. "I'm sorry. I have something to do later."

"Really? Fuck you got going on?"

"Malik, I'm actually about to go get my lunch. I'll talk to you later." Camy hung up before he could say anything else.

"Fuck!" Malik barked, hitting the steering wheel.

Camy went to eat with a few coworkers, but her attention was elsewhere. She couldn't help but stare out the windows, wondering if Malik was watching her.

"Earth to Camy," Jennifer said, snapping her fingers.

"I'm sorry. What's up?"

"We were all talking about going out tonight. Do you wanna join us?"

Camy gave Jennifer a funny look. "I don't know about all that."

"You're such an old lady. Come out, have some drinks, and shake your ass! Come have some fun with us, girl."

Camy thought about her life, and they were right. All she did was work and watch TV. She was really living like an old lady. "I'm down. Just tell me where we're going and what time we meeting up."

"Send me your address. You can ride with me," KeKe yelled over the table.

"It's okay. I'll drive my own car."

Later that night, Camy stood in the mirror. She had to admit she was looking too damn good to be sitting around the house, not doing anything. Camy added a little gloss to her lips.

"Damn, girl, you so fine," she said, walking away from the mirror.

Just as planned, Camy met up with her friends from work. It had been a minute, but she was enjoying herself without being up under Malik.

"Let's not spend the night babysitting these drinks. Let's go dance," KeKe yelled.

It had been a minute since Camy actually danced, but the way she moved on the dance floor, she still had it.

"Aye, nephew, look at your girl over there."

Malik set his drink down. "I see her ass. Trust me. I see her."

Rell looked across the room. "Damn, that is her over there with them thick-ass hoes."

Davon watched her hard, dancing like she had something to prove. "You gonna go get her?"

"I'm enjoying the show for now, but I'm seconds away from snatching her punk ass up."

Rell laughed. "Leave that girl alone and let her have some fun."

"Fuck that shit. I am her fun," Malik said, getting up.

Rell peeped a nigga walking up on Camy and knew what his brother was on his way to do. He stood up. "Don't start no shit in this bitch. The tool's in the car."

"I'll use my hands with a bitch-ass nigga. I ain't never scared to box with a nigga."

Rell knew how his baby brother could be, so he followed him but didn't make it obvious that they were together.

"So, what's your name, shorty?" the guy asked Camy.

"Camy." As soon as she gave the dude her name, she saw Malik walking up.

"Can we exchange numbers or something?" dude asked.

"No, the fuck y'all can't. Not as long as I'm paying her phone bill," Malik yelled. "Now, get the fuck out her face, nigga."

The guy clearly didn't want any problems, so he backed up. "My bad, nigga. Didn't know she had a man."

"I don't. You don't have to leave," Camy said.

Malik gave Camy a death stare. If he didn't love her so much, he would have choked her ass up right there in front of everybody. Instead, he snatched her up by the arm. "What the fuck you doing? Bring yo li'l ass here."

Camy tried to break free, but Malik's grip was too tight. "Let me go!"

Malik pulled her into the women's bathroom. "You must want me to knock yo' fucking head off. Why the fuck you in here acting wild and shit?"

"Malik, let me go! You don't own me and can't be mad when somebody else talks to me."

"But I love you," he said, placing a kiss on her neck.

It had been a minute since Camy felt his lips and hands on her, and as badly as she wanted to push him away, she couldn't.

"I need you, Camy," he whispered in her ear.

Camy wasn't sure what happened, but the next thing she knew, Malik had her in one of the stalls, holding her up on the wall, giving her some long, hard strokes.

"I love you, baby."

"I love you too, Malik," she moaned out.

After they were done, Malik and Camy walked out of the restroom, holding hands. Malik walked her straight out the front door. He wasn't about to let her out of his eyesight.

"Where you parked at?" he asked.

"Over there," she said, pointing toward the back.

"I'm gonna take you to your car. Tell your girls you started to feel sick and needed to leave, then follow me."

Camy did as he told her. It wasn't a surprise when he pulled up to his house.

"Malik, why are we here? I wanted to go home," Camy said as they walked in.

Malik started laughing. "Man, shut yo' fake ass up. If you really wanted to go home, you wouldn't had followed me. You knew I wasn't going your way."

Camy looked at the floor, knowing he was calling her out on her bullshit.

"Come get in the shower with me."

Just like a little lap dog, Camy was right behind him. It was something about him that she just couldn't shake.

Chapter 12

The next morning, Malik woke up to Camy gone.

"This girl on some real bullshit," he mumbled, walking through the house.

Malik went to his car to get his phone. As he looked through it, he saw that she had not called or left a text message. Malik then called her.

"Hello."

"When I see you, I'm putting yo' punk ass in the head-lock."

Camy giggled. "What I do now?"

"Why you not here? Who the hell told you to just get up and leave like that?"

Camy walked outside so the girls wouldn't be all in her business. "Malik, I do have a damn job. I don't have time to lay up with you all day like I did before. Besides, we are just friends, and I'm not trying to overstay my welcome."

Malik shook his head. "Why the fuck you keep saying that shit? You on some weak-ass shit right now."

Camy giggled. "I'm on the same shit you on, friend."

"Pull up so I can beat yo' ass."

"Bye, Malik. My client just walked in."

"Aye, you know you my baby, right?"

"Whatever. I gotta go," she hurried and said before hanging up.

Camy walked back into the shop with all eyes on her.

She called her client over so she could get to work.

***

Camy avoided Malik as much as possible, even with him sitting on his mama's porch watching her. It was weird, especially when she found herself watching him through her window. Malik had no idea how hard it was for her not to call or text him to come over. Camy closed her curtain after watching Malik smoke with his uncle and brother. She shook her head. He was sexy as fuck, even smoking and talking shit with his people.

Her phone rang, and she saw that it was her friend KeKe from work. When Camy talked to her about her situation, KeKe told Camy that the best way to get over an old fling was to get a new one. Camy highly doubted another could do her the way Malik did.

"Hello."

"Hey, KeKe, what's up?"

"I know you were against the whole finding a new man, but I have a cousin that I think you'll like."

Camy rolled her eyes. "KeKe, I swear you don't listen, girl."

"I know you ain't ready to fuck a new nigga, but I'm thinking that maybe y'all can just go out and see what the night brings. He's a real nice guy."

"KeKe, I don't know, man. I'm not sure if I'm even completely over my ex."

KeKe popped her lips. "Just one date. Please do this for me."

Camy finally gave in. "All right, just give him my number, and we'll go from there."

Not even a whole ten minutes later, Camy received a text.

JoJo: Hey, is this Camy, KeKe friend?

Camy hesitated to respond. She hated how he was texting her phone already. Only because she was doing KeKe a favor, she acted like she had some sense.

Camy: Yes, I'm Camy.

Right after sending that text, Camy's phone started ringing.

"I know this nigga not FaceTiming me."

"Hey."

"Hey. I should have asked if it was all right before FaceTiming you, but I just had to see how beautiful you were. My cousin didn't lie when she said you were fine as hell."

Camy tried not to, but she blushed. "Thank you."

JoJo wasn't bad-looking himself, she had to admit. At first, she wasn't even going to give him the time of day, but after sitting on the phone with him for damn near two hours, she realized that he was really a cool guy. He was able to hold her attention with a good conversation. JoJo didn't make her laugh as much as Malik, but Camy agreed to let him take her out the next day.

The next day at work went by too fast for Camy. It was like she was getting off as soon as she got to work.

JoJo: Hey, beautiful, are we still on for tonight?

Text Camy smiled at her text. She was actually excited to go out and have some fun.

She quickly texted back, letting him know that she hadn't changed her mind.

After her shower, Camy went through her closet to find the right outfit. She didn't want to look like a Plain Jane, but she also didn't want to give him the wrong impression of her.

"Where you going in that?"

Camy jumped before turning around and seeing Malik standing in the doorway.

"Didn't I tell you to give me my damn key back?"

Malik took a seat on her bed. "This my key, muthafucka. I'm paying the rent over here."

"Boy, shut up 'cause I didn't ask you to. Shit was getting paid before I started dealing with you."

Malik gave her a strange look. "Where you going?"

Camy stood in her full-body mirror, checking herself out.

"Get yo' big-headed ass out of the mirror and come talk to me."

Camy ignored him as she fixed her hair.

Malik stood back up, walking over toward her. He stood behind her, feeling her up. "You looking good as fuck, baby. Let me help you take this shit off."

Malik had her mind gone. Camy stood there, allowing him to slip his finger in and out of her pussy while sucking on her neck.

"Malik," she moaned, not realizing how he was once again about to have her caught up in his shit.

Her phone ringing knocked her back to reality.

"Malik, stop. I'm not doing this with you," she said, pushing him away.

"Damn, why the fuck you tripping? I can't have you tonight?"

Camy walked away and went into the bathroom. Malik followed right behind her.

"What the fuck wrong with you?" he asked, watching her wash her neck off.

"Malik, I'm about to go and need you to go as well."

"Where the fuck you going?"

"Out! Now, leave me alone!"

Camy then went back to her room to get her phone. "Hello."

"Hey, do you want me to pick you up or just text you the address?" JoJo asked.

"Text me the address and I'll meet you there," she said right before hanging up.

Malik tried to be calm, but there was no way he was going to let her play in his face like that. "You got me fucked up!"

"Okay, Malik, but I don't have time for all that shit right now. I'm about to go."

Camy tried to walk away, but he grabbed her by the arm. Pushing her up against the wall, he got close to her face. "You got me real fucked up if you think you about to go out with some lame-ass, bitch-ass nigga. You must want yo' ass beat."

Camy tried to snatch away from him. "Boy, get the hell out of my face. You not running shit."

"I'm running yo' ass. Now, whatever the fuck you thought you were doing, cancel that shit."

Camy laughed in his face. "Malik, I'm single and free to do as I please. I don't have a man, and we're just friends, remember?"

It took everything in him not to knock her fucking head off. "So, you really think I'm about to let you go out and fuck another nigga?"

"I'm about to go out to eat, not fuck, but that's my business. Now, get out my way so I can finish getting ready."

Malik paced her floor with his mind on a million.

"Malik, just leave."

"Man, fuck you. You lucky as fuck I don't fuck you up right now!" he yelled.

Camy laughing didn't make the situation any better. "Fuck me? Really, Malik? You didn't want me, remember? I was just a friend while you fucked around, and now you mad 'cause I got a date? You ain't shit, Malik."

He hated hearing that shit. The truth really did hurt. "I bet you ain't going nowhere," he calmly said before walking out of the house.

Camy didn't pay him any mind as she finished getting ready. He was acting crazy because she wasn't waiting around for him to decide if he wanted her or not.

Malik went straight outside and took the battery out of her car. He wasn't playing when he said she wasn't about to go out with another nigga.

"Malik, what the fuck you doing?" Ms. Patt asked, watching him toss the battery in the field.

"Aye, bro, come sit your crazy ass down somewhere," Rell yelled at him.

"This mine. I paid for this bitch!" Malik yelled.

Ten minutes later, Camy came out, looking too damn good for Malik. He didn't know if he wanted to eat her up right there or stomp her head in, knowing she was looking like that for another nigga.

Camy jumped in the car, knowing Malik was watching her every move, but she didn't give a fuck. Shit was never funny when the rabbit had the gun.

Malik laughed loudly as she tried to start her car.

"What the fuck?" she yelled, jumping back out of the car. Camy lifted her hood as if she knew what she was looking for.

"What's wrong, baby? You need me to see what's going on?" he teased.

"What did you do to my car, boy?"

Malik laughed. "Figure it out."

Camy didn't know what he did, but she knew he did something. Not wanting to argue with him, Camy went into the house to call JoJo.

"What's up? I hope you ain't calling to cancel on me."

"No, actually my car acting up, and—"

JoJo cut her off. "You can't make it?"

Being petty toward Malik and not thinking clearly, Camy asked JoJo to come pick her up instead. After sending him the address, Camy chose to wait inside until he arrived.

Malik sat on the porch, happy that he had ruined her plans.

"Bro, that was fucked up. Why you do that girl like that?"

"'Cause she ain't about to go on a date. That girl got me fucked up. She lucky I ain't beat her ass for even thinking that shit was cool," Malik explained.

Davon butted in. "But nephew, you said that wasn't your woman."

"She ain't, but she ain't about to be going out with no other nigga. If she wanted to go out, she should had called me. I would have took her ass out."

Rell was cracking up. "Bro, you serious as hell. That's the killing part about all this shit. You can't do her like that."

"Fuck you mean? I'm doing it, ain't I? She can't have no fucking friends but me."

"Nephew, look."

Malik's face turned stone, seeing a nigga walk on her porch and knock on the door.

"Bro, chill," Rell said before Malik could even get up from his chair.

"Fuck that. This bitch really done lost her fucking mind."

Camy walked outside. "I told you to call when you got here. You could have stayed in the car."

JoJo ignored her. "You ready?"

Camy saw Malik walking off the porch and soon regretted having JoJo pull up. "Look, you gotta go now."

"What? I just got here."

Camy heard him, but her attention was on Malik. He was just standing there, and that scared her. Not knowing what he was planning to do was terrifying.

"Malik, just go," she yelled.

"Didn't I say you wasn't going out with no bitch-ass nigga?"

JoJo turned around to address Malik. "We got a problem, nigga?"

"Nigga, fuck you!" Malik yelled.

JoJo started to walk off the porch, but Camy grabbed him. "Please just get in your car and leave. I should've never invited you over here in the first place."

"I ain't never scared of no loudmouth bitch." JoJo continued to walk toward his car.

"Malik, he leaving. Just let him go home," Camy yelled.

Malik paid her no mind. He felt like the nigga was trying to challenge him, but only because Camy had asked, he was going to let him leave the block in one piece.

Being on some slick shit, JoJo opened his car door, but instead of just getting in, he stopped to talk shit, thinking he was going to be able to hop in afterward and drive off. "Pussy-ass nigga wanna cry over a bitch," he teased.

Malik was quick to attack and beat his ass. Rell and Davon jumped in the shit, just because they needed something to do.

"Okay, y'all. Stop, please," Camy yelled, trying to break the shit up.

Rell and Davon stopped after Ms. Patt finally came out to break shit up. When Camy tried to pull Malik off JoJo, his wild ass hit her in the mouth. Seeing her lip bleeding, Malik finally stopped. "Damn, baby. I'm sorry."

JoJo hopped in his car, barely making it. "I'll be back," he yelled before driving off.

Camy rushed into the house, not wanting to be around all that bullshit.

After making sure his family was good, Malik unlocked Camy's door. "Baby, let me see you. You know I didn't mean to hit you, right?"

Camy held a wet towel on her mouth. "Get the fuck out my house, Malik. You have really lost your damn mind."

Malik pulled her into a hug, not caring what she was talking about. "I'm sorry, baby, but you should know that when a nigga fighting, you ain't supposed to break that shit up. Anything could happen."

Camy broke loose from him and then walked out of the bathroom, making sure to bump into him.

"What the fuck is yo' problem? I apologized, didn't I?" he asked, following her back into the bedroom.

"Go home, Malik."

"Why?" he asked, confused.

"It's like you going out of your way to make sure I'm miserable. Why do you hate me so much?"

"I don't hate you. Why do you say dumb-ass shit like that?"

Camy was frustrated and began to cry.

"What's wrong?"

"I just wanna be happy, Malik."

"What the fuck you think I'm trying to do? I know you ain't think that bitch-ass nigga that just got his ass beat was gonna make you happy. Did you?"

"I don't know, but you for damn sure didn't give me a chance to find out."

Malik kissed her forehead, feeling bad that she was crying but not for what he did. "I couldn't let you go out with that bum, Camy. I actually did yo' ass a favor."

Camy snatched away from him again. "You gotta stop doing shit like that. We are friends. That's it. That's the way you wanted shit, so you shouldn't care what I do. Let me move on from you in peace."

Malik wasn't scared of anybody or anything but Camy leaving him. He couldn't help but think about the conversation he had with his brother not too long ago. It was time to tell her the truth so that she could be his for real. "You can't live without me, and I, for damn sure, can't see you out here with another nigga. I don't know what you did to me, but I can't let you go."

Camy shook her head. She was tired of hearing the same shit from him with no changed behavior. "Okay, Malik. I get it. You love me, blah, blah, blah, but now what? We fuck then go back to being just friends? I want more out of life than just that. As long as you try to hold on to me, I'll never be able to live my life to the fullest. I wanna be a wife someday. I wanna grow old with kids and grandkids, Malik. I can't live if you try to fight everyone that tries to talk to me. Release me."

"You know I don't wanna do shit else but be the one to make you happy. A nigga like me ain't never been in love until you came around. I'm learning how to be your person, baby. I'm sick of all this back-and-forth shit too. I don't want anybody else but you."

"And what does that mean, Malik?"

Malik knew it was now or never with her ass. "That shit means I want you to my fucking self. I don't want you as a friend. I need you to be my woman. I don't wanna go another day without you as mine completely."

Camy couldn't hold back her tears. You would have thought that Malik proposed marriage the way she was in her feelings. "You for real, baby?"

"As a fucking heart attack. You know a nigga love yo' ass." Malik grabbed Camy's face to give her a kiss.

"Baby, be careful. It still hurts a little," she said, talking about her lip.

The couple ended the night making love until the early morning. As Malik slept, Camy smiled, happy to finally have her man.

The next morning, Camy jumped up to the sound of her alarm.

"Damn, baby, you can't call off? I wanted to chill with you today."

"Nope. I got three heads, so I won't be gone all day unless I get a walk-in."

Malik pulled the cover off him. "Look, you gonna leave me like this?"

Camy looked at how hard his dick was and smiled. "Meet me in the shower."

Malik got out of bed, then followed his baby into the bathroom. He'd be a damn fool to miss this opportunity.

Camy got to work, happy that her life was starting to fall into place. As soon as she walked in, she spoke to everyone, but from the way everyone was looking at her all funny and shit and the dry talking, she could sense the vibe was off. Camy went to her station with a fuck-it attitude. She wasn't about to let anybody stop her money.

It wasn't until Krystal and KeKe walked out of the office that Camy put shit together.

"You a bold bitch. How the fuck you get my cousin jumped then walk in this bitch like I wasn't gonna walk your bitch ass like a dog?"

Camy stopped setting up for her first client. "Ain't nobody get him jumped. Him running his mouth too much caused that. And as far as you dog walking me, I think the fuck not." One thing about Camy, she was never scared to fight a bitch.

"Y'all not about to fight in here and tear my shop up."

"We can go outside if this bitch wanna go a round," KeKe said, walking closer.

Camy peeped out the scene and knew this wasn't about to be a fair fight at all. She could see Jennifer on the side, ready to pop off. Krystal's statement about no fighting in her shop was just to get Camy to walk past the girls so that she'd be surrounded.

Camy laughed. "It's whatever, bitch."

KeKe tried to run up, but Camy was on it. She ducked the first hit, but when she swung, she had her curling iron in her hand. Thankfully, she had a client who wanted her sew-in curled, and she had come straight in and put them on. Hitting KeKe with the hot curlers caused her to scream and back up. At the same time, Jennifer ran up, but Camy was already on it. Before Jennifer could get too close, she was catching a chair to her face. Camy didn't care if she wasn't fighting fair. She wasn't about to let anybody jump her.

"All right, that's enough! Camy, you're fired!" Krystal yelled.

Camy didn't say shit. Instead, she picked up her phone to call Malik while the rest of the girls helped KeKe and Jennifer to the back.

"What's up, baby?" Malik answered.

"I need you now. Some shit just popped off up here."

Malik shook his head. "All right, give me about four minutes."

"Baby, don't hang up, just in case." Camy packed her shit up but was still watching her back. She didn't trust them at all.

Five minutes later, Malik walked in. "What's going on?"

"I got fired," Camy quickly said, handing him a box full of her supplies.

Malik gave her a crazy look. "What the fuck happened?"

"We can talk when we leave here. They might call the police, so I gotta get out of here."

Hearing that the police might be on their way, Malik hurried to grab her shit and take it to the car.

Camy followed Malik back to his place. Once they got in, they chilled on the couch.

"So, why the hell you get fired?"

"One of the girls that work at the shop had begged me to go out with her cousin. You and your people jumped on him."

Malik cut her off. "Fuck that nigga. His bitch ass told on me?"

Camy laughed right along with Malik before telling him how them hoes at the shop tried to get down on her.

"So, you got fired for protecting yo' self? That shit crazy as hell."

Camy lay back on Malik. "I'm sad. I really liked working back at the shop."

Malik kissed her forehead. "What you need me to do?"

"Shoot her shop up so that everyone gets scared and stops going there."

Camy laughed at her joke, but Malik looked her dead in the eyes. "How soon do you need this done?"

Camy got serious. "Stop, Malik. Don't do that shit. I was just playing," she yelled.

"I was playing too, crazy-ass girl."

Camy was cracking up.

Malik went into his room and returned with a shoebox. He then handed it over to Camy. Camy looked at the outside of the box.

"This ain't my size, Malik."

Malik smirked. "Open the box, girl."

Camy's eyes lit up, seeing stacks of money. "What you need me to do? Count it?"

Malik laughed. "You bet not ever call me slow again. You a little touched too," he teased.

"How?"

"Look, fuck all them bitches. I want you to take this money and buy you a building. You don't need them. Open yo' own shit."

Camy smiled extra hard. "I swear I love you so much. You my Mr. Make It Happen."

Chapter 13

For the next few days, Malik was on Camy's ass about finding the right building. He wanted nothing but the best for her, and it showed.

"You still ain't found shit that you like yet?"

"No, baby, not yet. I did see one that was nice, but the neighborhood was terrible."

"What you need, some more money to look in a better neighborhood?"

"No, baby, I can work with what you gave me. I'm just trying to take my time so that I can do this the right way."

Malik planted a kiss on her lips. "Let me know if you come across some problem and need my help."

"All right. Where you about to go?"

"I'll be back, nosy ass."

Camy giggled as he walked out the door. She really loved that man.

Malik went straight across the street to his mama's house to talk to his brother.

"What's up, bro?" he asked, hopping into his car.

"Damn, nigga, you finally came up for some air?"

Malik was confused. "Fuck you talking about?"

"Since she took you back, you been buried in her ass."

Malik laughed. "That's exactly what I've been doing too, nigga. How you know?"

Rell snatched the blunt away from his brother. "Nasty-ass muthafucka."

Malik continued to laugh. "Don't be sitting over there fronting like you ain't neva ate Tiffany's ass before."

"Bro, but I ain't sitting around talking about that shit."

"Anyways, let's roll out and get this over with."

Rell drove off. "Are you scared?"

"Hell yeah, bro. But I can't lie. That girl came into my life and got me looking at shit so differently. I used to say I didn't believe in all that love shit, but thinking about it, I just needed the right one to love. Since the first time that I've told her that, I haven't been able to stop saying it, and I never wanna feel differently."

Rell shook his head in agreement. "You was fucking with the type that wanted you to take care of them. Camy doesn't ask you for shit for real."

"And that's why I'm gonna give her crazy ass the world. And I've been trying to put another baby in her too."

Rell gave him a crazy look before looking back at the road. "Is that what she wants?"

"I guess."

"What you mean, you guess? Did she tell you that shit?"

Malik passed the blunt. "Nah, but when I say I'm cumming, she don't loosen the grip her legs be having around my waist. She knows what happen when a nigga nut in the pussy."

It amazed Rell how shocked he still got hearing some of the bullshit that came out of his baby bro's mouth. That nigga was a real-life clown.

"Damn, nigga, you passed the store up," Malik said.

"See, listening to your crazy ass got me all fucked up," Rell said, making a U-turn.

Inside the store, it took Malik all of twenty minutes to pick out the perfect ring.

"You sure, bro? You think she'll like that one?"

"Hell yeah. I know my baby's taste. She likes cute, little, simple shit. Nothing too flashy."

Rell had seen some other nice-looking rings in a different showcase that Malik hadn't paid any attention to. "Man, come look at these over here."

Although he had made up his mind, Malik went to see what Rell was talking about. "Damn, she might like this one."

"What you gonna do?" Rell questioned.

Malik went back and forth, looking at the two rings. "Maybe I could buy both and just let her pick."

Rell chuckled. "That ain't how that shit go. You gonna fuck around and spoil that girl."

"What's wrong with that? That's my fucking baby. She deserves everything."

After giving it some more time, Malik ended up getting the first ring that he picked out for Camy.

The brothers pulled back up to their mama's house.

"What's your plan now?"

"We're supposed to be having dinner with her daddy and his wife. I'm gonna do this the right way. When she goes to the restroom, I'm gonna ask for his blessing first. Then, I'm gonna ask her to marry me when she gets out of the restroom."

Rell smiled. "Damn, bro. I'm so fucking proud of you. I see you on your grown-man shit now."

Malik wanted so badly for everything to work out for them but was nervous as hell.

"Aye, bro, I'm gonna need you to hold onto this ring for me. Hide that bitch in your crib."

"Fuck nah! If Tiffany find that shit, she gonna think it's hers. Then, I'll have to explain that it's yours, and then, she gonna wanna beat my ass 'cause I ain't asked her to marry me yet. I'm not about to fuck up my household for your Black ass."

The brothers shared a laugh.

"All right, bro. I can understand that."

"Aye, where Unc ass at?" Rell asked.

Malik gave it some thought. "Shit, come to think about it, I ain't seen him all day. What if that nigga got a li'l bitch stashed off somewhere?"

They both thought about that shit, then laughed.

"Man, let me get out of here and go get ready for this dinner."

Rell gave him a strange look. "Bro, you doing that shit tonight?"

"Hell yeah."

"Good luck, my baby."

"Thanks, bro."

Malik got out of the car and then went across the street.

"Damn, baby. You look so damn good. I don't even wanna leave the house now."

Camy turned around with a big smile on her face. "Thank you, baby, but we missed the first dinner, and he ain't having that shit again."

Malik held Camy from the back, placing kisses on her neck, causing her to let out a little moan.

"Hell no, Malik. I'm not going there with you. You still gotta get ready," she yelled, pushing him off of her.

"Damn, Camy, you the one walking around here smelling and looking all good and shit. You can't blame a nigga for trying."

Camy giggled as she walked away.

While Malik was in the shower, Camy thought about how she used to cry, thinking she wasn't beautiful enough for a man to truly love, and how Jason used to make her feel so bad about herself, just to be the one to tell her that he loved her later. Finding out that it was all a mind thing to make her feel like she needed him and him only, then meeting Malik, was really the best thing that could have happened for her.

Malik walked into the room to find her crying.

"What's wrong, baby?" he questioned as he remembered that he didn't get a chance to hide the ring. For a minute, he thought she knew what his plans were.

Camy wiped her tears. "Nothing, baby. These are actually tears of joy. I'm finally completely happy."

Malik placed a kiss on her lips. "I hope I played a part in that."

"You know you did."

"Just know shit only gonna get better from here," he warned her.

Instead of going to his house, David had them meet him at a nice restaurant for dinner. He was actually excited to see his baby girl with her boyfriend. At first, he wasn't sure if he really liked the guy, but when she got into that accident, David witnessed him break down and cry for her and their baby that didn't make it. Every time David went to the hospital or called up there to check on Camy, Malik was there. David once had to beg him to go home to change clothes and get some rest. Malik did go home to shower but was right back up there. David saw that he really loved Camy, and his actions changed how he felt about Malik.

"So, Malik, what do you do for a living?" David asked when they were at dinner.

"Umm, I work at my uncle's shop. I fix cars there."

Camy gave him a strange look, remembering him telling her the same shit in the beginning. She smirked, thinking about how the only car he ever fixed was hers, and all he did was replace her battery.

"Malik, whatever you're doing, just be careful," David said, giving Malik a strange look.

As they all sat around talking, Malik nervously shook his leg. The way Camy was drinking her wine, he knew it was only a matter of time before she excused herself from the table.

Camy placed her hand on top of his. "Baby, are you all right?"

Malik sipped on his drink. "Yeah, I'm good."

David and his wife, Sarah, also wondered why he looked so nervous.

"Aye, son, this not our first time meeting and talking. You already passed my test. Calm down."

Everyone laughed, including Malik.

"Please excuse me," Malik said.

Once Malik went off to the restroom, David looked across the room at his baby girl. "That boy not on drugs, is he?"

"No, Daddy, stop talking like that. He just nervous."

"For what?"

"Long story short, I'm really his first girlfriend, and all this meeting the parents stuff is new for him. Just be nice, Daddy."

"That boy poured his heart out to me about how much he loves you. I like him and not trying to start no mess. Let me go talk to this boy."

David caught Malik pacing the floor. He was stuck in the hallway by the men's restroom. looking crazy.

"Malik, you need to talk to me about something?"

Malik looked up from the ground. "Huh?"

David chuckled. "Years ago, I fell in love with Camy's mother. I remember being a nervous wreck when I felt like it was time to settle down and make an honest woman out of her. I was so nervous to ask her father for his blessing that it felt like everything that I ever ate since birth was gonna come out. It's okay, son. You have my blessing. Just treat my baby right and always love her."

Malik smiled. "Thank you, sir, and you have my word on that."

The fellas shook hands to seal the deal.

Once they returned to the table, Malik placed a kiss on her forehead.

"Hey, baby, you good?" she asked.

Malik gave her a smile. "I'm good. How's your food?"

"When have I ever complained about food?"

Camy had everyone at the table laughing.

"Malik, do you know this girl always was a big eater growing up?" Sarah asked.

"I can tell, but it's cute on her," he admitted.

"Okay, enough about me. Daddy, when are you taking your next trip, and where are you guys going?"

"It's about to start getting cold in Detroit, and you know I hate the winter. So, for our next getaway, we haven't decided yet, but you know it's gonna be somewhere nice and warm."

As they talked about trips, Malik came up with the bright idea to take her somewhere and then pop the question. He knew she would love that.

Dinner came to an end, and instead of letting David pay for the meals, Malik paid. He felt like David needed to see that he wasn't no bum-ass nigga.

"Baby, tonight was perfect."

"Yeah, it was cool. I like yo' people and wouldn't mind chilling with them again."

They had just gotten out of the shower and were cuddled up in bed. Camy's head rested on his chest as usual.

"Are you gonna tell me what was going on with you at the dinner table?"

"No, just know that we are good."

That answer wasn't good enough for her, but she decided to be nice and let him sleep in peace.

Camy ended up waking up early and was surprised to see that Malik wasn't in the bed. Going into the front room, she saw him at the computer, looking things up.

"What you doing, baby? You not up looking at some nasty hoes, are you?" she asked, trying to be funny.

"Why would I when I got you?"

Camy giggled. "Shut up, boy."

Malik saw her trying to get across the room to where he was at. "I'm trying to handle something. Why don't you get back in the bed, and I'll be there in a minute?"

Camy trusted him, so she didn't question him. Instead, she did what he asked.

Malik climbed into the bed ten minutes later. He had everything booked and was ready to go. He knew she was going to be so happy.

"Good morning, baby. You want some breakfast?"

"I'm gonna get some in a minute," Malik said, pulling her closer toward him.

"You're so crazy."

"Shit, you're the one doing early morning offerings."

Camy giggled. He was crazy, but she loved his crazy ass.

Once Malik was done eating and smashing, they ended up in the shower.

"So, what do you have planned for today?" he asked.

"I was actually thinking about sitting in front of this computer, looking at these shops."

"Let me take you out today."

Camy smiled. "Where are we going?"

"Just know I'm gonna spoil you and feed you."

Camy jumped up. "Sounds good to me," she said, laughing.

Malik wasn't playing about spoiling her. They went into so many stores that Camy lost count. Malik made sure she grabbed something out of each store, too. Malik's truck was filled with bags at the end of their shopping spree.

"You said food would be involved."

"Calm down, girl. We on our way now."

"Good. I'm starving."

Malik gave her a weird look. "You pregnant again?"

"No, Malik. I'm hungry. Why would you ask me that?"

"I'm just saying. I've been putting in overtime on that pussy. You sure?"

She shouldn't have, but Camy laughed. "You so fucking crazy. But no, I'm not pregnant."

Malik did a quick look over at her. He was wishing to see a sign of her being pregnant again.

"My favorite spot," Camy said as they pulled up to what was Malik's favorite spot.

"Yeah, this is where it all started between us. Our first date was here, and I knew that I needed you in my life."

"Really, baby?"

"Hell yeah," he admitted.

Camy was mad that they couldn't get their favorite table but decided not to bitch. "I love this place. Every time I come here, I try something new, and nothing seems to disappoint me."

"That's why this is my spot. I wasn't gonna say shit, but you really took that bitch to my spot?" he asked.

Camy's face screamed guilty. "Baby, I was just hungry, and that bitch don't be going anywhere but Applebee's. I had to show her what good food was."

"Hell nah, this is some fucking bullshit," Malik mumbled.

"What? Is it your food?"

Malik looked across the room, causing Camy to look.

"Are you fucking serious? Them muthafuckas together," she said.

Malik tried to keep his cool, but he had to let Camy get at Mona for what she did. "What you wanna do?"

"I wanna beat her ass, Malik."

"Go ahead. I got your bail money. You know these muthafuckas gonna call the hook on you. Look, don't let that bitch beat yo' ass in your favorite spot."

Malik was just playing, but Camy jumped up. "Watch me walk this bitch."

Camy was quick on her feet and was at the table as soon as Malik blinked an eye. Mona had just slid Jason the positive pregnancy test that she had stolen from Camy a while ago. She knew that it would come in handy sooner or later.

"Get the fuck up, bitch!" Camy said.

Mona gave her a fake smile. "What's up, girl? I was just about to call you. How have you been?"

Camy wasn't the one for the small talk. She was ready to fight, but she at least wanted Mona to get up first to make it fair.

"I know you drugged me and killed my baby."

Jason gave Mona a crazy look. "What? She did what?"

Mona stood up. "Bitch, you crazy. I—"

Camy cut her off with a few punches to the face. She wasn't about to let the bitch play in her fucking face.

Camy was getting the best of Mona, and Malik stood right there, watching his girl at work. "That's right, baby. Beat that bitch ass!" Malik cheered her on.

Jason finally yelled out. "Camy, stop. She's pregnant!"

Finally, Camy got off Mona. "Stupid bitch," she yelled, stomping her face one last time.

"Get the fuck on, Camy. Look at what you did!" Jason yelled, seeing that Mona was bleeding from the nose and mouth.

Camy looked Jason dead in the face and then spit on him. "Fuck you too, bitch!"

Jason's reaction was to attack, but when he jumped at Camy, Malik was standing right there. "I wouldn't do that shit if I was you, nigga."

Jason knew he couldn't do shit with Malik, so he threw his hands up, showing that it wasn't a problem.

"You good, baby?" Malik asked as they rode home.

"Just a little upset that I didn't finish my food first, but other than that, I'm good."

Malik had peeped some shit that he didn't like. As bad as he wanted to leave it alone, he couldn't. He needed answers.

"Aye, you know I would have killed that bitch-ass nigga if he would have hit you, right?"

"Yeah, but I probably would have grabbed that knife on that table and diced his ass up first."

"So, why you spit on him anyways?"

"Where you going with this shit, Malik?"

"I'm just wondering what was the point. Was it because he was out with that bitch?"

Camy caught an attitude. "Leave me the fuck alone, Malik."

"Who the fuck you talking to? I'm not that li'l bitch. I'll fold yo' punk ass up."

Camy turned to look out the window. She wasn't trying to give him any more of her attention.

"I know you beat her ass because of that ho shit she did, but what he do other than fuck with her?"

Camy was happy that they had just pulled up to her house. She couldn't wait to get the fuck away from his ass. While Malik waited for an answer, Camy ignored him and stormed into the house.

Malik sat in the car, rolling up. He figured he'd give her a minute to cool down, but he still wanted answers. Malik wanted to know if seeing them together had been the reason why she went after Jason. Before he continued with his plans, he needed to know if she still had any feelings for that nigga. It was going to hurt, but he was going to cut her loose if she did. He wasn't into playing second to any nigga.

Later, Camy had just gotten out of the shower and was ready to go to bed. She would always stand up for herself, but she felt crazy having to keep fucking bitches up because they loved trying her.

"Can we talk now?"

"About what?"

"You still got feelings for that nigga or something?"

Camy sat up with an attitude. "What the fuck are you talking about?"

Malik stood at the doorway, watching Camy's movement. He needed to know what was on her mind.

Camy looked up from her phone. "Malik, if I still wanted him, I would be with him. That nigga begged and cried for me to take him back, but I told him that besides my daddy, only one other man had my heart, and that other nigga is you. Don't ever, in this life or next, think it's somebody else. Your Black ass won the pot of gold. Now, come hold me so I can go to sleep."

Malik had a smirk on his face. She said everything that he needed and wanted to hear. Malik undressed, then climbed in the bed. "I was gonna have to kill you if you were trying to play with me."

Camy laughed. "Go to sleep with all that crazy shit. Even when you were on your bullshit, it was still about you."

Malik gave her a kiss. "A nigga had you like that?"

"Yeah, now let's go to bed."

Malik got up early to get their bags out of the truck. He was so caught up in his feelings that he had forgotten the shit was in there.

Camy walked into the living room and looked at all the bags. "Where the hell is all this shit gonna go? You might have to take this shit to your house."

"All right, but I need you to do something for me first."

"What? What do you want, some breakfast?"

"Nah, I need you to pack up some clothes for like a week."

"Don't tell me you in some more shit and I gotta stay at your house again," Camy said, not knowing what was going on.

"Nah, girl, we're going on a vacation."

Camy was so excited that she started jumping up and down. "Oh my gawd, baby! Thank you." Camy raced over to the couch where he was seated then straddled his lap. "Baby, you're the best! I love you so much, baby."

They shared a kiss. The look on her face was priceless. If he had never done anything right in his life, he knew that he would make her happy.

"Baby, when do we leave? I need to get my nails and shit done. Oh my gawd. I can't believe this."

"Calm down, baby. You got enough time for everything. As a matter of fact, get dressed and go handle all that. I gotta meet up with bro anyways."

Camy gave him one last kiss before jumping up.

"Aye," Malik called out before she disappeared to the back.

"Yes, baby?"

"Do that thing I like before I get up out of here."

Camy giggled as she made her booty cheeks jump. "Now, gone before you be trying to fuck."

Malik walked out of the house with the biggest smile on his face. He had a real one on his team, and if everything went as planned, she would be his wife soon.

Malik jumped in his car and then drove off. He needed to take care of a few things before they left.

"Damn, Malik, you really outdid yourself with this one. I love it here. It's so beautiful."

"I think you're even more beautiful."

Camy laughed. "You corny for that one, boy."

Malik laughed right along with her. "Shut yo' ass up. Look at that smile on yo' face. You love my corny ass."

"Yes, I do, baby."

Malik sipped on his drink. "You do, huh?"

"For sure, fool," Camy said, still laughing.

"Goofy ass," Malik mumbled. "That's the dress you're wearing tonight?"

Camy picked the dress up from the bed. "Yeah, what's wrong with it?"

"That muthafucka looking short as hell. Is it gonna cover your whole ass?"

Camy laughed. "Stop playing with me, Malik."

"I'm just saying."

"It might. It might not. Now what?"

"I guess it doesn't matter. Either way, you getting this dick tonight."

This was their third day in Barbados, and Malik was still nervous to pop the question. Every night, he planned for them to go out for dinner, thinking that would be the night that he asked, but no. At dinner, Malik would eat slowly, trying to get his shit together so that they could move forward, but the more he stared at her, the more he became nervous. Every time he thought it was the right time, he would start to feel sick to his stomach. But tonight was the night.

"Why you staring at my food like that? You already know I'm not sharing my food," she said.

"I wasn't even looking at your food. I was looking at you."

"Why?"

Malik smirked. "Because I want you to marry me."

"Yeah, okay," Camy said, stuffing her mouth with more food, not taking him seriously.

Malik didn't take his eyes off her. He was so serious, and she was sitting there, taking him for a joke. "Camy, I'm serious. Marry me?"

"Stop playing with me, Malik. I know we play a lot, but please don't play with me like that." Camy started to cry a little. Part of her believed him, but the other half protected her feelings, saying he was joking. She had made up her mind that if he was playing, then she was going to fight him. It was only when Malik pulled out the ring that she truly felt he was serious.

Malik stood up from the table and then got down on one knee. "Camy, will you marry me?"

It took Camy a minute to answer because she couldn't stop crying.

"Damn, baby, you gonna give a nigga an answer or leave me hanging?"

Camy nodded her head before yelling out, "Yes, baby. Yes, I'll marry you!"

The people who were in the restaurant started cheering the two on as they shared their first kiss as an engaged couple.

Camy looked over the balcony, thinking about her life. Since being with Malik, her life had completely changed, and it had been for the best. He made her feel loved and beautiful. At first, things were rocky because he was stuck in his ways, but over time, he had proven to be the man that she needed. His proposing to her was just the icing on the cake.

"What's on your mind, baby?" he asked, stepping onto the balcony and wrapping his arms around her.

"You, me, us, just everything."

"That all sounds so good together. Just a year ago, muthafuckas couldn't tell me that this would have been my life."

Camy smiled as he kissed and sucked on her neck. "I love you so much, baby. I can't wait until I become your wife."

"I can't wait either. I want this so bad. Let's just say fuck waiting and get married while we here."

"My daddy would kill me and you. He don't play that."

"Yeah, you right. Why don't you come play with me?"

Camy cheesed hard. "What you got in mind?"

While his hands were under her dress, Malik pulled her panties down. Camy quickly stepped out of them.

"What if somebody sees us out here?" she asked.

"Fuck it. Let's give them a show."

Camy went from being bent over on the balcony, getting her cheeks slapped, to riding Malik's dick in the chair that was out there.

That night, Camy slept well in her fiancé's arms, but Malik couldn't sleep for shit. All he could think about was going home, marrying Camy, buying her a dream house, then, of course, popping a few babies into her.

The next morning, Camy jumped on the phone to call her daddy. Waiting until they got back to Detroit to tell him she was getting married wasn't something she could do.

David saw her number pop up on his phone and knew just what she wanted, but he was going to play it off. "Good morning, my beautiful daughter. I know you're not bored. Why are you calling me?"

"Daddy, Malik asked me to marry him, and I said yes!" she blurted out.

"That's great, baby girl. I'm so happy for you two. When's the big day?"

"We haven't decided yet, but I'm so happy, Daddy."

"I can hear it in your voice. I'm happy that you found someone to make you so happy."

"Thanks, Daddy. I love you and will talk to you later."

"Love you too, baby girl."

Once Camy got off the phone, she sat on Malik's chest. "Baby, wake up."

Malik opened his eyes just a little. "Either slide up or slide down if you want me to get up."

"This is why I call you crazy all the time," she teased.

"I was up most of the night and tired as hell." Malik forced her to lie down with him. "Let's go back to sleep, then we can get into some shit later."

Shay watched Malik's page with a face full of tears. Never in a million years would she have thought that Malik would be getting married to someone other than her. She had been following Malik's and Camy's pages all day, hurting her own feelings. That morning, she saw them go live on vacation, living their best lives. She was pissed he had never taken her anywhere but to the fucking abortion clinic. It really hurt her when the couple shared to the world that they were engaged. That alone killed her soul.

"I hate you so much!" she cried, rubbing her growing belly. "I can't let this shit go down, and I'm not."

Camy couldn't wait to lie in her own bed. She loved her vacation, but home was where the heart was. While Camy slept, Malik went to visit his mama. He was one of the main ones complaining about her mouth, but after not hearing it for a few days, he was missing it.

"Hey, Ma, what's good?"

"Hey, Malik. Where's my new daughter-in-law?" Ms. Patt asked with a huge smile on her face.

"She over there knocked out. That vacation got her drained."

Ms. Patt got up to check on her food. She then walked back into the front room. "You want a plate? Everything will be done in about fifteen minutes."

"Hell yeah. I was gonna have to go pick up something anyway. She's so tired that I know she ain't gonna get up and cook shit."

"I'll put her up a plate too."

"Thanks, Ma. I appreciate you so much."

"So, are you really about to marry that girl? You sure this is what you wanna do?"

"Yeah, Ma. I feel it in my soul that she's the one. I can't imagine being in this world without her. She got a nigga heart for real."

Ms. Patt smiled. She was happy that her son was out of his old ways and had finally found the right one. It felt good knowing that he wasn't going to be an asshole for the rest of his life.

Not even an hour later, Davon, Rell, Tiffany, and Camy were sitting around Ms. Patt's house, eating and talking. Everything felt perfect.

"Damn, I did wanna take everybody out to celebrate our engagement, but I guess this is it," Malik said, holding up his cup.

At once, everyone yelled out congratulations.

All night, Camy couldn't stop smiling. Malik was amazing, and his family seemed to really like her.

While they were celebrating, there was a knock at the door. As Davon got up to see who was at the door, Malik called out to Camy, "Aye, baby, you want some more wine?"

Shay pushed her way through the door. "Sorry, baby, but that wine ain't good for the baby." Once again, Shay had popped up to start some shit.

"What the fuck? I thought you got rid of that," was the first thing that Malik yelled.

With a grin on her face, Shay rubbed her big, round belly.

"Really, Malik? So, you just gonna keep doing this shit to me?" Camy cried as she started swinging on him.

Ms. Patt had let that shit at his birthday go down, but she had to stop this. With the help of Rell, they pulled Camy off Malik.

"Man, Camy, let's go talk. This all some fucking bull-shit!" he yelled.

"No, fuck you, Malik. What the fuck you even come into my life for when all you were doing was playing me?"

Malik tried to grab her hand to prevent her from leaving, but she swung on him again. "Stay the fuck away from me before I fuck around and kill your dumb ass."

Malik tried to go after her again, but Ms. Patt stopped him. "You can chase after her later, but you need to handle this situation right here."

Malik gave Shay a death stare. The more she rubbed her stomach, the more he hated her. "What the fuck you lie about getting an abortion for? Do you know how bad you just fucked my life up?"

Shay laughed in his face. "Did you really think I was gonna get rid of your baby, so you could run off and play house with that bitch? I told you we were gonna be locked in forever, nigga."

Tiffany shook her head as she told Rell that she was ready to go. She felt so bad for Camy that she could cry for her.

"Aye, we gone. Bro, call me in the morning," Rell said.

Rell wanted to stay, knowing that his brother would need him, but he had to keep the peace in his home. He had planned on dropping her off, and after making sure that she was good, he would head back out.

Malik sat in the recliner with his head buried in his hands. The way he looked at things, his life was over.

"What we doing now, Malik? We do have a baby on the way."

Ms. Patt felt bad for Malik. He had been on his bullshit, but Shay was wrong for the game that she played. "Listen here, little girl. You wrong as fuck. You see he already pissed because you lied, but you not about to bring your funky ass around here and get on his nerves. Why the hell would you lie about getting an abortion, just to pull this bullshit? Why would you do that?"

Shay started to feel bad. "I wanted my baby. I told him from jump that I wanted my baby, and he tried to force the whole abortion shit on me. He didn't care about how I felt. His main concern was Camy. Why should I be the one without his child, and that bitch get to carry his baby? Malik played with me for too long, so I played my own game."

Malik jumped up. By the look in his eyes, Ms. Patt knew that shit was about to get uglier. She and Davon had to use everything in them to stop Malik from beating Shay's ass that night.

"Bitch, take yo' ass home. Don't fucking call me until that baby born!" Malik yelled.

Shay cried, not for herself, but for him. After all that plotting and shit, she felt bad after seeing the pain in his eyes. "I'm sorry, Malik. I'm so sorry, baby."

Ms. Patt damn near had to drag Shay out of her house.

Malik sat back down on the couch. He rested his head on the pillow, and for the first time in a while, he cried. "Ma, I fucked up for real this time."

Ms. Patt took a seat next to her son. "It's gonna be all right, Malik. Go over there and talk to that girl. Just explain what happened."

Malik tried to calm himself down. "This time, I don't think that shit gonna work."

Ms. Patt hugged her baby boy. She had always warned him about playing these games with these girls, and now look at him. Stuck crying over the only girl that he had loved for real.

Chapter 14

For three days straight, Camy buried herself in her bed, under the covers. The thought of ending it all even crossed her mind, but she knew better than that. Malik had broken her down for the last time, and after the whole baby thing with Shay, there was no coming back.

Malik was at home, feeling the same way. Only the thought of bringing a baby into this world saved him from doing something stupid. He didn't give a fuck about Shay, but he was going to do right by his child.

Malik knew that not hitting Camy up after everything jumped off that night only made shit worse, but he was trying to give her some space. She at least deserved that before he stepped up to her, trying to explain everything.

Malik used his key to get into Camy's place. It was the middle of the day, and he was surprised to see her still in the bed. Malik sat on the edge of the bed, contemplating whether to wake her up. Giving it some thought, he slid closer to give her a few kisses. Pulling the cover off her face, he planted a few kisses on her cheek and neck.

Just like magic, she was opening her eyes. "I don't want you around me. Please leave and return that key."

Malik heard her but wasn't trying to. Instead of arguing, he started to tell his side of the story. "I was happy as fuck when the doctor told us that you were carrying my baby. I knew that I would forever love you and our baby for life. I wanted to be a real dad. I wasn't gonna run out on the baby or nothing like that."

Camy cut him off. "I don't wanna hear all this. I want you to get away from me. Malik, you have repeatedly hurt me, and I can't be a dummy by keep accepting the fucked-up shit that you do."

Malik knew she was pissed, but once again, he didn't respond to what she was saying. "Soon after we found out about the baby, Shay called me over, saying it was an emergency. At this point, I had cut her off, so I was curious to see what was up. I got there, and she showed me a paper from the doctor, saying that she was pregnant."

"I don't care shit about her or that fucking baby! Fuck them!"

"Camy, chill. I know you are mad, but watch yo' mouth. My baby ain't got shit to do with this."

"Get the fuck out!"

Malik got back to his story. "I was mad, and all I could think about was you. I never wanted to hurt you in any type of way, so I paid her to get an abortion. I might have been wrong for telling her to do it, but it was all for you. I couldn't let that shit stress you out. Just like everyone else, we all found out that she lied about the shit. Camy, you gotta forgive me for this. I tried to make everything right for you."

Camy cried. He cried. She wanted so badly to hug him, but she was tired of him making her look stupid. "I can't do this shit anymore, Malik," Camy said, sliding off her ring.

Malik felt his heart break. He kept trying to stop his tears from falling, but his emotions got the best of him. "Please, Camy, don't do me like that. I'm sorry, baby. What do I gotta do to fix it? Just tell me please."

They both continued to sit on the bed, crying.

Malik refused to leave, and she refused to put the ring back on, no matter how hard he tried to force it back on her finger.

"No, Malik. I don't want it anymore. Give it to the mother of your child."

"Stop being like that. This yo' ring. I bought it for you."

Seeing that he wasn't leaving, Camy jumped out of the bed, packing up a bag.

"Where you going?"

"I'm getting the fuck away from you until I can get my locks changed."

"I just told you the truth about everything, and you still gonna leave me? We can work this shit out. Please."

Camy left him in the room as she walked to the front door.

Malik wiped his face and then went after her. "I paid that bitch to kill my baby, just so yo' feelings wouldn't be hurt, and you still gonna leave me?" he yelled, trying to take her bag from her.

Instead of fighting with him outside while everyone watched, Camy jumped in her car and then drove off. She didn't give a fuck about her clothes. All she wanted was peace of mind.

Malik locked her house back up and then left. He now wished that he knew exactly where her daddy stayed so that he could go get her. He didn't care what she was saying. She was going to be his forever.

"Bro, chill out. We dragged your ass out the house to have a good time."

Malik gave Rell a weird look. "I'm not feeling this shit. I think I'm just gonna call it a night and head home." Malik had taken his breakup with Camy hard. For the last two weeks, he had been in a funky mood, not even wanting to be around anyone.

Davon shook his head. "Nephew, it's some bitches over there for you," he said, pointing.

Rell slapped his hand down. "Unc, stop pointing. You know better."

Malik then looked at his uncle weirdly. "Fuck them bitches. I want Camy back."

Rell picked his glass up. "Come on, bro. At least act like you feeling tonight. She'll come back home in due time."

Malik prayed that what Rell was saying was true. It had been a few weeks since he last saw or spoke to Camy, and not knowing how she was doing drove him crazy.

Davon got up to go to the restroom while his nephews stayed at the table.

"Still ain't heard shit yet?" Rell asked.

"Nah, bro. I call and text her every day, though. I swear the next time I see her ass, I'm gonna kidnap her li'l ass."

Rell started to laugh. His brother was a fool.

"For real, bro. She got me fucked up, playing with me like this. I'm gonna snatch her ass up and go out of the country on a private jet or something. We're gonna live on a private island and never come back to this muthafucka."

"What about your baby?"

Malik gave Rell an evil look and then shook his head.

"What, nigga? You can't say fuck your seed, no matter how you feel about the mama."

"Yeah, I know. I'm gonna have to set up an account and send her money every week for it."

"Your baby will never know you."

"Bro, chill on me. How the hell am I supposed to relax and have a good time if you asking me all these damn questions?"

Before Rell could respond, Davon returned to the table.

"Guess who here?" Davon asked.

Malik looked around. "My girl here?"

"Nah, but that nigga we jumped that day over there," Davon said, pointing across the room.

"Unc, what I tell you about pointing?"

Davon put his hand down. "My bad, Rell."

Malik could see the nigga, JoJo, staring their way. "What y'all trying to do?"

"We chilling tonight, bro. Fuck that nigga," Rell explained.

Malik tried to chill, but he found himself mugging JoJo for fifteen minutes straight. That was his way of daring the nigga to do something stupid.

"Bro, leave that nigga alone. I see you."

"Fuck that pussy-ass bitch," Malik barked.

JoJo wasn't stupid, and just like he was being watched, he was also watching them. Knowing how them niggas got down, he was ready to fight dirty just as well.

JoJo looked at his brother's text, saying he was outside. After giving Malik one last look, JoJo walked out of the club. JoJo saw that his brother, Trey, had his baby mama drop him off.

"What's the deal?" his brother asked.

"Them bitch-ass niggas in there partying and shit like I wasn't gonna come back for they ass," JoJo said as they walked to his car.

"Aye, let me pull up on these niggas, and you slide on them."

JoJo agreed to his plan and now understood why his brother had let his baby mama drop him off.

Waiting for what seemed like a lifetime turned out to be an hour before Malik, Rell, and Davon walked out of the club.

"There them bitch-ass niggas go right there," JoJo announced.

"Aye, bro, you sure you wanna do this shit?" Trey asked, to make sure.

"Hell yeah. I ain't call you out here for nothing."

Being drunk and caught up in conversation, Rell and Malik never noticed that they were being watched. Rell had parked two rows over from Malik and went on his way to get his car. Malik was going to drop Davon off because he was going that way anyway to check on Camy's house.

Rell pulled up on the side of Malik's car. "Y'all niggas be safe and call me in the morning."

"All right, bro. You be good."

Davon waved bye to Rell right before he drove off.

"All right, Unc. Let me get yo' ass home."

As soon as Malik started his car, Trey pulled up on the passenger side of Malik's car.

"Bitch-ass niggas!" JoJo yelled while letting off a few rounds.

"Ahh, shit!" Malik yelled, trying to get away.

Chapter 15

Camy couldn't sleep for shit that night, so she was up scrolling through social media, something she rarely did. "Oh, no. Oh my god," she said, jumping out of bed and getting dressed. She was two days late, but knowing how much Malik loved his Uncle Davon, it was only right for her to put her personal feelings aside and be there for him.

Camy found herself crying on the trip to Malik's house. Davon had always been nice to her. Once Camy got there and pulled up in his driveway, she noticed all the lights were off. She kicked herself for not calling first.

Camy rang the doorbell, praying that he would answer. After waiting and then ringing it again, Camy was walking off the porch when the front door opened.

"Aye."

Camy turned around to see Malik standing in the doorway. She quickly walked back to the porch. Malik didn't say shit, but he did hold the door open so that she could come in. Camy didn't know what to say. It was clear that he had locked himself in the house with bottles of Henny and weed. It was obvious that he had been trying to numb the pain. For a second, they just stared at each other.

"Malik, I'm so sorry."

Malik didn't have to say anything. The way his body basically fell on her told Camy just how hurt he was.

"He's gone, man. My fucking unc is gone," he cried.

Camy held onto him tightly as she cried right along with him. "I'm so sorry, baby," she repeated as she helped him back onto the couch.

"That nigga killed my fucking uncle, man, and I couldn't do shit to save him. He died because of me."

Camy held Malik while rubbing his back, the same way he did to her whenever she got upset. "It'll be okay, baby. It's not your fault. Don't do that."

Malik rested his head on her, letting out all the crying he had tried to hold in. Camy wished she had found out about Davon's death when it first happened because Malik smelled like nothing but alcohol. She thought that she could have been there to help him without the drinking.

Time flew, and they were soon knocked out on the couch, still holding onto each other. Camy woke up first. She looked at her phone to see that it was 3:40 a.m.

"Damn," she whispered as she tried to get off the couch.

Malik felt her movement and woke right up. "You leaving me?"

"No, I need to go to the bathroom and put on something to sleep in."

"Your shit still where you left it."

Camy hurried to shower and change clothes. She knew that it would be a minute before she would be able to go anywhere. When she went back into the living room, Malik was back up, smoking and drinking.

"Malik, give me this," she said, taking the bottle out of his hand.

"You know I haven't been to sleep since that shit happened. Bottle after bottle, blunt after blunt, my ass been up. I was scared to close my eyes because every time I did, all I saw was Unc being killed. All I can see is Unc getting hit in the head and his brains all over me."

Camy held her head low. "I'm so sorry, baby."

"I know we are going through whatever, but I really need you right now. You helped me get a little rest."

Camy couldn't imagine leaving him right now when he was going through so much. She held him as he cried.

"I'm here, baby. I'm not gonna leave you."

The two soon climbed into bed to go back to sleep. Instead of Malik holding Camy, she held him, letting him know that everything would be all right.

The next afternoon, Malik woke up to an empty bed. Not seeing Camy in the bed, he called her a lying bitch. She had just told him that she wasn't going anywhere, and now, she was gone. Once opening the bedroom door, Malik quickly took it all back. Camy was still there. She had woken up that morning, cooking and cleaning up his place.

"Good afternoon. Did you sleep all right?"

"Yeah, I did. Thanks for being here with me. I appreciate that."

"No problem. Now, why don't you have a seat so that you can put something on your stomach?"

Malik took a seat at the dining room table but wasn't about to eat. "I'm good. I'm not hungry."

"Malik, you've been smoking, drinking, and not taking care of your body the right way. Please just eat for me," Camy begged.

Usually, Malik would have said some freaky shit, but he wasn't himself. Camy didn't wait for him to change his mind about eating. She fixed him a plate and then gave him a bottle of water.

"Where this shit come from?" he asked.

"I went to the market."

They sat there in silence for a while. Camy knew that his uncle's death would hit him hard, but she still wanted him to take care of himself. "Baby, please just eat a little for me."

Malik tried not to break down, but he ended up crying again. Camy stood in front of him, holding him in her arms.

"It's okay, baby. It'll be all right."

"I don't know if I can eat. I just keep seeing Unc brains laying in my lap. My stomach might not be able to hold shit in," Malik warned her.

Camy ended up sliding down to sit on his lap. "It's okay, baby. Just take your time and try a little at a time. I got you."

Malik sat there for a minute, holding onto his girl. He knew she only wanted what was best for him. After a while, Malik started eating while Camy went into the bedroom to clean up and put some sheets on his bed.

For the next few days, Camy stayed at Malik's house, helping him cope with everything. They had even gone to visit Ms. Patt. Camy tried her best to be a helping hand in any way possible. The whole family was fucked up behind his death. It broke Camy's heart, seeing how hard everyone was taking Davon's death.

One morning, Camy got up so that she could go home and get something to wear to the funeral the next day.

"Where you going?" Malik asked, following her out the door.

"Baby, I gotta go home and get some clothes. I'm coming right back."

Instead of going back in the house, Malik followed her. Malik hadn't talked to anyone about who killed Davon, but knowing who the nigga was had him on edge. He didn't want Camy too far away from him, just in case them niggas came back. He'd be damned if anyone else he loved got killed.

"Camy, I was thinking that maybe you should move in with me," he said when they were at her house.

Camy walked out of her closet. "I like having my own space."

Malik didn't respond. He was going to respect her decision so that he wouldn't run her away. Malik chilled while she packed a bag.

Once they got back to Malik's house, Camy made sure that everything was together for the next day. She knew she had to be strong to hold Malik together.

The morning of the funeral, Malik woke up, throwing up.

Camy stood at the bathroom door, worried. "Malik, baby, are you all right?"

"Every time I think about that shit, I get sick to my fucking stomach."

Camy hated hearing that.

Just as he was finishing brushing his teeth, Camy walked in. He didn't say shit to her as he climbed into the shower. Camy stood there, thinking about how she had been there for a few days, and because Malik was taking his uncle's death hard, he hadn't tried anything with her. She wondered if she was wrong for wanting dick. Could this be them finally leaving each other alone for good? As much as Malik had hurt her, Camy's body was craving his touch, and she could no longer control her true feelings.

Undressing, she slowly stepped into the shower. Malik could sense that she was behind him. He turned around to see his girl standing there.

"Fuck took you so long?"

"I was scared," Camy admitted as he picked her up.

Malik held her up on the wall before plunging into her. "What was you scared of?"

"I didn't want you to think I was only thinking of myself while you were going through this hard time."

Malik gave her a passionate kiss. "I need you so much right now. I need a friend."

"You got me, baby," Camy moaned out, taking his hard strokes.

Camy was dressed and ready to go, but when she went out into the front room, Malik was on the couch, dozing off.

"Malik, baby, you gotta get dressed. We have about twenty minutes to get there."

Malik stared at her for a second. "I can't do this shit. I'm not going."

"Malik, please don't be like this. Get up and get dressed. You have to go say your final goodbyes to Davon. Besides, Rell and your mom are gonna need you."

"I just can't believe my unc gone, man. He ain't fuck with nobody for real."

Camy stood there with her arms folded, waiting for him to get dressed. No matter how he was feeling, she was going to make sure he made it to the funeral. "Malik!"

Malik finally stood up to get dressed. "You know I love you, baby, and I wouldn't have been able to get through this shit if it wasn't for you."

"Baby, you know I'll always be here for you."

During the funeral, Camy stayed by Malik's side. Every time he broke down, she was there.

Camy heard the female voice cry out, "Oh my God. Why him?" and instantly got irritated. Camy and Malik looked up to see Shay standing over the casket, putting on a show.

Shay then walked over toward the front row where Malik was sitting. As soon as she started to talk, Malik gave her a crazy look. That was the only warning that he wanted to give her to get the fuck away from him.

"I told you when to reach out to me. Get the fuck on," he whispered as he pulled her down to his level.

During the repast, while Camy went to fix Malik's plate, Rell went to sit down next to Malik. "Aye, bro, you good?"

"Not really. That was my nigga, bro. Shit will never be the same," Malik admitted.

"I feel that shit. I just wish I would have waited to pull off that night. That shit wasn't supposed to go down like that."

"Man, I was right there. Shit happened so fucking fast, bro. I couldn't get my shit fast enough to bust back at them niggas. Unc ain't deserve that shit."

Camy walked over with their plates, so the brothers ended their conversation.

Tiffany and Ms. Patt joined them at the table. Everyone was in their feelings and barely talking or eating.

"Man, who the hell cooked this bullshit?" Malik said.

Everyone then looked up at Malik before cracking up, laughing. No matter what the situation was, Malik knew how to make folks laugh.

Camy laughed but was the only one who continued to eat.

"Camy, stop eating that. That shit gonna fuck yo' stomach up."

"What's wrong with it? My plate good."

Malik shook his head.

"Malik, you always said she was greedy," Tiffany reminded him.

The family was able to talk and actually smile for the first time since Davon's death. It was like a load had been lifted off their chests.

"Malik, I really need to talk to you about something," Shay said when she approached them.

"Shay, it's not the right time or place," Ms. Patt warned her.

"When is the right time then? He don't answer my calls or texts. I need to talk to him now."

Malik stood up from the table. "Bitch, I just buried my fucking uncle. Ain't shit more important right now. I told you to call me when you have the baby."

Camy grabbed hold of his hand. Sometimes, her soft touch calmed him down. She knew why he was pissed but didn't need him fucking Shay up in them peoples' building.

Shay opened her mouth to say something else, but Malik cut her off. "Now, get yo' ass away from this table. Over here is for family only."

Shay looked over at Camy, wondering why she got to sit over there when Shay was the one carrying a child that was part of the family.

Before everyone went their own way, Camy sat in the car, waiting for Malik to get done talking to Rell.

"Bro, are you sure it was that nigga we jumped?" Rell asked. Malik and Rell had promised each other that they weren't going to get back at JoJo until after they got Davon in the ground.

"I'm positive. I'm ready to pop that nigga right now. Today."

Rell gave him a dap. "Fo' sho, bro. We gotta do this shit for Unc."

"I'm about to get her to the crib, but I'll call you when I figure out where that nigga stay or be at."

Rell and Malik hugged before going their separate ways.

Malik climbed into the passenger seat. "I'm ready."

"Okay, baby," she responded before taking off.

Malik had a smirk on his face. The sound of her still calling him baby was music to his ears.

After sitting up all night, playing detective, Malik climbed into bed, pulling Camy closer toward him.

"You okay, baby?" he asked.

"Yeah, it's been a long day. I'm just so tired. How are you holding up, Malik?"

"To be honest, I would be better once that nigga dead."

Camy gave him a strange look. "Malik, you know who did that to Davon?"

"Hell yeah. And yes, I'm gonna put that nigga on the news."

Camy didn't want to hear the details, but she still wanted to know who was responsible. "Who was it?"

"That shit don't concern you. Let me handle my business, and you just stay beautiful."

Camy tried not to blush, but he had her open. "Malik, I just wanna know, so maybe I could understand why this happened."

Malik gave in, just like that. "You remember that bum-ass nigga that you invited to your house, and we jumped?"

Camy sat up, clutching her invisible pearls, then started crying. "Oh my gawd, is this all my fault? Did I get him killed?"

Malik quickly grabbed Camy, holding her in a tight hug. "Don't say that shit. Ain't none of this your fault, baby."

Camy heard what he was saying, but she couldn't shake the feeling of blaming herself. "I shouldn't have invited him over, thinking that you were playing with me."

"Calm down. I picked with the nigga and dared him to do something about it. Now shit is what it is."

The couple held each other, trying to calm one another down. Malik held her tight, making her the first to fall asleep. He then reached over to the nightstand to get his phone to call Rell.

"Aye, bro, when we got home, I did some investigating bullshit and found some shit out."

"Damn, really? What did you find out?" Rell questioned.

"All this shit was a setup. The bitch that Camy worked with was that nigga Tim cousin. That's why she begged Camy to go out with that nigga. And the nigga we jumped was her baby daddy."

"Damn, bro. It ain't no telling what they had planned for Camy ass that night. Tim and his people hated your ass so bad that they tried to go after your girl."

"Man, I'm not even trying to think about what they had planned. I'm ready to go hunting and knock this nigga noodles loose."

Camy started moving around, causing Malik to sneak out of the bed and go into the front room. His leaving made Camy wake up, but she didn't move or make a sound. She wanted to hear what he was up to.

Malik got off the phone and then returned to the room shortly after. He went straight to the closet to grab some clothes.

"Where are you going?"

"Stop asking stupid questions. You already know what tip I'm on."

"No! You can't go," Camy ordered.

"Go back to bed, girl. You already know why this shit got to be done."

Camy started crying. "Malik, I'm scared!" she screamed out.

Malik sat down by her on the bed. "Fuck you got to be scared for? I'm gonna handle this shit, then come home and hold you for the rest of the night."

"That's the thing. What if you don't come back to me? What if something goes wrong? I don't wanna be in this world without you, Malik."

"I'm coming back. I promise. You know a nigga ain't never lied to you, and I'm not about to start now. Please don't be mad, but I got to get this shit over with. These niggas been alive one day too many."

Camy sat there, still in his arms, crying. Her body trembled, letting him know just how scared she was.

Malik didn't want to scare her, so he decided not to tell her the truth about JoJo and Tim. To protect her sanity, he told her to trust that he'd be back.

Camy knew that no matter what she said, Malik would do what he said he needed to do. She lay back down, allowing him to handle his business. At this point, she couldn't do shit but pray.

Chapter 16

"Shay, you gotta talk to that boy. This is his baby, right?"

Shay sat on the couch, fat and miserable and crying. "Ma, he won't talk to me. He said I can only call when I go into labor."

Shay's mom, Kim, paced the floor, worried about her daughter. "Fuck that shit! And you a damn fool for listening."

"Ma, I can't," Shay told her again.

Kim was so pissed off that she lit her cigarette. "I don't know why you thought having this baby was a good idea when you ain't worked in years and ain't got no money saved. Now look at your dumb ass. You are behind on your rent and bills and shit."

"Malik was paying my stuff, Ma, so I didn't have to work or worry about shit. He got mad and took his card off all my accounts. I don't know what to do now."

Kim watched as her daughter cried. She really didn't want to move her daughter back into her home, but because the baby was due soon, she felt like it was only right.

"Ma, what am I supposed to do?"

"I'm gonna help you pack this shit up before your ass is on the damn streets. You can come back to my house until you have the baby and get on your feet."

Shay shook her head in agreement, although she didn't want to leave her own shit. Saying, "Fuck what Malik said," she tried to call him again, but this time, she used her mama's phone.

"Hello, please don't hang up. It's an emergency," she quickly said.

Malik wanted to hang up, but he had to remember that she was carrying his child. "Fuck you want, Shay?"

The sound of him saying Shay's name made Camy look up.

"Malik, I'm behind on my bills and rent. They about to cut my lights off and put me on the streets."

"Look, I gave you five thousand to get an abortion, and you didn't. What the fuck you do with that money?"

"I spent it."

Malik shook his head. "How the fuck you blow through all that money when I had all your bills and rent on autopay? I told you that the money train was over."

"So, you just gonna say fuck me and our baby? That bitch over there probably controlling you and telling you to keep us in this fucked-up situation."

"You about to be homeless, and you worried about who is over here with me? You weird as fuck. Anyways, it sounds like you need to figure some shit out." Malik hung up the phone.

Looking over at Camy, he could tell that she was pissed. Thinking him talking to Shay had fucked up his day, Malik tried to get back on her good side. "You cool?"

"No!"

"I told her not to call me until the baby was born. I don't know why she being hardheaded. I'm sorry about that."

Camy shook her head. "It's not that, Malik. She's carrying your baby. You can't have them on the streets."

Malik was surprised by how Camy was taking things. "You sure you won't be mad at me for looking out?"

"Hell nah. You gotta make sure your baby is good. I would be pissed if you didn't help them. The baby may not be here yet, but it's due soon, and it can't come home to no home."

Malik gave her a kiss. "You know you a real one, right?"

"Yeah, I know. Besides, if the tables were turned, I would hope that she, or any other female, would say the same thing." Camy didn't give a fuck about Shay, but she was being nice, only because the baby's father was Malik.

"You know I really wish that it was you that was carrying my baby."

Camy didn't respond. She was now caught up in her emotions and started to cry. Malik tried to hold her, but she pushed him away and then went into his room.

Malik wanted to give her some space, but hearing her break down had him storming into the room. "Baby, it's all right. I got you," he said, holding onto her.

"This shit hurt so bad, Malik. I tried to move on, but the closer it gets to what was supposed to be my due date, I can't help but to cry."

"It's all right, baby. We can't replace that one, but I can put a new one in you."

Camy didn't respond. Just him saying that reminded her of why she had broken up with him in the first place. His ass was out there passing out babies like candy on Halloween.

"I think it's time for me to go back home. I've been here long enough," she said.

"So, you really about to be on that bullshit again? We been doing so good this whole time. What the fuck you tripping for?"

"I was trying to be supportive and try not to think about why I left you, but I can't. I'm still hurt about a lot of shit that happened between us, and I'm tired of just letting shit slide."

Malik paused for a minute, trying not to say the wrong thing. "Did you tell yo' daddy what happened?"

"What you think? You're still breathing, ain't you?"

Malik smiled. "That mean you still love a nigga, and I could get another chance, right?"

Camy shook her head. Malik would always be a smooth-talking asshole.

"You gonna always have my heart, and I'm gonna have yours. You can act like you don't want me, but I know you'll forever be mine."

Camy got up to walk off, but Malik grabbed her. "Where you going?"

"I need to go home."

Malik pushed her up against the wall. As he gave her sweet kisses on her lips and neck, he lifted her up while snatching her panties off from under her T-shirt. "You not about to leave me."

Camy wanted to go home to clear her mind, but feeling him slide into her was something that she wanted as well.

The next morning, Malik went ahead and put his card back on Shay's accounts. Camy was right. He couldn't just have his baby mama all fucked up and shit like that.

"Hello," Shay said, excited that he called.

"Aye, I put my card back on yo' shit, so everything is taken care of. And you need to stop talking shit about Camy 'cause if it wasn't for her, yo' lying ass would have been in the streets."

"I'm sorry. Can you tell her I said thank you? And thank you for looking out."

Malik hung up. They had talked long enough. As he sat there, looking at his account statements, he shook his head at all the money he spent monthly. Not only was he helping Shay out, but he paid for Camy's shit and went half with Rell on his mama's house expenses.

"They better be lucky I'm a nice nigga," he mumbled.

Camy had just stepped out of the bathroom, looking crazy.

"What's wrong with you? Fuck you looking like that for?" he asked.

She climbed on Malik's lap to rest on him but didn't say a word.

"You good?

"Just hold me."

Malik noticed how sad she sounded but didn't want to press the issue. He figured she'd talk when she was ready.

Camy knew she would eventually have to talk to Malik about their situation, but she wasn't sure how to feel, and she knew he was going through a lot at the time.

"I took care of Shay like you said. She said thank you."

"Oh, okay. Malik, we have been cooped up in this house for a while now. Can we go out?"

"Yeah, it has been a minute, but not today," he said, placing a kiss on her forehead.

Camy had an attitude. "Why not?"

Malik never told her the whole story behind Davon's death, but he really kept her locked in to protect her. Just them dealing with each other had muthafuckas coming for their heads.

He was taking too long to answer. "Why not, Malik? I'm going crazy in this house. You won't even let me go to the gym," Camy complained.

"Don't I work out yo' body every day?"

"I wanna go somewhere. Or at least let me go home to my own shit," she whined.

"Man, sit yo' ass down somewhere," he yelled as she stormed off to his bedroom. Malik followed behind her. "Why the fuck you can't listen?"

"I've been saying I wanted to go home, and you been acting like I can't leave, but at the same time, you leave the house and . . ." Camy paused, realizing what she was saying. "Malik, am I in danger like last time? Is this why you been keeping me locked up in this house?"

Malik's head hung low. "You know I can't chance shit when it comes to you. Please just chill for a few more days. I promise I'll make it up to you."

"Why this time?"

Still trying to hide the truth, he tried to switch the conversation. "Let's chill and watch a movie. What's new out?"

Camy snatched her bag from the closet. "Stop playing with me, Malik."

"You too pretty to be so worried. I got everything taken care of."

All that shit didn't work this time. Camy started packing her clothes.

"Why the fuck you gotta be like that? Why you can't just chill out until shit dies off?"

"Until what dies off? Why you can't just tell me what's going on? Let me decide if I wanna leave or not."

Malik was getting pissed. "No matter what, you ain't leaving this bitch until I say so."

"Wrong, bitch!"

"What the fuck that mean?" he yelled, now snatching her clothes back out of the bag. "If these niggas try to get at you, what the fuck I'm supposed to do all the way over here? I can't let you go home right now. I can't even imagine how I would feel if someone was to hurt you."

"I remember telling you the same shit, and you still left. I'm not a damn baby, Malik, and I can hold my own." Camy snatched her bag and started walking out of the room.

Malik wasn't going for that. He had never hit her before, but today, he was ready to knock some sense into her stubborn ass. Grabbing her by the back of the neck, Malik forced her to stop walking before tossing her on the couch. "Sit yo' ass down! Why the fuck you won't fucking listen?"

Camy cried. "I just wanna go home!"

Malik released her. He had only been trying to stop her and not hurt her. Her tears were his weakness. He took a seat on the couch. snatching her into his arms. "I'm sorry, baby. I know you might hate me right now, but I can't let you walk out that door. Can you please wait a few more days?"

Camy was still crying. "Why? Why is someone trying to hurt me?"

There was a silent moment between the two. Camy got comfortable, resting her head on his chest.

"I told you what happened with me and that nigga Tim. Well, Tim's cousin is that bitch KeKe, and JoJo was her baby daddy. I don't know what they had planned for you that night, but we stopped it by fighting him that night."

"Damn, baby. I didn't know. No wonder she was pressing the issue so tough."

"That's not it, Camy. Shit get worse."

"What?" Camy asked, confused. It was a lot to take in.

"JoJo killed Davon, and we got back at them. Do you see why I need you to chill? Too many people playing roles, and can't nobody be trusted. But I do trust you here with me."

Camy didn't say shit. She was shocked by all that was going on around her that she didn't know about. She lowkey felt stupid for flipping out when he told her that it was for her own good from jump.

Malik heard her crying. Instead of being in her face, yelling at her, he just held her and let her know that he had her.

While she slept, Malik packed his and her bags. He had decided to take her on a last-minute trip to ease her mind. It wasn't anything big, but getting out of Detroit for a minute sounded like a good plan.

Malik had just come in from the garage when she walked into the front room. "Where were you?" she asked.

"Garage. Go put some clothes on."

"No!"

Malik shook his head. "Why are you so fucking stubborn? You wanted to get out the house so bad, but now, you won't even go get dressed."

"I'm scared now. I don't need to do shit but sit my ass down like you said," she said, taking a seat on the couch.

Malik stood there, watching her. She was so fucking beautiful and stubborn at the same time. "Please, baby."

Camy didn't fight with him. She got up and then went into the bathroom to take a shower. Not even a whole five minutes later, Malik was in there, clapping her cheeks.

"I love you, baby," he whispered in her ear.

"I love you too, baby," she moaned out.

Malik thought something was different, but instead of mentioning it, he kept going. Shit was too good to miss the moment.

All while she got dressed, Malik couldn't help but keep looking at her weirdly. Something was indeed different.

"What now, Malik?" she asked.

"I don't know. You tell me."

Camy giggled. "Boy, you tripping for real."

Camy continued to get dressed, ignoring his stares. He was the one being weird now. "Okay, I'm done. Where are we going?"

"Let's just say somewhere warm."

Camy's face lit up. "Oh my gawd, baby. Are we going on another trip?"

"Something small, but I don't want you to be bored in the house anymore. Now, come on!"

As Malik drove, he kept his hand on Camy's thigh.

"Don't be rubbing my thighs, thinking about having me bent over on a balcony again."

Malik started laughing. "You a fucking fool, girl. As long as that's my pussy, I'll hit it any way I want to."

"Who said it was yours again?"

"Me, dammit. Fuck you thought? Besides, you told me it was last night, unless you a fucking liar."

Camy was still laughing, "Whatever I say during sex don't count."

Malik turned the music up, not paying her any attention. He said what he said, and that was final. Camy kept laughing. He knew that she wasn't going anywhere any time soon. He was her rock.

"Damn, Camy, we been here for two days, and we ain't did shit yet." Malik had a whole schedule for them to relax and have fun in Miami for a whole week, but Camy had gotten ill the first day there.

"I'm sorry, baby. I don't know what's wrong with me. Let me take another nap, then I'll be ready to do whatever you wanna do."

Malik smirked. "Anything?"

"Anything, baby. Now, give me an hour," she said before rolling over.

While she slept, Malik got on the phone with Rell. "Hey, bro, what's good?"

"Shit, just got done dropping the kids off to Ma, about to head home to Tiffany and the baby."

"All right, nigga. As long as y'all good."

"So, how you and the missus doing?"

"I don't know, dawg. Something's up with her. That muthafucka been sick since we got here. Honestly, she could have stayed her sick ass at home."

Rell laughed. "I told you that you were gonna have her spoiled as hell before it even started."

"Man, she's spoiled, but I love her and wanna give her whatever she wants. I didn't tell you this, but I brought that ring out here. I was thinking about trying this shit again since I fucked up last time."

"I already know she gonna say yeah again. Congratulations, bro. Just don't fuck it up this time when y'all get back."

Malik shook his head. "I put everything on the table. Ain't no secrets between us anymore. All loose ends are tied."

After talking to Rell, Malik always felt better about all his plans. Having a personal therapist on call should have been something that everyone had.

Malik then got up to put his plan into motion. As soon as Camy woke up, Malik already had her dress laid out on the bed with her shoes and accessories.

Camy felt a little better and wanted to go out and have some fun with her man. After taking a shower and getting dressed, Camy stared at herself in the mirror. She then started to wonder if Malik saw what she saw.

"You look so fucking beautiful."

Camy jumped before turning around. "Malik, you scared me."

Malik wrapped his arms around her, placing kisses on her neck. "You feel better, baby? Because you sure do look good."

"Yes, baby, I'm feeling a little better. So, what are we about to do?"

"Dinner and whatever comes along with it."

Camy grabbed her purse. "You sound like you buying me dinner for some pussy, nigga."

Malik laughed. "You must be feeling better with yo' silly ass."

***

After dinner on the beach, the couple walked barefoot through the sand.

"I know this ain't shit fancy, but I knew being in the house was driving your spoiled ass crazy."

"Baby, this place is fine. You already won me. You ain't gotta go all out to impress me."

Malik placed a kiss on her lips. "You my everything."

Camy kept walking while Malik stood there. Once again, her ring was screaming in his pocket, and he was freezing up. He learned that dealing with this situation, shit never got easy.

Camy turned around with a smile that outshined the moon and stars. "Come on, baby. What's wrong?"

Malik smiled back at her. "I'm coming." He did a little jog to catch up with her.

"Let me get on your back."

"Hell nah, you heavy as shit," Malik jokingly teased.

"Whatever, boy. You always holding me up when you hitting this in the shower, but now I'm heavy?"

They both laughed. Malik let her get on his back as they walked toward a vacant area.

"Malik, we gotta turn around. This is where people go to get killed and dumped in the water."

"Why do you be saying crazy shit like that?"

"Because I watch a lot of TV. Now, let's go back."

"Shut yo' scary ass up. You know I got you."

Camy laughed as she climbed down off his back.

"Let's get in the water."

"Boy, are you crazy? It's dark and scary."

Malik wrapped his arms around her from the back. "I'm not gonna let shit happen to you. Take this dress off and get in the water with me."

This time, Camy did as he asked. He had that type of effect on her.

"Malik, I love you, baby," she said when they were in the water.

Malik had Camy's mind gone as her legs wrapped tightly around his waist, taking long, hard strokes.

"I love you too. You need to go ahead and be my wife for real."

Camy buried her face into his neck, but only moans came out. Malik didn't take her not answering as a no. He figured that she would give him an answer later.

Once the couple got back to where they were staying, Camy jumped in the shower while Malik sat on the balcony, smoking.

"You wanna hit this shit?" he asked when she came out.

"Nope. I came out here just to let you know I was about to go to bed."

Malik was low-key pissed but didn't want to ruin their vacation. "Good night. I'll be in there in a few."

"Good night, baby. I love you."

Malik pulled from his blunt. "Yeah, okay."

Noticing his tone, Camy stormed off into the bedroom.

Soon after, he jumped in the shower, but instead of joining her, he lay on the couch. Malik wanted this vacation to help them clear their minds from all the bullshit that was going on in the streets and rekindle their relationship. He wanted her to be his, but shit wasn't going as planned.

Malik awoke the next morning to Camy lying on him. He gave her a kiss on her forehead. "Yo' little ass gonna make sure you come find me."

Not wanting to wake her up, he decided not to move. He eventually ended up falling right back asleep, rubbing on her booty.

"You say I'm weird, but you are sitting over there, watching me sleep," Camy said, opening her eyes.

Malik sat up in the chair. "I'm just trying to figure you out."

Camy caught his tone and could tell that he was seri-ous. Her smile quickly left her face. "What are you trying to figure out, Malik?"

"Why the fuck you playing games with me?"

Camy sat up, feeling confused. "Malik, baby, what's going on? What are you talking about?"

Malik sat there, holding his tongue. He always tried to spare her feelings, never wanting to hurt her, but she had pushed him to this point. "We've been back together for a minute now, and at first, I kept the ring on the nightstand by your side of the bed, hoping you would put it back on. I know yo' punk ass seen it, but you ain't put that bitch back on yet."

Camy cut him off. "Malik— "

"Man, let me finish."

Camy didn't finish her sentence. Instead, she let him finish.

"I brought you out here to chill with me, and you spent the first couple of days in the bed, pretending to be sick. We had fun last night, but when I asked you to be my wife, you acted like you didn't hear me. What the fuck are we doing?"

"So, now I can talk? We being friends, right?"

Malik jumped up. "You know what? Fuck it. Pack yo' shit. We're going back to Detroit. We could have stayed home if you were gonna be on this bullshit."

Camy started to cry as he walked away from her. She had so much to say but decided to wait because her emo-tions were everywhere. Camy could hear Malik throwing shit around in the room, and she was scared. She hadn't been trying to piss him off. She wanted to have a good time, too.

"Malik, stop making all that noise," she said, finally getting up from the couch.

Malik turned to face her. "Come pack yo' shit up!"

"No!"

"Why the fuck you don't listen? You always trying to challenge me and shit."

"Malik, calm down. Let's talk. Why are you so mad at me? What did I do?"

Malik took a seat on the bed, trying to calm down. "You know I've been trying to do right by yo' ass, and you're bullshitting. You really ain't trying to marry a nigga?"

"Me not answering wasn't a no, Malik. You know I still love you so much, but after everything, I thought that maybe we should slow down on marriage right now. Besides, when I came back to you after Davon's death, we were playing it safe. You were the one that said you needed me as a friend, not a wife, in the shower that day. So, I've been just that, a friend."

Malik stood back up, throwing the pair of shorts he had in his hand at her. "You so full of shit, Camy! You knew what the fuck I meant and what I needed. And to be clear, no answer is a fucking no. Man, get the fuck out my face!"

Camy tried to walk toward him to calm him down, but he backed up. "Get the fuck away from me before I kill yo' ass and have yo' daddy searching for your body," he threatened.

Camy grabbed her chest. "I'm sorry, Malik. You gotta understand where I'm coming from."

"Fuck you and wherever you coming from! I do whatever for you, and you gonna sit up and play in my face like that. Fuck you! When we get back to Detroit, I'm done."

Camy cried harder. "Malik, please don't do this."

Malik walked past her, making sure to push her out of his way. Camy turned around to follow him, but as soon as she got to the front room where he was, she raced off to the bathroom. Malik heard her vomiting, but since he was so upset, he didn't even go check on her.

When Camy finally came out after showering, Malik had her bags packed and already at the door. "Get dressed so we can go," he ordered.

"I don't feel good, Malik. I don't think we should leave yet."

"Sounds like you need to find you a muthafucka that gives a fuck because I'm done caring."

Camy paid no attention to his attitude. She went into the room and then buried herself under the covers. Malik went into the room to start more shit with her. If he wasn't getting a wife, she wouldn't be getting any sleep.

Snatching the cover off of her, he started yelling. "Get the fuck up, Camy."

"Malik, I told you that I don't feel good. Please just give me a minute," she begged.

Malik took a seat at the end of the bed, thinking about his behavior. Putting his feelings aside and thinking of hers now made him think he was wrong. "You've been telling me how much you love me and shit this whole time. Why won't you marry me? I know I fucked up with that baby situation, but I thought we were getting over that shit."

"Malik, shit is different, and I have a lot to think about now. You gotta give me some time."

"That shit not good enough. I need a final answer now."

"Malik, that's not fair, and you know it. You can't bully me into doing nothing."

Malik stood back up. "Fuck you. I'm not about to beg yo' ass for shit. You don't have to marry me, funky-acting bitch."

"Bitch? Really, Malik? You really that mad? You need to grow the fuck up, boy."

"I am grown. You grow the fuck up. Matter of fact, get the fuck up before I leave yo' ass here."

Camy laughed, pissing him off more. "You really doing all this because you have fucked me up so bad in the head that I'm scared to be like that with you again. Us being friends and fucking was fun, but look at how you embarrassed me when I did try to be on that level with you."

"Man, fuck you," was all that he could say, knowing she was right.

Not giving a fuck if she was ready, Malik started taking their bags downstairs to the car. She was going to have to hurry the fuck up or get left.

Chapter 17

"Malik, can you pull over please? I'm feeling so sick."

Malik didn't respond but pulled into a McDonald's parking lot. As Camy stepped out, he started talking shit again.

"Hurry the fuck up before I leave you."

Camy rushed into the restroom, feeling sick again.

Malik was irritated but knew he had to calm down and give her some time to decide if this was what she really wanted. Killing the engine, he went into the building to check on her.

"Camy, you good?" he asked, knocking on the women's restroom door.

Just then, she walked out, looking tired as hell. "I'm good for now. If I'm taking too long and you need to go, just go. I'll call my daddy to come get me."

He noticed her playing along with his game, so he ignored her. "When you due?"

Camy walked past him and ignored his question. Malik followed her as she went toward the truck.

"Come on. Let me help you get in. Do you need some food or something?" he asked, trying to be nice.

"Malik, just get me home."

As they drove home, Malik kept placing his right hand on her stomach, causing her to be irritated. "Why you ain't tell me? You know how bad I wanted this for us. I prayed for this shit and put in that overtime to make shit happen."

"Ain't shit official yet, but do it even matter?"

"What the fuck that mean? And I suggest you watch what the fuck you say to me."

Camy ignored him. She wasn't sure why she said that other than to get on his nerves. He had pissed her off, and now, she was acting like him.

"I know I talked a lot of shit, but I'm happy about the baby, and I wanna give you all the time in the world to make up your mind about marrying me."

"You called me a bitch, Malik."

"How was yo' ass acting? Like a funky bitch, right? I didn't lie about shit."

Camy rolled her eyes.

Malik soon pulled up into his driveway. "Home sweet home. I'm gonna get you in, then come out to get the bags."

Although he said he would help her, she got out on her own.

"Punk ass!" he yelled, jumping out of his ride.

Once in the house, Camy went into the bedroom to grab her keys.

"Fuck you doing?"

"Going home."

Malik leaned against the wall. "I'm sorry for tripping, but I want you to stay with me. All bullshit aside, be my girl again, and come stay with me."

"Now, why would my funky bitch ass do that?"

"Come on, Camy. I was wrong for flipping out. We both know I can't live without you, and you, for damn sure, can't live without me. Let's do this shit by the books and build a home for our baby."

Camy didn't respond. What he was saying was somewhat true, but not being able to shake the fact that someone else was having his baby soon was tearing her apart.

"I need time to think about this all. Shit different now, and I need time to figure out what I wanna do."

"What's different? Do you still love me, or have that changed? And what the fuck you need to figure out?"

"My love for you will never change," Camy calmly said.

Malik placed a kiss on her lips. "So, you just been bitchy all day for what?"

"Feed me," she said, trying to get off the situation that they really needed to talk about.

Malik chuckled. "Man, I got you, baby."

After eating and showering, the couple cuddled in the bed.

"This time, I'm gonna be there for every step of the way. I don't even want you going out, being around those fake-ass hoes or nothing."

"Malik, the only females I hang around are really your mom and Tiffany, and lately, I've been under your ass twenty-four seven. But I told you ain't shit official yet."

"The way you been sick, and the way that pussy been gushy, you pregnant, girl," he assured her, smiling.

"You so silly, boy."

"Because I love you and like to see that smile on yo' face."

"I love you too, Malik."

The next morning, Malik woke up to an empty bed. He shook his head, feeling like Camy had run game on his ass the night before. "Slick-ass muthafucka," he mumbled as he hung the phone up. She wouldn't even answer the phone for him.

Pacing the floor, Malik decided to call his mama up.

"Hey, Malik, how was the trip? Y'all good?"

"Ma, Camy car over there?"

Ms. Patt shook her head, knowing that it was some bullshit going on. "Yes, son, she pulled up a few hours ago."

"Aye, do me a favor. If she come out the house, call her over there to talk to her."

"What's going on, Malik?"

"Just talk to her for me," Malik ordered before hanging up.

Camy missed being at home. Although she just wanted to sleep all day, she decided to clean up a little. It had been so long since she had been there, and she had no idea when the last time was that she had actually been home to get shit in order.

Malik decided to let her have her space and not pressure her. Instead, he hooked up with Rell on some money shit.

"So, when the big day?"

"I don't wanna talk about it," Malik snapped.

Rell rolled up the blunt before they could drive off. "Don't tell me she said no."

"Hell yeah, bro. I almost killed her ass and buried her on that damn beach."

"Damn, that's fucked up, bro. I thought y'all were doing so good."

Malik puffed on the blunt. "Me too, bro. And she pregnant again and acting like she don't want me around her. Punk ass snuck out my bed this morning."

"Damn, bro. Y'all sure she pregnant? Did Mama give her the test?"

Malik chuckled. "I told Ma that if she saw her to invite her over to talk to her."

The ride was silent until something hit Malik.

"How could Mama tell us about Tiffany and Camy but never Shay bitch ass?"

"I don't know, man. Maybe she wasn't around her like that."

Malik decided to leave it alone, although something didn't sit right with him.

Camy woke up, remembering that she had done everything but take the garbage out. After throwing on some black stretch pants and a T-shirt, Camy grabbed her coat to take the trash out.

"Camy!"

Camy looked up and saw Ms. Patt standing on her porch.

"Hey, how are you?"

"I'm good."

Remembering what Malik asked, Ms. Patt jumped into action before Camy went back into the house. "Come on over. I just took dinner out."

Camy heard food and damn near ran over to her house. After washing her hands, she sat at the table, waiting on her plate.

As the ladies began to eat, Malik walked in the door. Since Camy's seat wasn't facing the door, and she was so into her plate, she didn't see him.

Malik leaned down, placing a kiss on Camy's cheek. "Thanks, Ma," he said.

"This was a setup?" Camy asked.

"No, baby. I love having you as company. Go ahead and finish your plate," Ms. Patt said.

Malik went into the bathroom to wash his hands so that he could join them for dinner.

"Why you dip on me?" he asked.

"Because I wanted to go home, and you wouldn't let me."

Malik turned his attention toward his mama. "Ma, what you think?"

Ms. Patt knew what he was talking about without him saying anything else. "Yeah, it's clear as day."

"You sure?

"Positive. Have I ever been wrong about this?" she asked.

Camy looked back and forth between the two while eating. "Are y'all talking about me like I'm not right here?"

Malik gave her another kiss. "Thank you."

"For what, Malik?"

"Everything," he answered.

Ms. Patt got up from the table to let them talk.

"What's going on?" Camy asked.

"You're pregnant for real. My mama just confirmed that shit."

Camy thought back to when he told her how his mama was able to tell when one of her sons had a baby on the way. Camy sat there in silence. She wanted to be happy, but the bullshit that happened last time replayed in her head. She was scared to celebrate too early.

"Baby, that's a good thing. Smile." Malik could see the tears starting to build up. "What's wrong? You don't want this?"

"Just scared. I just keep thinking about what happened last time, and it's fucking with me."

"I already told you I'm gonna be on yo' ass this time. Shit gonna be different. Ain't none of that going out and shit gonna be happening. You ain't got no damn friends but me."

Camy giggled. "That's all you wanted anyways, me to yourself."

"Damn right."

Malik washed up the dishes once they were done eating. Afterward, they went to Camy's house. Malik ran her some bath water so that she could relax.

"You need anything else?"

Camy smiled. "Just you."

Malik shook his head. "You know we two bipolar-ass muthafuckas, and we about to populate the world with this shit?"

Camy was cracking up as he climbed into the tub with her. Camy rested her head on his chest.

"You know we need to get our shit together before the baby gets here," she said.

"I know. I don't like how shit went down before we came home, but I'm sorry for flipping out like that."

"I'm sorry too, baby." Camy turned over a little to share a kiss with her man.

"I love you, Camy."

"I love you too, Malik."

"Caught yo' ass," Malik yelled as Camy was getting dressed.

"What are you talking about?"

"Where you sneaking off to?" he questioned.

"Ain't no food in this house, and I'm hungry. I was on my way to the market."

Malik stood up. "Give me a minute. I'll go with you."

"Okay, hurry up."

As the couple got in his car, Camy started to panic. "Baby, I forgot my purse. I need my purse."

"Calm down. I'll go get it."

Camy sat there, watching the door, waiting for Malik to return.

Malik grabbed her purse off the table, wondering what the hell she even needed it for. She did the cooking, and he bought the food. Not putting too much thought to it, he shrugged his shoulders, thinking that maybe it was a chick thing.

As Malik stepped on the bottom step, he saw a van pull up and knew it was nothing but trouble. "Camy, get the fuck down!" he yelled just as the first shot hit the porch.

Malik didn't know if he was the target or her, but he was willing to risk his life to save her and their baby. Racing to the car, Malik ended up being hit twice before the car drove off. His body dropped right at the passenger-side door. Everything happened so fast that Malik didn't even see this shit coming.

Camy was crying and thought the worst as she jumped out of the car, not knowing if they were coming back or not. "Malik, baby, please don't leave me," Camy cried.

Ms. Patt managed to call for help before running out of the house to check on her baby boy. "Malik! I called for help. You gotta fight this shit."

With tears in his eyes, Malik looked at two of the most important women in his life. He prayed that that moment wouldn't be his last time seeing them.

Surprisingly, the ambulance was there in seconds to work on Malik.

Someone on the block had called Rell, and he pulled up right before they put Malik in the back.

"What the fuck happened to my brother?" he yelled, pushing his way through the crowd.

Ms. Patt grabbed Rell, stopping him from jumping on one of the EMTs who wouldn't allow him to ride with Malik. "Rell, please calm down before they try to arrest your ass."

Rell then went over to the side to see what Camy was saying to the police. She was so broken that she could barely get her story out.

"Ma'am, what did you say happened to him when he came back outside?"

Camy tried to calm down, but her mind was all over the place. With her head buried in her hands, she tried to explain what happened again. "He went to get my purse, and they shot him. They shot him. Oh my gawd, I need to see him." She cried harder.

Rell grabbed Camy. "Come on. Let me take you to the hospital."

Camy, Ms. Patt, and Rell got in his car to ride to the hospital. Everyone was fucked up, but Rell thought that he was the one that should do the driving at a time like this. "Camy, I need you to pull it together and tell me everything you saw," Rell said.

Ms. Patt wiped her tears. "Not now, Rell. Please, let's just use this time to pray for my baby boy."

Camy sat in the back, crying her eyes out. After all the shit that she and Malik had been through, she couldn't believe that there was even a chance that it all could end like this. "I'm so scared."

"It's okay, baby. My son is a fighter. He will be all right."

Ms. Patt's words didn't help Camy. She was in the back seat, trembling and crying, making herself sick to her stomach. By the time they arrived at the hospital, Camy was racing to the bathroom to vomit.

While Ms. Patt checked on Camy, Rell talked to someone at the front desk to see where they were supposed to go.

"You all right?" Ms. Patt asked Camy.

Camy started back crying as she washed her hands. She could see Malik's blood on her from when she was holding him.

"Come on, girl. We can't spend all day in the damn restroom."

Camy followed Ms. Patt, who followed Rell, to where they were told to wait. The women took a seat, but Rell paced the floor. He had never been so scared in his life. Malik and he had grown up so close that they really were each other's best friends. He had already lost his uncle and would really lose it if Malik didn't make it. Life without his bro was something that he could never imagine.

When the doctor finally came out hours later, all that he could tell the family was that Malik was rushed in for emergency surgery after being shot two times.

"So, what now, Doc?" Rell asked.

"That young man is a fighter and is very strong. It might be a little too early to say this, but we believe that he'll be all right."

Camy and Ms. Patt both cried and spoke out at the same time. "Thank you, God."

As the doctor walked away, Shay walked in.

"Oh my gawd, Ma, how is Malik doing? What are they saying?"

The sight of her big-ass belly irritated Camy, but it wasn't the right place or time for her to act up.

"Shay, he's going to be all right. The doctor said that he is a fighter."

Shay wiped away her tears. "I knew he wouldn't leave his son like that."

Camy sat up, forgetting what she had just told herself, but Ms. Patt caught the shade as well.

"Malik has a mother, brother, fiancée, and two kids that needs him alive," Ms. Patt said.

Shay looked over at Camy and then rolled her eyes. She didn't know that they had another baby on the way or that their wedding was back on.

"Aye, Camy, you want me to drop you off at home?" Rell asked.

Camy gave him a funny look. "What?"

"My bad, sis. Malik's house?"

Camy shook her head. "No, I wanna be here when he gets up. I'm not gonna be able to rest until I see him."

Shay continued to roll her eyes. After three years, she didn't even know what street Malik lived on, let alone ever chilled at his house.

It seemed like every other minute, Shay was saying shit, trying to get on Camy's nerves. Camy didn't even give a fuck about what she was talking about and really wanted her to leave.

"Ma, your first grandson from Malik will be here soon. Are you excited like I am?"

"Shay, me and you had this same conversation the other day. Right now, my mind is on Malik's recovery. We get it. You are carrying his first child. Now, please be quiet."

Shay sat back, feeling embarrassed.

Camy got up to go back to the restroom. After washing her hands, she stared in the mirror. "Come on, Camy. You got this. Malik gonna be all right, and y'all gonna move on from all this bullshit."

Once she stepped out, Rell was standing right there. "Let's talk."

"What's up, Rell?"

"I need you to tell me exactly what happened. Me and my brother always ride for each other, and right now, bro needs me."

Camy took a seat and then started from the beginning. "When he stepped on the bottom step, he yelled, telling me to get down, so I did. Some more shots went off, and I heard him yell out. I peeked, and at the same time, they drove off. I saw Malik falling. He was closer toward the truck."

"Damn, did you at least get the color of the car?"

"It was a black soccer mom van. That's it." By this time, Camy was crying again. "He was shot, almost killed, trying to make it to the truck to save me. I'll never be able to repay him for that."

"No matter what you might hear or feel, that nigga really loves you."

Camy buried her face into her hands as she cried. "I love him too. I just wish he would have noticed that even though I was in the truck right in front of them, they never tried to hit his car, only him."

Rell nodded as he walked back over toward his mom. He still didn't know who was responsible, but he was going to get to the bottom of shit. "Ma, we have been here for hours, and you look tired. Want me to take you home, or you good?"

"We have been here all day, and it's time for me to take my medicine. I'm about to see when we can see him."

Ms. Patt making that move pushed things in their favor. First, Ms. Patt went to the back to see Malik. He was still out of it for the most part, but she made sure to tell him that she loved him. Next was Rell. He showed much love and told him he was on it. He knew Malik would have wanted him to handle whoever. Camy decided to go last, but Shay tried to make a big deal out of it.

"I'm carrying his first child. I'll go last because I wanted to stay up here with him."

"Shay, stop trying to get on that girl nerves. We all know, just like you do, Malik would want you to take your ass home," Ms. Patt said.

"Ma, I'm just saying. I've known him the longest and—"

Camy was finally at her breaking point and decided to stand up for herself. "Please just take your dirty ass home. You know that nigga don't give a fuck about you. That was an oops baby. Now, instead of trying to get on my nerves, you need to be thanking me for telling him that it was all right for him to keep your bum ass off the streets."

Both Rell and Ms. Patt gave each other a crazy look. They couldn't believe what they were hearing.

"That's enough. Now, both of y'all are having Malik's baby and need to get along, especially while he is laying up here, fighting for his life," Ms. Patt said.

Shay then stormed off to go see Malik.

While she was in the back, Rell tried to make some plans with his people.

"Camy, I know you staying, so just call me if you need anything. I can have Tiffany drop off some clothes and shit."

"Okay, thank you."

"Y'all know he's gonna need help once he gets back home."

"I'll be there with him. I'm not going back to my place. Besides, he wanted me to move in his house anyways," Camy said with a smirk, seeing that Shay had walked back out and was listening to them talk.

"All right, cool. Don't forget to call me or Tiffany," Rell reminded her.

Ms. Patt gave her a hug. "Listen, baby, you make sure you call me if anything changes. I also want you to relax and try not to stress my grandbaby out, worrying so much. Malik will be all right. He's surrounded by love and prayers."

They all hugged again before everyone went their separate ways. Camy went to see Malik. She could feel her heartbeat jumping out of her chest as she got closer toward Malik in the bed. She kept hearing those gunshots and him screaming out in pain. Each time, she felt like it was her that was hit.

"Baby, I love you so much, and I'm gonna need you to pull through one hundred percent. I promise if you make it, I'll marry you and let you put a shit load of babies in me."

Camy bent down to give him a kiss but could see that Shay had left her lip prints on his cheek. "I hate that stupid bitch," she mumbled, walking into the restroom to get something to wash his face.

Being there that first night was the hardest for Camy. It seemed like every ten minutes, someone was coming in to check on him or take blood. How was he supposed to get any rest when they kept fucking with him?

Camy moved the recliner chair closer to his bed. She held his hand and stretched out in the chair before she finally fell asleep.

When Camy woke up, the nurse was taking Malik's vitals.

"How is he doing?"

"Good morning. I'm Sarah, and I'll be his nurse until three p.m. He is actually doing better than we thought he would do. This guy is a true fighter."

Camy smiled. "Yes, he is."

She thought about how hard he had fought to win her every time he fucked up. She knew he'd fight for what he truly wanted.

As soon as the nurse walked out, Camy called his mom.

"Good morning, baby. What's going on?" Ms. Patt asked.

"The nurse said he is doing so much better this morning. Hearing that was like music to my ears."

"See, God is good, and He will protect his children. Now that he's in the clear, I need you to get you something to eat. I know you've been worrying and not eating, but feed my grandbaby."

"Okay. I'm gonna get something soon."

They soon got off the phone in better spirits. Camy did say she was going to get some food but ended up falling back asleep. She had woken up all night every time they came in.

Camy ended up waking up an hour later to Tiffany holding a bag with clean clothes and food.

"Here you go, girl. Rell told me not to even wait for your call. How are you holding up?"

"Thank you so much, Tiffany. I really appreciate you."

"No problem, girl. You're part of the family. I got you."

"The nurse said he was doing much better, and hearing that sort of took a load off me."

"You know you can't be stressing out like that," Tiffany reminded her.

"I'm trying. Malik would have a fit if he saw how I've been."

They both laughed.

"Hell yeah. That boy is crazy, but it's all love."

The girls ate and talked for a while. Camy liked her because she was cool and down to Earth like her. Not to mention, she had dealt with this family and knew all the tea.

"Camy, what did you do to get him fully?"

Camy giggled. "Let his ass tell it, I did voodoo on his ass."

Tiffany was cracking up, remembering that whole story about him running away from Camy. "Girl, y'all crazy as hell. Anyways, Shay crazy ass ain't try to come back up here, did she? I heard about all that shade she was throwing."

"I handled that shit. I told the hospital that I was his fiancée, and she wasn't allowed to come up here or call to get any information about him. That bitch got me fucked up for real."

Tiffany was cracking up. "You and Malik were meant for each other. Both of y'all are crazy."

"Damn, girl. You let me talk you to death. It's after twelve p.m. now."

It's all right. This was my vacation away from them kids. But for real, I just wanted to make sure you were good. I'm about to head home before Rell starts calling," Tiffany said, laughing.

The girls hugged and said their goodbyes. Once Tiffany was gone, Camy hurried to shower and get dressed. Even though they said he was all right, she still didn't like leaving him alone.

Camy went over to Malik's bed. "Come on, Malik. Wake up, baby. We need you here with us," she said, holding his hand. She then placed a kiss on his forehead. As she cried, Camy continued to talk. "Malik, can you hear me, baby? Get up, baby. I swear if you die, me and this baby will be right behind you with our other baby. We would just be a happy family in the afterlife."

Camy jumped up, feeling him squeeze her hand. She quickly pressed the button for the nurse to come in. When the nurse arrived, Camy was sent out of the room, so they could check on him. Camy got worried and started to regret saying what she said. For some reason, she could hear Malik asking why she was saying stupid shit like that.

Chapter 18

On Malik's last day in the hospital, Rell kept him company while Tiffany and Ms. Patt took Camy back to Malik's house to get the house in order for his return.

"Aye, bro, I see that you good and all 'cause they letting you come home, but I'm still fucked up behind this shit."

"Me too, bro. I was almost outta here."

"What's the plan when you get home?" Rell questioned.

"I wanna go home, give Camy some dick, then probably beat her ass."

Rell didn't mean to, but he laughed. "Bro, what the fuck, dawg?"

"When they had me knocked out, high on all them meds, I heard her talking to me. She said some crazy shit. I woke up squeezing her hand, wishing it was her neck."

Rell was cracking up. "What the fuck she say? Some shit about her being with somebody else?"

"Hell nah. She was talking crazy about killing herself and the baby to join me if I didn't make it. Since I've been up, I haven't even talked to her about that shit yet. I'm gonna wait until we get home, just in case I have to hurt her crazy ass."

Rell shook her head. "Wow, yeah, that shit crazy for real."

Malik couldn't do shit but be happy to see another day, but after all that bullshit, he felt like it was time to change his life around.

***

Malik had been home for a whole week, and he was getting tired of Camy being on his ass. "Camy, please, baby, go away."

Camy giggled. "No, Malik, you supposed to eat and take this pill. You need to stop being hardheaded."

"I'm doing better. I don't need that shit no more."

Camy punched Malik in his left shoulder.

"Man, what the fuck wrong with yo' crazy ass?" he yelled, holding his shoulder.

"See, you still in pain, boy. Take your pills."

Malik shook his head. "I need a new nurse. Yo' crazy ass fired."

Camy stood over Malik, holding his bottle of water, watching him take the pill. As Camy tried to walk off, Malik slapped her ass.

"Boy, that hurt."

"Instead of me taking a pill, you need to let me give you this dick."

Camy laughed. "You need to heal all the way. I can't have you popping shit out of place. I can't handle seeing you in pain like that again."

"You really love a nigga?"

Full of excitement, Camy yelled out. "Hell yeah!"

Malik paused to stare at her for a minute. He tried not to say anything to her about what happened at the hospital, but it was eating him alive not to talk to her about the shit she said.

"Is that why you said that crazy shit?" he asked.

"What are you talking about, baby?" Camy asked, slowly sitting on his lap.

Malik drank some more of his water. "I heard what you said as I was waking up. What the fuck do you be thinking?"

"I don't want to talk about it." Camy tried to get up, but she couldn't get out of his grip.

"Why you say that crazy shit? Is that how you really feel?"

Camy had tears in her eyes as she answered. "Malik, my true feelings are not crazy. I don't wanna be without you. If I ever have to, I don't think I would be strong enough to handle it. Since we met, my life was no longer mine. It's always been about you."

Malik was shocked. "If I ever leave this Earth, you better continue to live your life to the fullest and take care of my babies. Do you understand me?"

Camy cried, shaking her head. "I don't want to."

Malik had people say that they loved him before, but he had never heard someone cry, believing that if he were dead, they would be happier if they died right along with him. "Stop talking like that, Camy. You're stronger than you think. Trust me."

Camy cried in his arms. No matter what he said, her feelings could never change.

"Don't cry, baby. It's all right to love me, but don't ever think you gotta go with me."

"Okay," she mumbled.

"Anyways, fuck all this death talk 'cause I'm here and alive. I can't let no bitch-ass niggas take me from you and mine."

Camy had been denying Malik sex since he was home, fearing him hurting himself, but that night, she rode him to sleep.

When Camy woke up the next morning, Malik was sitting up, staring at her.

"What's wrong, baby?"

"Marry me."

Camy smiled. "Okay, Malik. I'll marry you."

"You for real?" he asked with a huge smile on his face.

"Yes, baby. I love you too much to keep you waiting. Besides, knowing you risked your life for me, it's only right."

"Come give me a kiss," he ordered.

Camy jumped out of the bed. "Damn, baby, wait a minute. I gotta go brush my teeth."

Malik laughed as she left the room. When she came back in, Malik was down on one knee, holding her ring.

"Baby, you didn't have to do all that. Now, who's gonna help you get up?"

"I had to do it the right way."

Camy stood right in front of him with her hand out.

"Camy, will you marry me, baby?"

Camy quickly answered. "Yes, baby. It wouldn't be right if I didn't."

"Baby, it's three in the morning. Who blowing your phone up like that?"

Malik grabbed his phone, reading the name. "Hello."

"Aye, Malik, this Kim. Shay is in labor right now."

"All right, I'm on my way," he said, jumping out of bed.

Malik flicked the light on, causing Camy to jump up. "Everything all right, baby?"

Malik turned around with the biggest smile. "My baby on the fucking way. Man, I can't wait to see him."

Camy sat there, ready to cry. That day was also her original due date, and the fact that their baby didn't make it still hurt her. It also hurt seeing how happy Malik was. Camy didn't even feel bad for not being happy for them.

"You leaving?" she asked.

"Hell yeah. Did you hear what I said was going on? Baby, where yo' keys at?"

"I don't know," she coldly said, lying back down.

Malik stared at her for a minute, catching her attitude. "Man, Camy, don't be like that. What the fuck you want me to do, not go see my son?"

Camy sat up for a second. "Turn the fucking light off!" she barked.

Malik grabbed her car keys off the dresser before leaving. Not even his love for her could stop him from being there for his baby, and all this had nothing to do with Shay.

Camy couldn't help it, but she cried hearing the front door shut and her car driving off.

Malik drove like a bat fresh out of hell to make sure he got there in time to see his baby boy enter this world. Once he got to the hospital and was directed in the right direction, he raced down the hall to the room.

"Damn, this is it," he mumbled, walking in.

"Malik, where you been? It's almost time."

"Stop talking to me. I came as soon as you called." Malik didn't care for Shay's mama and didn't care too much about paying her any respect.

"Malik, chill on my mama," Shay said.

"I tried to chill on yo' ass, but you lied about getting that abortion. Now, I'm gonna need both of y'all to leave me alone, so my son can come out without hearing all that bullshit y'all talking."

Kim gave Malik a weird look. She wanted to go off but decided to stay quiet because this was who her daughter had to deal with.

Two and a half hours later, Malik was the proudest man on Earth, holding a healthy baby boy. As Shay breastfed the baby, Malik kept staring at him. With the baby being fresh out into this world, Malik couldn't tell who he looked like, but he loved him already.

"Damn, I really got a son in the world. I know I don't fuck with you like that, but my son ain't gonna never want for anything. I got him until I leave this Earth, and I put that on my unc."

"I know, baby. You're gonna be a great daddy," Shay said, reaching out for his hand.

"You know how shit is. All that 'baby' shit out the window. Chill on that shit."

Kim couldn't stand Malik, and every time he opened his mouth, she got irritated. "Okay, I saw you give birth. Now, I can leave. I'll be back tomorrow to check on you, Shay," she said.

"Bye, Ma. Thank you."

Shay was happy that she was gone. She needed some alone time with Malik. Fuck what he was talking about. She wanted him still. "Malik, I know you were mad at me, but look at our son. He looks just like you. You should be happy that I decided to keep him."

"I'm gonna love all my kids, no matter what, but I hate the way you went about doing shit. I'll always hate you for that shit. Just know I'm only here because of that li'l nigga right there," he said, pointing at the baby.

Feeling his phone vibrate in his pocket, Malik answered it, seeing Camy's name across the screen. "What's up, baby?"

"Is the baby here yet?"

Malik could tell that her conversation was dry. "Yeah, baby, he's been here for about an hour now."

As Malik started telling her about how much he weighed and how he had a headful of hair, she cut him off. "What time are you coming back home?"

"Come on, Camy. Don't be like that. I promise I'll be that way soon."

"Our baby got me feeling sick as hell. I need you."

Malik shook his head. "Damn, can you try a warm bath like you tried last time? Remember you were able to sleep right after that."

"But you were here to hold me, Malik. We need you to sleep."

"Okay, I'll be there in a minute," he said, hanging up the phone and returning it back to his pocket.

"I see she still running shit."

"Shut the fuck up and worry about taking care of my son the right way. That's the business you need to be worried about."

Shay started laughing. "Don't play that tough shit with me."

"I'm about to get out of here. You gonna be good?"

Shay decided to play the same game that Camy's spoiled ass was playing. Knowing that Malik's weakness was his baby made her job even easier. "No, Malik. I'm a new mother and scared. I don't know what I'm doing. You can't just leave us. We need you." Shay pretended to whine. Shay then lifted their son off her chest, causing him to whine.

"What's wrong with him? Fuck you do?"

"Pull that chair up and come hold him."

Malik did exactly what Shay wanted, and that was to stay longer to piss Camy off.

Malik walked in around eight a.m. He knew Camy wanted him home the night before, but once he got to holding his son, he was too attached to put him down. Malik walked into the room to see that Camy was still asleep. Trying not to wake her up, he undressed and then climbed into the bed with her.

"Get the fuck away from me!" Camy tried to get up, but Malik snatched her back down.

"Man, lay back down. What the fuck wrong with you?"

"Leave me alone, Malik. We needed you last night, but you were too busy for us."

Malik didn't feed into her bullshit. One thing for sure was that he wasn't about to play with either baby mama on all that drama.

Camy saw that her acting out wasn't working, so she stormed out of the room, making sure she slammed the door.

"Fuck!" Malik jumped back up, chasing behind Camy's spoiled ass. "Man, what's up?"

"I'm feeling like we're becoming a burden on you, and maybe I should just go back home."

"You already know you can't go back over there. This is your house until we find a new house. I see you're bored and think fucking with me is about to be a new hobby, but you better go find something else to do with yo' time. I told you to start back looking for a building."

Camy sat there, rolling her eyes, with her arms folded. "I can't find anything that I like right now."

"It's been a minute since you looked. Maybe they added some new shit on the site."

Malik tried to play it cool, but no matter what he said, her attitude didn't get any better. "What's all this attitude really about?"

Camy started to cry. "I don't like playing second to that bitch."

Malik shook his head. "Second to who, Camy? You already know where my heart at."

"Do I?"

"Hell yeah! Look at your fucking finger. You the only one running around with a ring from me."

The truth finally came out.

"But I'm not the only one with a baby. This shit hurt, Malik, and I feel like she's gonna be using this baby as a way to get you back."

"Stop being insecure."

"How, when I know how you were, Malik?"

"Listen to what you saying. You said *were*. Baby, you should know, out of all people, that I've changed so much to be the right man for you. I'm only dealing with Shay because of my son."

"So, what's his name?"

"We haven't thought about it yet. She needed me to come back later, so we could handle all that. That's why I was trying to get a nap in before I have to go back up there."

Camy jumped up, storming back to the room, slamming the door. Instead of chasing behind her this time, Malik got comfortable on the couch to get some rest.

Malik ended up sleeping for four hours straight before he woke up to Camy throwing his phone at him.

"How the fuck me and my baby supposed to get any sleep when that bitch keep calling?"

Malik looked at his phone and saw that Shay had called him seven times. "Why you ain't answer? It could have been an emergency with my son or some shit."

"I'm not your fucking secretary."

Malik ignored her as he called Shay back. "What's up?"

"I was just calling to see if you were coming back up here."

"Look, Shay, let's set some rules now. You know Camy about to be my wife, so don't blow my damn phone up like that. Only call me if my son needs anything. We are not friends and don't need to sit on the phone chitchatting and shit. Do we have an understanding?"

Shay knew Camy had to have been over there bitching, trying to run shit. "Okay, Malik. I understand, but I wanted to name the baby today and thought that maybe you wanted to be here so that your name could go on the birth certificate."

Malik smiled. "All right, I'll be up there in a minute."

Shay smiled, knowing that she was winning.

"Camy, baby, can we talk?" Malik said after he hung up the phone.

"Sure, since it seems like I'm not gonna get any sleep anyways."

"Look, chill on all that attitude shit. We about to take care of this birth certificate shit, then I'll be right back. Do you wanna ride or something? We can go eat afterwards to get out of this house."

"No, go deal with that baby and his mama," Camy said with much attitude.

Malik snatched her out of the bed. "Stop doing that punk-ass shit! You know damn well ain't shit going on between me and that girl, but I'm gonna be there for my baby."

Camy started to cry again. Malik had done so much to get her back. He risked his life for her, but the fact that he had to spend time with Shay was killing her on the inside.

"I'm sorry. I just don't wanna lose you, Malik."

"And you not. Just put some trust in me. I don't want Shay, but I'm gonna take care of my son with her. You know how I feel about this type of shit. You know I have to be better than my daddy."

Malik wrapped Camy up into a tight hug. "Baby, I love you so much. I'll never put our relationship in jeopardy. I worked too fucking hard to get you. Now, do you understand me?"

Camy wiped away her tears. "Yes, baby."

Malik grabbed her face, planting nothing but sweet kisses on her. That quickly turned into them making love, causing Malik to leave the house a whole two hours later.

"Listen, baby, when I get back, we can go out. I know you'll be ready to smash then."

Camy giggled. "You already know."

While he was driving to the hospital, Ms. Patt called her baby boy.

"Hey, Ma."

"Hey, where you at? Are you at the hospital?" Ms. Patt asked while riding with Rell.

"I'm pulling up now. Why? What's up?"

"Me and Rell just pulled up. I wanna meet my grand-baby."

Malik, Ms. Patt, and Rell all met up at the elevators to surprise Shay.

"Camy ain't wanna come?" Rell asked.

"Hell nah, bro. She been acting so crazy lately. It's ridiculous."

While the brothers laughed, Ms. Patt shook her head. "Get ready for this jealousy bullshit for the rest of your life. And I hope you marry that girl and never go back to your hoeing ways. You don't need a bunch of women stressing you and me out with a bunch of babies."

"All right, Ma. Chill out on me."

Shay was burping the baby as they all walked in. She wasn't in the mood for all of them. She wanted personal time with Malik again.

Ms. Patt gave the baby one look and frowned. "What's his name, Shay?"

"Me and Malik was gonna try to come up with something today."

Rell came over from washing his hands. "I wanna hold my nephew."

Malik was a little too happy for Ms. Patt, but to keep the peace and thinking it was the wrong time and place, she just took a seat.

"Aye, bro, who do you think he looks like?" Malik asked.

Rell looked over his nephew again. "Shit, I don't know. It might be too early to tell. Wait for a couple of weeks to see what he change into."

Malik laughed. "You talking like he a damn Transformer."

They all laughed at him.

"Well, I know how much y'all loved Davon and thought that maybe it would be okay to name him after him," Shay said.

Before anyone could say anything, Ms. Patt jumped up. "Rell, take me home before I go the fuck off on this girl."

Malik went after his mama. He didn't understand why she snapped like that. "What the hell going on, Ma?"

"Not once when she was pregnant did I feel anything. That's not your baby, Malik."

"Ma, that fake-ass psychic bullshit you be doing might not work all the time. You actually think that girl fucked somebody else?"

"Don't be stupid, boy."

"If it ain't mine, then who the fucking daddy?"

Rell noticed a few people watching. "Aye, we can talk about this shit later. Boy, you know Ma be on her shit. Don't sign shit until we talk and you get that test done."

Rell and Ms. Patt left, leaving Malik in his feelings. As he returned, his smile was gone, and he was giving Shay a death stare. "I don't like being lied to, Shay, so I'm gonna ask you this shit one fucking time. Who yo' baby daddy?"

Shay instantly got an attitude. "Here you go with this bullshit. What's really going on? Did Camy call crying about my baby being here first?"

"This gonna be my last time telling you this shit too. Don't bring my wife's name up no more."

Shay rolled her eyes. "Come hold him. You can look at him and see that he's your fucking twin, Malik. Don't do him like that."

Malik took a seat next to her hospital bed. Shay handed him their son. Malik stared at the baby, trying to make himself see somebody in the baby. As he stared, the baby opened his eyes, staring back at him. That caused Malik to smile. He wasn't about to let his mama put that bull-shit in his head.

"Hey, Daddyman."

Shay lay in the bed, watching Malik talk to their son.

"Malik, that's your baby. You know how your family don't fuck with me because you never made it official with me but with Camy. They trying to fuck this up for us. Look at how he's holding onto your finger and watching you. He knows you are his daddy."

Malik looked her way. "Don't play me, Shay. You know how I get down."

"Malik, I love you too fucking much to even play that type of game with you."

Malik thought about what she was saying and decided that she had a point. Shay talked a lot of shit, but he could never see her stepping out on him. She was his loyal side chick.

"So, what was that shit you was talking about naming him after Unc? You really wanna do that?"

"Yes, you know Davon was my nigga."

"All right, I can fuck with that."

When it was time to do the birth certificate, the baby ended up with the name of Davon Malik Simmons. Only because of the love he had for his uncle and the fact that he was no longer alive did Malik not trip about his name being last.

On his way home, Malik called Rell to tell him what they had decided to do.

"Bro, you should have got a DNA test done before signing shit. I told your hardheaded ass that," Rell yelled over the phone.

"Aye, chill, my nigga. I ain't never told you to get a damn test when Tiffany had a baby for yo' ass. I got this."

"I ain't never had to question Tiffany's loyalty either."

"And when did I ever have to question Shay's? You already know how she was about a nigga."

Rell hated how stubborn Malik could be at times. He was one of the only niggas Rell knew that loved to bump his head and learn the hard way.

"Hey, baby, what you doing?"

Camy looked up to see her man standing there, looking good as fuck. "Damn, baby, you looking like a snack."

Malik chuckled. "You must want some dick before we go eat?"

Camy cheesed. "Maybe."

"Freaky ass."

"Shut up, boy. You like that shit about me."

Malik chuckled. "Honestly, I love that shit."

Camy melted in Malik's arms as he planted kisses on her. Camy then quietly pushed Malik off of her.

"You smell like that bitch. Go take a shower so we can go eat."

"You on some real bullshit. You know that, right? I never even touched that girl."

Camy gave him a strange look. "If you didn't, you wouldn't smell like her. You back to lying?"

Malik walked off so that he could jump in the shower. He wasn't even in the mood to argue with her crazy ass.

Once out of of the shower, Malik got dressed and joined her in the front room. "You ready?"

"Yeah, I'm starving."

Malik rubbed her stomach as she stood up. "Let's go feed my baby."

Twenty minutes later, the two were pulling up to their favorite restaurant.

"Let's pray they let us in after you beat that bitch ass the last time you were here."

Camy got out of the car. "They better, or I'm gonna cry."

"I believe you," Malik said, laughing.

Once at the door, the couple had no problem getting in. "What you got the taste for?"

"I don't know. This baby got my taste buds everywhere. I'm about to just close my eyes and point at something on this menu."

Malik chuckled. "You know you goofy as hell. You better eat whatever you pick too."

"Everything is so good here, so I don't see a problem with that."

Malik laughed at her a little more. One thing that he loved about her was that he didn't have to be so serious all the time around her. She made it so easy to chill and enjoy himself.

"Malik, pick one—winter, spring, summer, or fall."

"Fall. You know I love the hoodie season."

"No, baby. We can't get married in no damn hoodies."

"If I'm spending my money, I can do whatever I wanna do," Malik said with a serious face.

"You not about to fuck up my day, boy."

"Shit, it's my day too."

Camy wanted to go off, but the waitress came over with their food. As soon as she walked away, Camy was on his ass.

"Malik, stop playing with me before I call this shit off."

"What the fuck you ask me for? This is why I told you to do the planning because I don't care about all that shit. All I wanna do is marry yo' ass."

Since they got back together, Camy had been trying to talk to him about the wedding, and all he ever told her was to make sure her ass was there. He didn't care about the rest of the shit. Whatever she wanted, he was going to make it happen.

"Okay, I wanna wear a lime green dress and wig."

"Find me a matching tie, silly ass."

"Malik, stop playing with me."

"You stop playing," he said, laughing.

"Okay, at least help with the colors, and I'll go from there. Can you at least do that?"

"Sure, baby. From here on out, I'm gonna help you more," he said, seeing how serious she had become.

Camy smiled, happy that he was now on board.

Camy's attitude quickly changed when his phone started chiming.

"Who is that texting you like that?"

Malik quickly texted Shay back, telling her that he was busy and would hit her up later. "Nobody."

Camy stood up. "Take me home."

Malik looked around to see if anyone was paying them any attention. "Sit yo' ass down and feed my baby."

"I can't enjoy my food with your baby mama blowing your phone up like that," Camy snapped.

"Stop trying to make a scene in this bitch. Sit down and eat," he ordered.

Camy took a seat, but her feelings were everywhere. She was actually starting to question whether she could deal with this shit for the rest of her life.

Malik tried to brighten up the moment, but Camy wasn't having it.

"That shit looks good. Let me taste some."

Camy looked up, giving him the craziest look ever before sliding him her plate. "Here, take it."

"You don't share food. What's wrong with you? I put my phone up. Now what?"

"The way shit going in my life, I'm gonna have to get used to sharing."

"What the fuck you doing all that for, Camy?"

Camy wiped her tears away. "I'm ready to go."

Malik pulled out the money to pay the bill and to tip the waitress. He had a shitload of questions, but he decided to at least wait until they got home. The ride home was very awkward. Camy was crying, in her feelings, Malik was getting mad because she wouldn't talk to him, and Shay was blowing his phone up after he told her to chill out.

"Camy, I'm sorry about tonight. I'll make it up to you. I promise."

Camy turned the radio up, still ignoring him. She was so angry that ignoring him was her being nice. He really didn't want her to start talking.

Malik turned the radio off. "Camy, talk to me."

"I don't like what's going on, and I—"

His phone started going off again, causing them both to look down at it.

"I thought you told the bitch you were busy!"

"I did. I'm about to answer. Maybe something wrong with the baby."

Camy popped her lips. "I bet."

"What the fuck that supposed to mean? I don't understand yo' ass. Do you want me to take care of my son or be a fucking deadbeat?"

Camy didn't respond. He was right. She did want him to take care of his son, but the fact that Shay was the mother bothered the fuck out of her.

Malik pulled up in the driveway.

"Do whatever you wanna do, Malik," she said, slamming the door.

Shay called back, which prevented him from getting out.

"Why the fuck do you keep calling me? Didn't I tell you I was busy?"

Shay rolled her eyes, thinking Camy had made him be mean to her. "Whatever, boy. When it comes to our son, you ain't too busy."

"What's wrong with him, Shay?"

"He sleep right now, but I was calling to see if you could take us home tomorrow when we are discharged."

Malik shook his head. "You was blowing my shit up for something you could have easily texted. Do you remember them lines I told you not to cross?"

"Yeah, I remember, but I'm not living to make that bitch happy."

"See, I am, and with that shit being said, stop calling my shit like that. I'll pick you up tomorrow. Just text when y'all ready, not before then."

Shay wanted to say so much more, but he had hung up. She set the phone down, pissed off because he really was in love with Camy's funky ass.

Once Malik got in the house, Camy was already lying down. Malik knew this whole baby with Shay was bringing down her spirit.

"Baby, shit gonna get better. I swear I'm trying to get shit in order. I know I fucked up in the past, but I'm not and don't plan on doing shit else to fuck up what we got."

Camy rolled over. She was so over everything.

"Damn, for real? That's how you gonna do me?"

"Malik, I don't know what to say or do. Everything that I wanna say is mad disrespectful, and I'm trying so hard to spare your fucking feelings."

"Damn," he said, giving her a strange look. Malik tried to give her a kiss.

"Go away, Malik."

"You mad, but I ain't do shit. I told her to stop calling. It's not my fault that she ain't listen."

Camy cut him off. "But it's your fault that bitch had that baby."

Malik watched as she broke down crying. Now, they were getting into what was really bothering her. "Camy, I did my best to stop that, and you know it. He here now. What the fuck you want me to do?"

Camy tried to calm down to talk. "I am trying to be mature about the situation, but the more she calls bullshit, the more it irritates me. I hate her so much."

"Me too, but I gotta deal with her. That's my son's mother."

That night, instead of them making love until they fell asleep, Malik held Camy in his arms until she cried herself to sleep. By the way she was acting, he started to feel selfish for asking her to stay with him if she couldn't handle him having a baby with another woman. It was too late to call Rell, but he was going to hit him up first thing in the morning.

The next morning, Malik got up and called himself making breakfast for Camy. He walked into the room, carrying a plate with some eggs and sausages.

"Good morning, baby. You wanna eat?"

Camy looked at him, then at the plate. Before she could say anything, she started to throw up all over the bed.

"Damn, my shit ain't look that bad," he said, helping her into the bathroom.

While she showered, he tossed everything in a big trash bag to throw away. There was no washing that shit. Malik walked into his room and cracked the window. He hated that smell. He then pulled out something for Camy to throw on so that she could be comfortable.

Before returning to the living room, Malik went into the bathroom to check on his big baby. "Yo' nasty ass all right?"

Camy laughed. "Yeah, baby. I'll be out soon. Is it some more food?"

"You really are nasty. You still wanna eat after that shit you just did?"

Camy continued to dry off. "Your damn baby just emptied my stomach. I really need to eat now."

Malik shook his head before walking out.

Camy tossed on the boy shorts and T-shirt he brought her. When she went into the living room, Malik had his mama on FaceTime while writing down what she was telling him. "Ma, slow down. You said I needed what?"

"Boy, leave the cooking to Camy."

"She sick."

Ms. Patt laughed "Well, I suggest you just buy her a can of soup. Boy, you don't know what you doing and gonna fuck around and give her food poisoning."

Malik didn't like her laughing at him. "All right, bye, Ma. You done pissed me off for the day."

Ms. Patt hung up, not paying her son any attention.

"Malik, you don't have to cook for me." Camy took a seat next to him on the couch.

"I was trying to make sure you and my baby were good. I hate seeing you sick like that. What can I do to help?"

"Just remember what you saw the next time you wanna cum in me, especially after this baby."

Malik laughed. "Shut yo' ass up. But for real, do you need anything?"

"Just hold me the way you are doing now. I swear when I'm in your arms, I feel at peace."

Malik planted a kiss on her lips. "I know that feeling, baby."

Chapter 19

While Camy slept, Malik called his mama back. He was determined to make her a pot of homemade chicken noodle soup.

"Okay, Ma, let's go over this shit again."

Ms. Patt explained to him three times what to do. She was irritated but proud that he was at least trying. Growing up, Malik would starve before he took his ass in the kitchen to fix himself anything, not even a sandwich.

"Why did I have to hear from someone else on what Shay named that baby?" she asked.

"I don't know. Maybe because I haven't had a chance to tell you yet. I told you Camy was fucked up over here."

Ms. Patt calmed herself down. She really wanted to talk some sense into her son and not argue. "Malik, I don't think that's your baby. Once that girl told everyone that she was still pregnant, she started coming around, and not once did I feel anything. I've always been right about this type of shit. Get that boy tested."

"Ma, that's my fucking son. Stop trying to plant that shit in my head."

"You so fucking hardheaded, but you gonna learn. That boy don't even look like you, stupid ass!"

"Ma, mind yo' fucking business and get the fuck off my line."

They both raced to hang up on each other first.

Malik played in the kitchen while Camy slept. Although he was pissed off, he wasn't about to let that shit stop him from taking care of his big baby.

Camy was knocked out, but once she started smelling food, she got up. "Malik, what are you doing in here?"

Malik was at the table, searching the internet for a home for them. He loved the house that he was in, but he wanted a house with his wife. Malik smiled. "It smells good, doesn't it?" he asked, proud of himself.

"To be honest, it does. You've been faking this whole time, boy. Had me thinking you couldn't cook and shit."

Malik laughed. "I called my mama back and watched some shit on YouTube. I wanna start helping out more."

Camy smiled. "You'd be surprised at what you can learn at YouTube University." Camy went closer toward the stove to get a better view of what he had going on.

"Get yo' ass away from my stove. I ain't forgot about that nasty shit you did this morning."

"Shut up, Malik. I'm better now. Yo' baby be tripping."

Malik grabbed Camy to hold her in his arms. As he placed kisses on her lips and neck, he rubbed her stomach. "When we go back to the doctor? You are growing like a muthafucka."

"Next week, Malik. I set a reminder on your calendar in your phone."

"My bad. I ain't see it. I can't wait to see what's going on. Can they put pregnant women on a diet or something if they grow too fast?"

"I don't know, Malik. He might can suggest that she slow down, but I'm not sure about making her diet. Besides, I don't think I'm growing too fast. I'm barely showing."

"Shid," he said, laughing.

"You calling me fat?"

"Hell yeah, but in a good way, so don't look at me like that."

Camy wasn't even mad. All she could do was laugh.

Being nosy, Camy sat on his lap, just so she could see what he was up to on the computer. "These are some nice houses."

"Yeah, and they'll be perfect for our family. I am serious about making everything perfect for you and whatever in here," he said, rubbing her belly.

"Baby, do you think I should wait until after the baby, wedding, and house for my building?"

"Why? I mean, it's all up to you, baby. That money ain't going nowhere."

"I was thinking that once I had the baby, I was gonna wanna be at home, being a mommy. The last thing on my mind would be combing a bitch head. I might even be walking around nappy-headed myself."

Malik listened closely to what she was saying. "I see what you saying, baby, but like I said, it's up to you, and the money will forever be available for you."

Camy giggled to herself.

"What's so funny?"

"I was just wondering how much do you actually make at your uncle's shop that you never go to?"

Malik laughed with her. "Man, shut up and don't worry about my job."

As they laughed, Camy's phone went off. She looked at the screen, wondering why Rell was calling her.

"Hello." She answered by putting the call on speaker.

"Hey, sis, my brother around?"

"Yeah, hold up," Camy said, passing Malik her phone.

"What's up, bro? Why you calling me on her shit?"

"Nigga, take your phone off Do Not Disturb. Anyways, Shay been calling me and Mama, talking about you were supposed to be picking her and the baby up. Go ahead and deal with that." Rell hung up. He was still pissed about how Malik dealt with Shay and her son, but he was really in his feelings after he talked to their mom.

Camy's whole mood changed, watching him grab his phone to call Shay.

"What's up?" Malik said into the phone.

"Malik, you said you were gonna pick us up and take us home today."

"Yeah, I did, but Camy got sick, and after that, I forgot. Where you at now?"

"I'm home now. You gonna stop by and see Baby Davon?"

Camy rolled her eyes, thinking Shay named her baby that just to feel like she was a part of the family.

"I told you Camy sick, and I need to make sure she good. If shit changes, I might be that way tomorrow."

Shay popped her lips. "So, I see you putting her before me and your son."

"She always came before you, and as far as my son, I love them both, and I'm dividing my time up between them until my other baby gets here. After that, the three of them will have to share my time. I'm about to get back to my fiancée. I'll check on my baby later."

"I hate you so much, Malik, and fuck that bitch."

Malik hung up before Camy could pop off.

"Why you do that? Call that bitch back," Camy said.

"Nah, you about to chill out and not upset my baby. Fuck that dumb shit she talking about."

"You still got that bail money if I wanna fight?"

"If you fight while carrying my baby, they won't let me bail out for killing yo' wild ass. Now, go sit the hell down."

Camy was pissed but chilled out.

Malik calmed himself down. "I'm sorry about that, baby. I know you don't like dealing with all this shit, but I promise I'm gonna get this shit together. I already set some rules for her, and by the way shit going, I'm gonna set some more. She might have my son, but you about to have my last name, and she gonna have to learn to respect that shit or get fucked up."

Camy giggled. Malik always talked about fucking somebody up.

"I love you so much, Malik."

"And I love yo' ass too."

After he got into it with their mom, Malik wasn't a tad bit surprised when Rell pulled up. Whenever there was a problem between them, Rell was always the one to calm everyone down. He was the glue to hold them all together.

"So, I take it you're mad at me or something too?"

Rell gave Malik a strange look. "I'm not mad at you, bro, but I do think you are moving too fast with this Shay shit. Not to mention, naming her baby after Unc really not sitting right with me."

The brothers sat in the truck, smoking while doing their normal therapy session.

"I believe in my heart that that's my baby. The way I had that bitch mind gone, I can't see Shay fucking on another nigga. You and Mama on some other shit for real. And that was my fucking uncle too. I don't see why my son can't be named after him."

Rell shook his head. "Not trying to be funny, but he doesn't even look like you, nigga."

Malik was getting pissed off. "Bro, shut the fuck up with that shit. He just got here a few days ago. He doesn't look like shit right now," Malik barked.

Rell passed him the blunt, then hopped out of the truck. He wasn't in the mood to argue with Malik. Malik watched as Rell got into his car and then took off. He didn't feel bad because he asked his brother and mama to stop saying that Shay's baby wasn't his, especially when he felt like it was.

Malik went back into the house to check on Camy. "Damn, baby, how many bowls are you gonna eat?"

Camy giggled. "Shut up, boy. This only my second bowl. Besides, I am eating for two."

"You sure? I mean, you are getting big as fuck."

Camy went to the table with her bowl, ignoring him. She was tired of him bullying her.

Malik watched her eat. This had been the first time that he had cooked, and her greedy ass actually enjoyed it. He felt like a proud husband-to-be. "Camy, I need your honesty on something."

Camy dropped her spoon. "What is it?"

Malik handed her his phone. "Do this baby look like me?"

Camy never wanted to see Shay's baby, but she looked anyway. "Umm, cute baby, but I can't say that he does or doesn't. It's too soon to say."

Malik took his phone then walked off. Making it to his room, he slammed the door. Everyone had him fucked up, and it was fucking with his mental.

"Where are you going?"

Malik was drying off from his shower and getting dressed.

"I figured since you were feeling better, I would go see the baby and see what's going on with him."

Camy rolled her eyes. "So, you going to spend time at that bitch house?"

"Man, cut that shit out. You already know what's up and why I'm going over there, so don't even start that shit."

Camy knew what was going on, but she hated Shay so much that she couldn't handle Malik being around her.

Malik noticed the look on his soon-to-be wife's face and knew that she wasn't happy. "Why don't you come see the baby with me? I know shit weird right now, but you're gonna have to get to know him anyway."

Camy wanted to yell, "Fuck that baby and his mama," but knew better. Malik would have beat her ass for real speaking on his child like that.

"You know I'm not about to go to that bitch house. I'll meet the baby when you start bringing him over here."

"Why you gotta be like that?"

Camy jumped out of the bed. "'Cause I don't like the bitch and never did. I'm only tolerating her baby because of you, because—"

Malik cut her off. "I'm giving you a chance to think about what you about to say before you piss me off."

Camy walked past him, making sure to bump him. "I wasn't even about to say shit smart."

Malik followed her out of the room. "Come here!"

"Fuck you, Malik!"

"Come the fuck here, Camy!" he yelled, finally catching up to her. "I'm sorry, all right? I know this is hard on you, and you stressing like a muthafucka, but I swear I'm trying to get shit straightened out."

Camy allowed him to hold her tight. She questioned if she was being selfish for wanting him all to herself.

"Look, I'm gonna go over there for a few. Then, when I come home, I'm all yours. We can do whatever you wanna do."

"That sounds like a plan, baby."

Malik planted a kiss on her forehead. "Maybe when I get back, I can give you a full body massage like you like."

Camy giggled. "See, you talking like that, I'm not gonna let you leave."

Malik gave her another kiss. "Let me get out of here. The quicker I get over there, the sooner I can come home to you."

Although Camy trusted Malik, she still didn't like him around Shay. She knew bitches like her didn't mind playing dirty to get a nigga to their self.

After Malik left, Camy jumped on her laptop to finish searching for wedding ideas.

Shay got up from the couch to let Malik in. Happy to see him, she couldn't control her smile. "Hey, I'm glad you got out of the house to come see him."

Malik shut the door. "Where my baby at?"

"He in the room," Shay said with an attitude. She was jealous of how much attention he showed Baby Davon and not her. No matter how badly he treated her, she still wanted him bad.

Malik walked back out of the room, holding his son. "Why the fuck he laying in your bed? Where his shit at?"

"He ain't got one yet."

Malik gave her a dirty look. "You so full of shit. I gave you five thousand dollars to get an abortion, but you spent that shit on partying and shit. After I found out you didn't do it, I still gave you money to go buy everything that he needed since he was coming. Where did all that money go?"

Shay didn't like the conversation, so she tried to change it. "You stressing, baby. Do you need your dick sucked or something?"

Malik was still standing up with Davon, and without saying a word, he walked over to her and slapped her. "Don't fucking play with me, Shay."

Shay was so pissed that she couldn't even say anything. Feeling stupid, she ran into her room, leaving Malik and the baby in the front room. Malik didn't care about her leaving. He wasn't over there to see her anyway.

Davon was asleep for most of the visit, which caused Malik to just hold him and stare at him. He wanted to believe that Davon was his, but what his mama and brother had been saying was getting to him.

"Aye, man, who you look like?" he said to the baby.

Shay had walked out of the room just in time to hear him asking their son that stupid question. "Malik, don't play with me. That's your fucking son, nigga."

"Don't come in here with all that yelling. Don't you see he sleep? Anyways, I'll ask him what the fuck I want to."

"If you don't believe he yours, get the fuck out then. I'm not about to let you disrespect me like that, and I know it's that bitch in your ear. She just don't want to share you."

Malik laid Baby Davon down. "Didn't I tell you to keep her name out yo' fucking mouth? You need to be thanking her because the old me would have had my foot up yo' ass by now."

"Get the fuck out, Malik!"

"So, what now? I can't come see my son? What bullshit you on?"

"I didn't say that. I just think you need to come back another day with a better attitude."

Malik went back to the couch to pick his baby boy up. "I'll be back, man." Malik then went to put him back in the bed. "Aye, when I come back, he better have his own bed."

After Malik left, Shay couldn't stop crying. She loved but hated Malik so much at the same time.

Malik prayed his attitude was gone by the time he got home to Camy, but Shay had really pissed him off.

"Hey, baby, how's little man doing?" Camy asked, trying to be nice.

"He all right," he dryly responded.

Camy could sense he was in one of his moods, but that only upset her. "So, she pissed you off, and you come home in a fucked-up mood. I guess my plans are off."

"Why do you do that stupid shit? If you see I'm mad already, why do you even fuck with me to make yourself mad?"

Camy knew he had a point, so instead of answering, she took a seat. "I'm sorry, baby. What happened?"

"That bitch really gets on my nerves. Even after I had to put hands on her stupid ass, she still was on some bullshit. She ain't doing shit for my son for real."

"It's gonna be all right, baby," Camy said, allowing him to express his feelings.

"I love my baby, but that bitch is trash. All that money I give her, and he don't even got a fucking bed. That bitch on some other shit."

Camy had so much to say, but the way her mouth was set up, he would have been pissed. In her eyes, that bitch hadn't just become trash. He was fucking her while she was trash the whole time. To be nice, she kept it simple.

"Baby, for now, just buy what he needs and stop putting money in her hand. All that stuff you bought him for over here might have to be divided up between homes."

Malik loved her way of thinking. He liked how she wasn't acting petty about the situation. "So, what do you wanna do?"

"I know we talked about going out, but I have another idea."

Malik gave her a strange look, wondering what she had up her sleeve.

"What tip you on?"

Camy got up, then went into the room. She needed to finish getting ready.

Malik followed her into the bedroom. "Where we going?"

"Out. Now, let me get ready, boy."

Malik watched as she made herself even more beautiful. If it had been up to him, they would have spent the afternoon in bed. He had never been so in love with a woman that he didn't want to share her with the rest of the world. He sometimes questioned if his way of thinking was a sign of him being selfish.

"What the fuck you doing?" Malik asked when they got out to the car. Camy jumping in the driver's seat threw Malik off. He was used to doing all the driving when they rode together.

"I'm driving, baby. Now, get in."

Malik got in the passenger side but didn't like it. "Why I can't drive?"

"Because you don't know where we are going, and I do. Now, please let me have this moment."

Malik leaned over, giving his girl a kiss. "You bet not be on no bullshit, Camy."

Camy laughed but still refused to tell him exactly where they were going. Twenty minutes later, the couple pulled up to a building that Malik had never seen before.

"What the hell is this shit, Camy?"

"Just come on. We are about to enjoy ourselves."

Malik was skeptical at first, but after realizing what was going on, he was all game. Earlier that day, he had mentioned giving her a full body massage, and now, they were both laid on a table with nothing on but a towel covering their lower bodies, getting full body massages.

"We gonna have to do this shit more often. I feel cheated like a muthafucka."

Camy giggled. "Why, baby?"

"'Cause I used to always do this to you and never realized how good and relaxing this shit is. I needed this in my life."

Malik looked over at Camy, expecting a response, but she had dozed off that fast.

The lady that was doing Malik's back put him to sleep ten minutes after Camy dozed off.

***

"So, how did you enjoy my surprise?" Camy asked an hour later as they climbed back in his truck.

Malik smiled. "I loved it. You must have told her to add the special to my service."

"What the hell you talking about?"

"That bitch massaged my dick more than my back. How much extra was that?"

Camy killed the engine. "Don't make me go back in there and fuck one of them hoes up, Malik. Did she touch you for real?"

Malik was cracking up. He was only joking, but the way Camy was ready to pop off was funny as hell. "Calm down, Baby Tyson. You wasn't about to do shit anyway, not carrying my baby."

Camy sat there for a moment. Even with him saying he was joking, she was still pissed just at the thought of a funky bitch getting her nigga off.

"You want me to drive?"

"Nah, just shut up so I can get my mind right."

Malik continued to laugh as Camy finally drove off.

"Ain't shit funny, boy. You must like when I'm bothered or something."

Malik reached over to rub her stomach. "Nah, I don't. I'm gonna need you to calm down and relax. Matter of fact, let's go get some food so we can go home and chill for the rest of the day."

"I'm good, Malik," she snapped.

"Nah, yo' ass ain't good. You tight as fuck right now. Pull over right here and let me drive," he ordered.

Malik got out so that Camy could slide over to the passenger side. When they had first found out that she was pregnant again, he told her he wasn't about to let shit slide, and he meant that shit.

Camy lay back and was soon dozing off as Malik stopped to get them some food.

After eating, the couple cuddled up to watch a movie until they were both back asleep.

The sound of Malik's phone going off woke Camy up first. She grabbed his phone and instantly got pissed seeing Shay's name pop up on the screen.

"Hello."

Shay had been waiting for this moment. She couldn't wait to fuck with Camy.

"Put my baby daddy on the phone."

Camy laughed. "Bitch, you gotta tell us the nigga name first."

Hearing Camy yell out "bitch" was enough to wake Malik up.

"Who the hell you talking to? Give me my damn phone," he said.

Malik tried to grab it, but Camy hung up. "It was the wrong number anyway."

"Man, who the fuck was that?"

"A bitch looking for her baby daddy!" Camy yelled.

Malik snatched the phone. "Why you play so fucking much? What Shay want? Was my son good?"

"I told her that she had the wrong number. Don't nobody know who her baby daddy is."

"Camy..." Malik paused to choose his words right. "You need to stop being like that. Then you hang up like she not the mother of my child. Anything could have been wrong over there."

Camy's attitude was now on a hundred. "Fuck that bitch. And you gotta be delusional to even think that baby is yours. Do you really think your mama ain't been telling me everything?"

"What the fuck she been telling you?"

"That's not your fucking baby, fool. So, now, I'm wondering if you still fucking her because you keep running your stupid ass over there like you going to see a baby that's not even yours."

"Have you lost yo' fucking mind? You must be on something 'cause I'm not fucking nobody but yo' stupid ass. When I say I'm going to see my son, that's what the fuck I'm doing. Ain't nobody fucking Shay ass no more. You really need to stop listening to my mama. She ain't always right."

Camy started putting her clothes back on. "Fuck you, Malik, 'cause you back fucking that bitch and still trying to string me along. Let's just end this shit. That way, you can stop playing in my fucking face with that bitch and her bastard-ass baby."

For the first time, Malik snapped on Camy and actually hit her.

SLAP.

Camy instantly grabbed her face and started crying.

"How many times I gotta tell yo' ass to watch your mouth when it comes to my fucking son? Why the fuck you always gotta run yo' fucking mouth?"

Camy stood there in shock, crying, trying to wrap her mind around the fact that Malik had actually hit her. Malik stood there, waiting for her to apologize, but instead, she picked up his shoe and busted him in the head with it. "Stupid muthafucka."

Malik shook his head as she stormed off. Instead of chasing behind her, he took a seat on the bed. They both needed a moment to cool off.

Camy paced the living room floor, wondering what her next move was going to be. She wasn't used to a nigga hitting her and hadn't planned on letting that be her life.

Even though it wasn't the right moment, when Shay called, Malik answered.

"What is it?" Malik was pissed. He could tell from her hesitation to answer that she didn't want shit.

"I was just calling to tell you how nosy your son is. He be looking around like he looking for you or something."

"Damn, for real? Tell him I'll be that way soon."

Camy stood in the doorway, pissed off. It was not because he had hit her but because he was too comfortable on the phone with the bitch that had been fucking up their relationship.

Malik looked at Camy, but instead of getting off the phone, he continued to talk to Shay.

"Look, you been fucking up on that money tip. I'm gonna bring him what he need. I gotta start treating yo' ass like a child and stop putting money in yo' hand."

Shay wanted to say some smart shit but decided not to because he was right. Once he placed money in her hand, she did everything but what needed to be done. "You right, and I'm sorry about that. I know I gotta do better."

"You damn right you do."

That alone made Camy feel like she was once again playing second to Shay, and she didn't like it. Without saying anything, Camy grabbed her car keys and then sneaked out the door.

It wasn't until he heard her car start up that he realized what was going on. "What the fuck! Aye, Shay, I'll call you back." Malik hung up before she could respond. He raced to the door, but at about the time his feet hit the porch, Camy was already gone.

"This stupid muthafucka," he mumbled as he walked back into the house. Malik ended up calling Camy over five times, and her funky ass refused to answer.

It had been a minute since he talked to his mama, but he dialed her number.

"Oh, so you do remember my number? I take it that you're not mad at me anymore for speaking my truth."

"Ma, I ain't got time for all that bullshit right now. Look, can you please call me if Camy pop up over there?"

Ms. Patt chuckled. "No!"

"Why the fuck not? This a fucking emergency, Ma."

"Didn't you just go off on me and tell me that I needed to mind my own fucking business? Now look at your crybaby ass. Now you want me in your fucking business."

"Ma, you ain't never mind yo' business, so what's up with all this bullshit? You been telling Camy that Shay baby ain't mine and shit? Do you know you and yo' big mouth got Camy thinking I'm cheating and shit?"

"Well, are you?" Ms. Patt questioned.

"Hell nah. Why would I go through all this shit to get her, just to cheat? This whole time, all I've been doing was kissing her ass and taking care of my baby. I don't even look at Shay the same way like I used to. Ain't shit she can do for me now but help with my son."

Ms. Patt believed her son, but she couldn't let him sit around and be nobody's fool. "Malik, that baby is not yours. I know you feel like you have to prove to the world that you're nothing like your daddy, but have your own kid and do that shit. Don't save a child that doesn't belong to you."

Malik was at the point of thinking that she just liked to piss him off and get on his nerves. Malik wanted to go off but decided to chill. "Ma, if Camy pops up over there, please call me." With that being said, Malik hung up. Anything else that she had to say wasn't important to him anymore.

Malik called Camy a few more times before getting dressed. She had him fucked up, thinking her leaving like that was cool.

***

Camy was in her feelings, but she couldn't run to her daddy with her problems with Malik. She still loved him but knew her daddy would hate the real Malik. Camy had never mentioned to her dad about how Malik was at the beginning with his "no title" rule, and she definitely hadn't mentioned his baby with Shay.

After driving around with nowhere to go, Camy ended up knocking on Ms. Patt's doorstep. Ms. Patt opened the door for Camy, knowing she needed someone to talk to.

"Come on in. I've been expecting you."

Camy walked in and then took a seat on the couch. "Really?"

"Yeah. Malik called me. He wanted me to call him if you showed up."

Camy started to cry. "Please don't call him. I just need a break to clear my mind."

Ms. Patt finally took a seat. "I'm not calling that boy. I don't know why y'all don't listen to me. I told you the first time you let that boy get you pregnant to get rid of it and go on with your life. Malik will never grow up. Look at you now, pregnant again. Do you think because he gave you a ring that things would be different? Listen, Camy, I'm telling you this because I like you, but my son is not the one. You might have got him to open up, but that li'l boy in him will never go away."

Camy used to get upset when his mama talked to her, but now, she listened. She hated hearing it, but at the same time, she needed to hear this. "I don't know what to do. I love him, but dealing with him is a lot," Camy cried.

"I know, but you got that baby, and it's too late to stop that, so you gotta figure out what's best for you and that baby. Don't get me wrong. Malik is an excellent provider, but ask yourself if he will ever truly claim your heart the way you want him to."

Ms. Patt got up to go into the kitchen. She had some food cooking and wasn't trying to burn it talking to Camy.

Camy was getting sleepy, but every time she felt herself dozing off, she jumped up. She knew how Malik and his mama liked to set her up. "I'm about to go home. I need to get some rest."

"Come on, Camy. I know you wanna stay for a plate. Go have a seat at the table."

Camy hesitated. "Did you call Malik and tell him I was here?"

"Nah, not this time. I know how that boy could be. Now that he believes that he found love in you, he expects you to move as he says because he is finally ready to settle down. Now, go feed my grandbaby."

Camy couldn't help but think that she was right. She just prayed that her greediness didn't cause her to be there so long that Malik popped up.

Chapter 20

Camy rolled over, trying to avoid the sun that was coming in from her window.

"You selfish as fuck."

Camy jumped, damn near falling out of the bed. "Malik, what the fuck are you doing here?"

"I keep asking myself the same thing. I've been sitting here, wondering why the fuck I'm back at yo' shit, where niggas tried to kill me, chasing behind yo' ass. It's selfish as fuck how you keep running back over here like you want something to happen to me."

"Malik, stop saying that shit. You know I don't want nothing to happen to you."

"I can't fucking tell. You got me chasing yo' ass all around Detroit."

"Stop then!"

Malik snatched Camy up quick as hell. "Stop fucking playing with me. You already know why I'm doing this shit."

Camy snatched away from Malik. "I don't know shit anymore. Tell me why you are here and not around the corner with that bitch."

Malik shook his head. If he didn't know any better, he would believe that Camy was trying to fuck shit up and push him away. Malik didn't give a fuck. He wasn't about to let her fucked-up ways mess things up between them.

"Camy, I love you, not Shay. I wanna marry you, not her. I don't understand why I gotta keep telling you that shit. Please tell me what I gotta do to fix this shit."

Camy looked him dead in the eyes. "I don't like being second. I can handle the baby. It's just her. I don't like how she using this baby to fuck with me."

"I talked to her about that shit before. I'm trying, baby. I'm trying. Just don't shut me out like that, and all that running away gotta stop."

Camy sat on the bed in her thoughts, not responding.

"Camy, I love you, and I'm not about to let you go that easily. You ain't learned that shit by now?"

Camy gave Malik a smile. "I can say that you don't give up on what you really want."

"I don't. Oh, and another thing, I'm about to stop paying the rent and bills over here. I'm not about to keep you a spot to run away to."

Camy laughed, but Malik was dead serious. He wasn't playing with her ass. "Come on. Let's get the fuck from out here."

Camy didn't move.

"Man, get the fuck up," he ordered.

"No, I wanna stay here, Malik. You already handled what needed to be done. I'm safe here. Besides, I need my own space again."

Malik wasn't trying to hear shit she was saying. "I keep telling you that all you need is me. Now let's go home."

"This is my home."

"No, the fuck it ain't. Not no fucking more."

Camy shook her head. "Your mama warned me about you and this control shit. Just because you love me doesn't mean that you can control me."

Malik wanted everything to go peacefully, but just her bringing up some bullshit that his mama said pissed him completely off. "So, this ain't about us. It's all about my mama? You trying to push me away because she don't want to see me happy?"

"No, Malik. It's not that. I do love you. I just want things to be different," Camy tried to explain.

"Different like what? Talk to me so I can fix this shit."

Camy thought about what her problem was and regretted bringing the shit up. Everything went back to what his mama said.

"Say something, dammit!"

"It's just that your mama said that Baby Davon wasn't yours for real, and you were using him for a reason to still fuck with Shay. I know what you told me, but she keeps telling me the same shit repeatedly, and I'm tired of hearing it."

Malik started pacing the floor. "I'm not about to talk about that shit. You know, just like Shay knows, it's all about us, and I stand on that shit. That's my mama, but you gotta stop listening to her about shit. That lady been bitter since my daddy left her ass."

Camy's thoughts were everywhere. A part of her wanted to believe his every word, but the shit that his mama had planted in her head had her confused.

"Please, baby, don't sit here and fuck this shit up. I've done everything in my power to prove to you just how much I want us to work."

Camy went over to Malik. He wrapped his arms around her. "I love you, girl."

"I love you too. And I'm sorry for giving you a hard time. For now on, I'm gonna ignore what she tells me."

Malik prayed she kept her word.

For the next three weeks, everything was smooth between Malik and Camy. She had stopped complaining when he had to go spend time with the baby, and Malik put his foot down and set out even more rules for Shay. Shay didn't like the new Malik but played along, so he wouldn't stop helping her.

"Malik, are you ready?" Camy asked. It was time for her doctor's appointment.

Malik brushed his head again. "Yeah, let's see what's going on with my baby."

The week before, Camy's doctor had to reschedule her appointment, and Malik was anxious to see his baby. After helping Camy in the truck, Malik got in to head to the doctor's office.

"Let's make a bet."

"What you thinking about, Malik?"

"Let's make a bet on the baby gender. 'Cause you big as hell. It gotta be a boy."

"Was Shay big with her son?"

Malik gave her a dirty look. "Fuck you bring her up for? Why you trying to start shit?"

"I'm not, baby. I really was wondering how you came up with that theory."

Malik thought about what she asked. "I don't know because she lied about that baby, and about the time she told me the truth, I didn't go around her ass. I just always believed that boys grew bigger in the belly."

"Okay, we can make a deal on that. You keep saying I'm big, but I don't see it."

Malik laughed. "Damn, I gotta take you to the eye doctor too?"

"Stop being a bully," Camy jokingly said.

At the doctor's office, they only had to wait ten minutes before getting called to the back. Malik stood over her, watching as the doctor used the ultrasound machine to check on their baby.

"How everything looking?"

Camy laughed. "Malik, let her do her job."

"It's all right, Mom. I was just getting some measurements."

After another few minutes, the doctor gave them both a weird look.

"Is everything all right?"

Malik's question had Camy trying to sit up. "What's going on?"

"Dad, I'm going to need you to calm Mom down. I have no bad news to deliver. I just need to ask if you want to know everything that I see today and the gender."

"Hell yeah. Tell me everything about mine," he blurted out, forgetting he was talking to the doctor.

"Okay. First, I need to show you both this. Over here is Baby A, and if you look over here, you can see Baby B."

"Twins?" Camy asked, confused.

Malik was all smiles. "Hell yeah. I've been putting in that overtime."

Camy started laughing. "Shut up, boy."

Without even trying, Malik had the doctor laughing with them.

"Okay, let's get to the sex. Baby A has a third leg right here, and Baby B is right here chilling with his legs wide open, showing off his goodies."

"Oh my gawd, two boys," Camy said, wanting to cry. She stared at Malik, trying to figure out how she could blame this shit on him.

After printing out a few pictures, the doctor walked out so that Camy could fix herself up.

Malik could tell that she was upset. "What I do now?"

"Nothing, Malik."

The two walked to the car in silence. She was pissed, and he was trying to figure out how to fix her attitude.

Before helping her into the truck, Malik gave her a kiss. "This is one of the best days of my life. Thank you for my boys."

Camy burst out in tears. "I wanted a girl. This not fair," she cried.

"Camy, get yo' ass in the car. All that crying shit gotta stop. You gonna make my sons soft as hell."

Camy started laughing. "Shut up. I'm supposed to be sad right now."

Malik rubbed her stomach as he drove off. "Damn, man, I can't stop smiling. I'm legit happy as fuck."

Curious to know where in the hell twins came from, Camy started asking questions. "Do twins run in your family?"

"Hell yeah. Unc was a twin, but his twin died at birth. That's why now that I know it's twins, I gotta really be on your ass. Oh, and I got like three sets of cousins that are twins."

Camy shook her head. "You should have told me that before nutting in me."

"Shut yo' ass up. You still would have got nutted in if I would have said something. Stop playing."

Camy laughed, knowing he was right.

"I knew you were getting big as hell too fast. My boys in that muthafucka, just growing and shit. I can't wait to hold them for real."

Camy was upset because she wanted a girl, but she smiled because of the smile on Malik's face.

"Aye, just tell me when, and I'll give you that girl that you want."

"Whatever, boy. You just wanna fuck."

Malik laughed. "You damn right. Every single chance I get with you."

Camy was about to say something smart, but his phone started to ring. Since his phone was connected to the car, Camy was able to hear his whole conversation.

"What's up, Shay?"

"Your mama called and wanted to know if it would be all right to keep the baby for a few hours. I know y'all haven't been talking, so I told her that I would see if it would be okay."

Camy could tell that he had really been getting Shay in order.

"Umm, you know what? Tell her she can keep him for a few hours. I know you need some free time anyways. Make sure you pack his bag up right."

"All right, I'll talk to you later." Shay hung up and then did a little dance. She was ready for a break.

Since Baby Davon was spending time with his grandma, Malik didn't have a reason to drive over to Shay's house. He was happy because he wanted to show Camy just how happy he was that she had blessed him with twin boys.

"Malik, what time will you be back?" Camy asked. Malik was over at Shay's house to visit his son.

"Hey, baby. I know I said that I'd be home in a few, but Davon keep crying, and he throwing up and shit. I don't wanna leave him like this."

"Okay, baby. I understand. Also, I hope he feels better."

"Me too, baby. Thank you. I love you."

"I love you too, baby."

As soon as Malik hung up, Shay started popping off at the mouth.

"Give me my son. He whining because instead of you holding him right, you on the phone caking and shit."

"Aye, don't start no shit."

Shay couldn't help but talk shit. Her heart was hurt every time he mentioned Camy and his twin boys. She was jealous, and they weren't even here yet. She hated how he came right over, talking about his twins.

"I'm gonna buy a bigger house. I want all my kids to have their own room at my place. I want them to live with me," he said.

"Hell nah, not my baby."

"Shay, we gonna have to work something out with him. Can I get him every weekend and the whole summer then?"

"I don't know about that, Malik. How would Camy feel about that?"

"About the time he old enough to really be away from you like that, me and my wife would have an understanding. She already knows how bad I wanna be in my kids' life, and she loved it. You the only one giving me a problem. Whether you like it or not, these kids are related and gonna be around each other as much as possible. I'm not raising my boys to be strangers towards each other."

Shay knew where he was coming from, but she was still bitter that she wasn't his number-one girl. Why couldn't it be her in the home with him and the kids?

Just talking to Shay about his boys, Malik felt like it was time to talk to his own brother. Life was too short to be mad over some bullshit words. "Give me a minute." Since Baby Davon had dozed off, Malik laid him down, praying that he stayed asleep this time.

Shay stayed on the couch as Malik sat on her bed, next to his son.

"Aye, bro, you good?" Malik asked when he called Rell.

"Yeah, how about you?" Rell responded.

There was a small pause between them.

"Rell, I know I be on some other shit, but we brothers, and life too short for us not to be talking. I love you, bro."

"I love you too, Malik. I've always had your back on shit, and I'd never tell you nothing wrong just to piss you off."

Malik knew he was trying to bring up the conversation about Shay's baby not being his, and he didn't want to hear that shit. "Aye, bro, I got some good news."

"What's up, bro?" Rell asked.

"Bro, Camy is having twin boys. Can you believe that shit?"

Rell was happy for them. "Boy, I'm happy for y'all. I'm just glad that twin shit hit somebody else besides me and Tiffany."

Malik joined his brother in a laugh. They stayed on the phone for a few more minutes, talking shit to one another, before getting off the phone. After hanging up, Malik felt much better. He missed his big bro/best friend.

Baby Davon slept all while he was on the phone, but as soon as Malik got off, he was back crying. Malik shook his head as he picked him up and placed him on his chest.

"You getting spoiled, Daddyman. You about to have two baby brothers, and I need you to be a big boy when they come. I can't have all y'all spoiled like this."

Malik didn't mean to, but he fell asleep holding Davon in the bed. Shay walked into the room with a big smile on her face. She had a master plan.

Camy woke up to an empty bed and instantly felt sick to her stomach. Picking up her phone, Camy dialed Malik's number. To her surprise, he didn't answer.

As soon as she set her phone down on the bed, she started receiving messages from Shay.

Before Camy could respond, Shay was sending picture messages.

The first picture of Malik and Shay in her bed together broke Camy into a million pieces.

"Malik, why?" she cried as if he could hear her.

Shay had sent Camy three pictures that she had staged to hurt Camy, knowing that, in real life, he was knocked out from the drink she made him.

Camy tried calling Malik's phone again, not knowing that Shay had placed it on Do Not Disturb right before posting their pictures on social media for the world to see. Camy left three voice messages, going off on him. Since he wouldn't call her back, she left him one last message before trying to pull herself together.

"Malik, I trusted you, and this is how you play me? You promised that you weren't sleeping with her, but you were in the bed with her with no clothes on. How could you do this to me? What did I do to deserve this hurt and pain?" she cried into the phone. Camy found herself holding the phone, just crying her heart out, even after the beep went off.

***

Malik jumped up, still tired and confused. "Man, what the fuck! Camy gonna kill me." Malik looked over at Shay, who pretended to be knocked out. "Get the fuck up! Why you ain't wake me up?"

Shay turned to face him. "I guess we both fell asleep last night."

"Nah, bitch, you on some slick shit," he said, putting his shit back on.

"Whatever. Hurry up and get out of my house. Go run home to that bitch."

"Shay, what I tell you about yo' mouth? Don't disrespect her. I'm trying not to fuck you up."

Shay giggled as she picked Baby Davon up.

Malik grabbed his phone and then placed a kiss on his son. "I'll call him later."

Shay had made sure to put his phone on Do Not Disturb, just so he could make it home without knowing what had happened. Malik tried calling Camy a few times, knowing that she was pissed, but she didn't answer.

It wasn't until he pulled up and actually went through his phone that he realized what the hell was going on. Between a million calls and text messages, Malik's phone was filled with notifications from social media. Clicking on it, he was shocked by the pictures that Shay had posted of them.

Malik instantly called Camy back. "Baby, I know them pictures look bad, but I can explain. The doctors said skin-to-skin would calm him. That's why my shirt was off. That bitch took them pictures, trying to make it seem like we fucked or something. I swear, baby. I swear I ain't touch that girl."

Malik didn't ease up. After seeing that Camy had already packed most of her shit, left the house, and wasn't answering, he kept calling and texting. He ended up back at Shay's house to beat her ass for real, but she had already packed her and the baby's shit up and left. She must have known he was going to hurt her.

Malik drove around the corner then pulled up to Camy's house. He knew she would pull up any minute now, and he would be able to explain it all. When it came to her, no fight was too big. Malik played the waiting game while calling Camy and Shay back-to-back. Someone needed to answer and fast.

Ms. Patt was happy to see her son. She had just received some important mail and needed to show him. "Malik, come here."

"I can't. I'm busy," he snapped.

Rell had pulled up after his mama called him, saying that she needed to talk to him.

"Hey, Ma, what's up?" Rell asked.

"Your stubborn-ass brother won't come talk to me. I don't know what's wrong with him."

Rell saw all the bullshit and knew his brother was going through it. "Ma, let me deal with him. Go back in the house."

She listened, knowing that Rell could handle his brother better than she ever could.

Rell jumped in his brother's truck. "Talk to me, bro."

"That bitch set me up. Camy gone, man, and Shay ran off with my son. I don't know what to do," Malik said, trying to hold himself together.

"Damn, bro, that's fucked up. I saw those pictures, and they did look bad."

"I fucked up, bro. One day, I was over there with Baby Davon, and we were talking. Shay asked me what happened with me and Camy's first baby. I told her, and boom, she turned around and slipped me something to get me to spend the night with her ass. I swear I didn't fuck or nothing, bro. You gotta call Camy for me. She ain't answering my calls."

Rell believed his brother because he wasn't the type to lie about shit, no matter whose feelings he was going to hurt.

Camy answered on the third ring.

"Hello," she said, holding back her tears.

"Aye, Camy, where you at? You good?"

"Rell, I know Malik sitting right there, and I'm on speaker phone. I don't have anything to say to him but fuck him. I trusted him, and he played me. This was the final straw. I'm done for good this time," she cried.

"Baby, I didn't do shit. Please just listen to me," Malik begged.

Knowing that he was her weakness, and not wanting to fall for his bullshit, Camy hung up. Malik then snatched Rell's phone out of his hand, trying to call her back. Camy tossed her phone in the back seat. She wasn't trying to hear shit.

"Bro, you gonna be all right?"

"Hell nah. I don't even got no purpose of being here anymore."

"Stop saying that shit. I already lost Unc. I'd go crazy for real without you, bro. Shit gonna be all right. You just gotta give her a few days."

Malik dug in his pocket and then pulled out Camy's engagement ring. "She gone for real this time. She ain't never took this ring off."

Rell felt bad and didn't know what to say. He kept saying shit would be all right, but he wasn't sure this time.

"You know when she mad, she come back to her place. She'll be pulling up in a minute."

That was when reality kicked in. Malik had really played himself.

"Not this time, bro. The last time she did that shit, I told her landlord that she was moving. I paid the rent up and paid him to pack her shit and move it into storage until I bought us a new house. Wherever she done ran off to, I don't know where that's at. I'm sitting here, waiting on something that ain't even gonna happen."

"Damn, bro, did you check with her daddy?"

Malik quickly searched through his contacts to find David's number. He called him.

"Hey, umm, David, have you heard from Camy lately?"

"She called this morning, but I'm out of town right now and couldn't really talk at the moment. I told her that I would call her back later. Is everything all right?"

"Yeah, I gotta go." Malik didn't wait for a response before hanging up.

"Man, where the fuck this girl at?" Malik yelled, hitting the steering wheel.

Rell was worried about his brother. He knew that, right now, letting him drive off and be alone was the last thing that he needed.

Malik finally jumped out of the car. "Let me go talk to Mama."

The boys walked in to see Ms. Patt sitting on the couch with a smile on her face.

"See, Malik, I told you that baby wasn't yours," she joyfully said, waving the letter that came in the mail.

"Man, it ain't the right time for that shit," Rell snapped.

Malik snatched the paper from Ms. Patt. "What the fuck you talking about, Ma?"

"Just leave it alone," Rell suggested.

Malik gave Rell a funny look. "What the fuck, bro? Davon ain't mine."

Malik looked over the paper, just to make sure he had read it correctly. "This paper says it ain't a chance in hell that he mine."

Rell shook his head, knowing that it was only a matter of time before Malik snapped. Their mom didn't even realize that he was already going through something, and she was only adding fuel to the fire.

"You believe me now, boy? I'm your mama. I know what I be talking about. That day I kept him, I did one of those home DNA tests and mailed it in. I called Shay lying, stupid ass yesterday and told her about the results, and she went crazy on me."

"Why you ain't call me?" Malik questioned.

"I did, boy. Your ass don't never answer for me. That's why I called your brother over here this morning. I knew you would answer for him."

Everything was making sense now. Malik now knew why Shay did what she did and got the fuck on. She knew that once he found out, he wasn't about to take care of a baby that wasn't his, so she had nothing else to lose.

"Yeah, I'm about to go ahead and head home," Malik said.

"Nah, bro. I know you don't wanna be over here, but you don't need to be by yourself right now."

Ms. Patt stood up from the couch. "Stop babying that boy. He's gotta learn to listen, or he's gonna bump his head plenty of days."

"Ma, chill out. It's a lot going on right now, and you need to chill on Malik."

Malik didn't say shit. He simply walked out the door. Rell chased behind him.

"Aye, bro, where you about to go?"

"Home."

"Bro, come ride to my crib or something."

"Rell, leave me the fuck alone. I'm gonna be good."

Rell didn't get mad. Making sure his brother didn't do shit to harm himself was his main concern. "At least call me, bro. You know I got you."

Malik didn't respond. Instead, he drove off, leaving his brother feeling hopeless.

Ms. Patt stepped on the porch. "Let his crybaby ass run off."

"Ma, you wrong as hell right now."

Rell went back in the house with his mama to explain how everything had played out and why he was trying to get Malik to not leave.

"Damn, I had no idea. I feel so bad. He ain't gonna harm himself. He gonna kill Shay first. Trust me. I know my son."

"So, did she tell you who the daddy was?"

"Nah, but it ain't my son's baby."

Rell chilled with his mama for a few more minutes before leaving. While heading to Malik's house, he gave him a call.

"Rell, I said I'm good. Please don't start calling me every ten minutes."

"You my little bro, dawg. I can't let this shit get the best of you. We already lost Unc. I can't lose you too."

"I'm not going anywhere. If shit changes, I'll call you first."

Rell started to respond, but Malik hung up the phone.

Rell drove by to make sure that he did make it home. Rell shook his head, seeing that Malik's car wasn't in the driveway. Rell didn't know what to do but to go home to be with Tiffany and their kids. He needed to try to clear his mind and wait for Malik to call.

Shay sat on her mama's couch, nervous as hell. She honestly thought about what she had done and wanted to die.

"Why would you do that to that boy? Are you fucking retarded?"

Shay cried. "Ma, he hurt me first, and nobody gave a fuck. To be honest, I didn't mean for this to spiral out of control the way that it did. I just wanted him to love me the way he loves Camy."

She couldn't believe the bullshit that her daughter was saying. She had to be on some type of drugs. "Look, I know how Malik is, so y'all can't stay here. That boy ain't about to come tear my shit up, and you know he coming."

"Ma, please."

"No, I wanna live. I didn't play these stupid games with these crazy-ass niggas for that very reason. Y'all gotta go."

Shay cried. "Ma, he gonna hurt me."

"Good. Maybe he'd knock some sense in ya."

Shay sat there for ten more minutes, crying and begging, but her mama wasn't having it. Finally tired of begging and not getting anywhere, Shay grabbed Baby Davon. "If something happens to me, it's your fault."

"Girl, don't do that shit. It's all your fault for playing with that crazy-ass nigga. You fucked his whole life up. You should had stayed in your place."

Shay knew her mama was right, but she wasn't trying to hear that shit. She walked out, not knowing what was going to become of her.

As soon as Malik saw her walk out and get in the car, he quickly pulled up and blocked her from leaving the driveway. Shay was scared but didn't try to run. Malik opened the passenger-side door to get in.

"What's up?"

Shay started crying again. "I'm so sorry, Malik. I'm so sorry."

"Sorry for what? Tell me what you've been up to," he calmly demanded.

"I'm sorry for lying. I just wanted you so bad. I'm sorry."

"What you lie about, Shay? What the fuck you been lying about?" He knew everything but wanted her to be woman enough to tell him to his face.

Shay was terrified but knew she had no choice but to tell the truth. "Baby Davon not yours. I'm so sorry, Malik," she cried.

"Who his daddy?"

Shay started crying harder. "Please, Malik, please don't hurt me," she begged.

"Who his daddy?" he repeated.

Shay was scared, and she knew that he would really hurt her if she told him. "I can't tell you, Malik. Please, baby. I'm so sorry."

Malik reached over and slapped her. "Stop playing in my fucking face, Shay. I asked you a few times if you were sure he was mine. I gave you chances to tell me the truth, and you still lied to me. Who baby is that?" he asked again, trying hard not to fuck her up.

"It doesn't even matter anymore."

"What the fuck that mean?"

"His real daddy is dead."

Malik instantly felt sick to his stomach. "So, you was the bitch Unc was sneaking off fucking and shit? You really played me like that."

As Shay cried, she covered her face, scared that he was going to attack her in front of the baby. "I'm sorry, Malik. I was lonely and missing you. He came over one day, talking about you and Camy, and I got jealous. You never looked at me the way you did her. I just wanted to be loved, and Davon was there to fill that void."

"You can go home now. I'm not gonna bother you," he said, climbing out of her car.

Shay's mom stayed in the window, watching and waiting for Malik to fuck Shay's stupid ass up. She was low-key disappointed when he got out of the car without showing his ass.

Malik was hurt. Never in a million years would he think that he would have ill feelings toward his unc. Instead of hurting Shay, Malik got out of the car in his feelings. Only knowing that he had two boys coming into the world saved her life and saved him from going to prison for murder.

Shay sat in the car, crying her eyes out. Although he said that she was free to go home without worrying about him, she knew that he would no longer provide for her or the baby.

Only because her voicemail wasn't full yet did Malik know that Camy was at least listening to his voice message. For the past three weeks, Malik had called Camy almost a hundred times every day, and that morning wouldn't be different. He refused to give up on them.

Ms. Patt had told Malik he was wrong for not wanting to help Shay with the baby, knowing that it was Davon's, but Rell could understand his pain. He vowed to help out, but only after the DNA test came back. Because Davon was deceased, they had to do a special test that would take a little longer:

"Baby, I see you took that money. I hope that's enough for you to start all over, no matter where you are. You know if you come back home, things will be better. I swear. I told you that Shay and her baby were no longer my problem. It's all about us. I know you listening to my messages. Please tell me what I gotta do to fix us. I need you, Camy."

Malik hung up, praying that day would be the day that she walked back into his house with her beautiful smile brightening up his heart again.

Camy so badly wanted to call Malik back but was tired of all the bullshit. Even though she heard his story about what supposedly happened, she didn't know what to believe. To her, it seemed like every nigga that she loved played with her heart. She hated it, but she was going to have to do him like she did Jason.

"Welcome to AT&T. How can I help you today?"

Camy gave the worker a fake smile. "I need to change my number again."

The End